The DATING DIARIES

The DATING DIARIES

KRISTEN KEMP

PUSH

SCHOLASTIC INC.

NEW YORK TORONTO LONDON AUCKLAND SYDNEY

MEXICO CITY NEW DELHI HONG KONG BUENOS AIRES

To Johan, for making life sparkling and new.

To David, for brilliant ideas and unrelenting encouragement.

ISBN 0-439-62298-0

12 11 10 9 8 7 6 5 4 3 2 1   4 5 6 7 8 9/0

Printed in the U.S.A.   40
First printing, July 2004

My ah-ha moment

Thursday, April 3

I looked better when I was Paul's girlfriend.

As I cried, the Muppet Babies on my thin pillowcase turned brighter than I'd ever seen them. Dancing Kermit went from faded green to the shade of a ripe avocado. Miss Piggy had been almost invisible for five years, but suddenly her flesh became peachy. I peered into the handheld woe-is-me mirror I kept on my nightstand. When I watched my face contort into sadness, I cried even harder. My skin was pale, zitty, and blotchy; my eyes were veined, swollen, and hidden under my unibrow; my hair was knotty and full of scalp grease. Under less insane circumstances, my complexion was decent. As things stood, though, my sparkle and shine were history.

Just like Paul and I were history.

My eyes sprung another leak, so I slammed my head back into the softness of the wet Muppet Babies. After crying on them for four days straight, I had memorized every thread of every character.

"Who do you think you are, Katie?" Mom berated from the hallway. "I didn't raise no goddamned nun."

I had hung a crucifix outside my doorway just after the breakup. My mother was about as devout as a turnip, so I bought the symbol to scare her away. She hated it when I threatened to pray, so I prayed loudly whenever I wanted to make her disappear. I wasn't religious, either, but I didn't think she'd figured that out yet. Her strongest beliefs were in cable television, drive-through windows, and airbrushed fingernails. She was not your average level of annoying, I swear to God. My mother was a manicure-obsessed, southern she-devil who lived for drugstore lipstick and drive-through dinners.

Clearly, since she was insulting me, she was no longer leery of the cross. Hoping for just a few more hours of peace with my pillowcase, I vowed to hang up a rosary the second she walked away. I'd bought the beads because I thought they'd make a sexy belt on a future date with Paul. Of course, that's when I used to care about how I looked. Recently, I'd had no plans to leave 142 East Main Street ever again unless it was through the valley of the shadow of death. I just hoped Mom would think to bury me in my favorite sheets.

"Do you think prayin' will help? You need to get up off your ass and wash your stanky self in the shower. You need to go back to Shitville High School and graduate. It ain't too late to get a life," she said, her three-inch fingernail pointed my way. "Remember, the less you got, the more there is to get."

Uh, right.

I had a remote control for my stereo, so I turned up my electronic monks CD. Luckily, I could get higher decibels on my woofers than she could in her larynx. My mom usually meant well — like the time she volunteered to hide eggs for the first-grade Easter egg hunt just so she could tell me where they all were. She wanted to win the grand prize for us, which was a year's supply of chocolate. We won, and then we ate twelve months' worth in one day. I ended up with hives. I can no longer eat chocolate — even in reasonable quantities — without welting up. My mother never has any in the house because the memory of me covered in those festering, malformed, scarlet blotches freaks her out.

The music vibrated through my brain and my windows, and for five-tenths of a second, I was almost able to forget that Paul had dumped me for a Swedish transfer student named Johanna (pronounced Yo-Hawnnah, also known as Ho-Hawnnah), a freshman no less. He wanted to be with a total cliché — a blondie with a rack and a sexy accent. To make it worse, she was a boy climber, which is what Matt and I called freshman chicks who try to move in and up on upperclassmen. A year ago, they were in training bras and getting used to tampons. Once in high school, though, they thought they were superstars with their new boobs and gleeful hormones.

It dawned on me that I had made progress — not by dissing the boy climber Swede — but for thinking about something besides my situation for a few seconds. Quickly, though, Paul popped back into my head. The feeling arose again — a dull, thudding pain that became sharp and sliced its way up my legs, torso, chest, and neck. It landed in my head with the weight of four thousand swaying monks. The pounding memories of Paul and our almost five years together burst through the weak dams in my eye sockets. Kermit turned avocado green again.

How could that much liquid possibly come out of my body? My eyes were weary and sore and dry like raisins. Oh, raisins brought on the pain again. Raisinettes were Paul's favorite candy, and he always ate them when we went to the movies. Toward the end of the seventh grade, Paul and I were assigned to the same science group for a project along with some quiet girl and my best friend, Matt. We all schlepped back and forth to one another's houses collecting different kinds of leaves, weeds, and dandelions that spring, forcing our parents to mingle. By then my mother had decided she was too old to dye her hair the color of backyard tomatoes, thank God.

While researching the origins of various plants (i.e., weeds), I developed a mad burning passion for Paul. I know some people would call it puppy love, but they would be wrong. The way he smelled, a mixture of Zest and smashed grass from playing soccer, has kept me awake at night ever since. His deep, dark eyes pulled me into his world and refused to let me go. Whenever he'd lean over me to glue a dead dandelion to our poster board, parts I didn't know I had would explode deep inside my body. He teased me, calling me Barney because I have freak-colored eyes that are purple. I lived for the seconds when he'd glance my way or speak to me. Flirting was easy, organic, fun. Matt, darn him, was the first to notice.

You are acting weird, stated the note he passed me during seventh-grade health class.

What else is new? I am weird. That's why you're my only friend, Air Jordan, I wrote back, complimenting him on standing tall after his mom allowed him to stop wearing his orthopedic shoes to school. He'd been strutting around the halls NBA-style that whole week.

4

I think you have it bad for Paul. When I read that line, I tingled, knowing it was true. I liked keeping to myself — my mom didn't even know I had started my period till six months after the big day. Normally, that was the bonus of having a best friend who was a boy. Girls pried too much, sharing the deepest darkest secrets as easily as they swapped lip gloss. Boys would rather sleep on broken glass than ask about female intimacies. Matt may have been the exception, once I thought about it, because he *did* like to gossip a lot for a guy. At least he waited patiently, sometimes for weeks, before diving into my business. And by the time he got around to asking, he already knew the answers. With one look into my eyes, he could tell if I was hungry, tired, or happy. He knew if I felt like taking on the tallest tree, or if I wanted to hide under the covers, or if I was hopelessly, insanely in love with Paul Green.

You are so lame, said the note I passed back. *I do not have it bad for ANYBODY.* He giggled and pointed at me when he read my lies. He had outed me. I wondered if anyone else knew, and bonked my pencil so hard on my desk that the teacher had to ask me to stop. We got a B on our plant project, and I left the seventh grade with the fluttery burden of having experienced my first big crush. I welcomed the summer and made moving on my main objective.

Matt and I spent June swimming and doing whatever we could outside. By July, we started feeling more mature and stopped asking each other to "play." We had already replaced the term with "hang out," and we wasted away the long days acting wise and unaffected, making wagers over games of Monopoly. Matt lived four doors down from me, which made it easier to isolate ourselves in our own little world. From playing

Barbies (I have pictures of him with dolls in hand) to climbing to daydreaming, we had a secret language only we understood.

When we went back to school for our final year of junior high, something had changed within me. I was ready to let someone else get into my head. One look at Paul in the hallway and I longed for him the way a bee wants to kiss a honeysuckle. At night, I'd fantasize that Paul and I were at an outdoor symphony holding hands and plotting ways to sneak off so we could roll around in the weeds. I'd wake up to the reality of life on Main Street again — with Matt, my mother, her boyfriend, and no Paul. I'd been having so many new sexy dreams about Paul that I even asked Matt to kiss me in my backyard on a warm, Indian summer afternoon. Matt almost gave in, then jerked away. To dull the awkwardness, he told me I was full of cooties. We went swimming instead.

It didn't matter. The first day of that October just happened to be the beginning of my *life* — well, my real love life, at least. Before sixth period, Paul walked up to me and said stuff like, "Katie, where have you been all year? Did you have a good summer? That was a cool science project we worked on, wasn't it? "

Our eyes locked and words couldn't say enough. I smiled. My heart did not do a loop and my stomach did not fill with butterflies or any other weird bugs. Instead, I had this sense that everything in the world was okay. I felt special, like when I was eight and Matt brought me Ivy League Barbie, the one my mother never remembered to buy. Matt had saved his allowance to surprise me. The gesture was sweet. When Paul visited my locker that first time, his voice was soft and gentle. He made me happy.

Once again, Matt thought I was strange. When I reluctantly told him after school about my encounter, he jumped up and down. "For goodness sakes," he said, never cussing. "What did you say? Did you freak? Did you pull a Cherry?"

"God! No!" I missed a lot of the school gossip, but Cherry's boy-toying was obvious even to me. Guys loved her like they loved ESPN — and she loved them in plain view all over Shitville Junior High. "No, Matt, calm down." Matt's ways — his utter earnestness especially — made him different from everyone else. Even if he had understood why other kids made fun of him — and he didn't — he would not have been able to change. "Paul just asked me to the movies Friday night. We're going to ride our bikes to the theater and share some popcorn or something. It'll be fun. It's no big deal," I told him. But I knew better: That date was going to change everything.

That was four and a half years ago. Paul and I had spent at least four days a week together ever since. When we had time apart, I hung out with Matt. My mother was more than supportive of the arrangement. "I'm so goddamned excited," she'd say. "You got yourself a steady honey in junior high. You're just like me — you ain't about to waste time. Anyway, you were turnin' my hair gray without more friends."

"They don't call them steadies anymore, Vikki J.," I'd reply. She had changed her name about the same time she'd started wearing her nails longer, which allowed for more elaborate airbrushing. She used to be Victoria Jones James, but she thought Vikki J. Jaymes suited her better and, most important, increased her chances of getting a job at a better Shitville hairdressing salon. She was still hot on the name today, and she still cut hair and did nails out of a spiffed-up room in our basement.

"Oh, whatever, honey pie," she'd answered. "That Paul is a young hunk of beef, I tell ya what. It's about time you had

7

friends — not that there's anything wrong with that Matt. You worried me with all of that bikin' and studyin' you two done. I just didn't want you to be a lonely little teenage freak like I was."

"Stop it." Had I spoken? She didn't hear me.

"You know that. Anyway, how were you supposed to become a cheerleader if you stayed the way you were? Now you might get more popular and have a better chance."

My eighth-grade self was not amused. "Vikki J., come *on*. What's all that supposed to mean?"

"Oh, you just needed more friends, that's all. Katie, you've never been invited to a goddamned birthday party in your life." The way she used cuss words, more often than other people blinked their eyes, irritated me. I did not want to be like her, so I did not speak the way she did, and I did not grow or paint my nails. She was right that I didn't care about socializing — the same way she didn't think about sophistication.

"That's not true. Matt invited me to his! His mom even made a mini upside-down pineapple cake."

She tightened her ponytail, unknowingly giving herself a face-lift, and shook her head. She gave up on me for the moment and focused on her appointment book. She and I were home together way way way too often, which made her cozy and me crazy. My mother never really made the effort to get a real job, even though she talked about it a lot. She was successful enough in her self-employment. I just wished she wasn't always around to get in my business and make me watch soap operas.

"By the way, aren't cheerleading tryouts the second month of school? With this new boyfriend, you just might make it."

She wasn't kidding when she asked that question, and I never saw the point of arguing. The only splits I liked were the banana kind. Why would anyone attempt such a feat when it's perfectly comfortable to stand up straight? Regardless, I had tried out every year since the third grade because Vikki J. had given me forty dollars each time. If she had ever realized how uncool it made me to jump around in public with the rhythm and coordination of a cadaver, maybe she would have paid me to *stop* trying. But I could always use the money, and I seemed to lack the gene for caring what other people thought. I couldn't even tell you who was the most popular kid in any of my grades, but I was fairly certain it was never me, boyfriend or not.

Now, memories of Paul, from the eighth to the twelfth grade, were my biggest enemies. Only from the safety of my bed could I stand to think about our past. For example, after we'd been dating for about a month, he told me I was the most beautiful girl in all of Shitville. He repeated it every day from then on, too. I never liked my looks, and he was the first person to make me feel good about them. He had that soft, gentle, protective way about him. Everyone liked Paul — he made people want to smile and cuddle, as if he were a mischievous kitten. But I was just plain old me. I could not consider myself cute in my overalls or baggy cargo pants, the uniform I wore nearly every day. I hated makeup because my mother had always been covered in it.

Sometimes Paul would take off my tortoiseshell glasses and just stare at me. "I love everything about you, Katie," he'd say. "You have inner and outer beauty; you're my hidden diamond. No one has discovered you but me." I acted as if these statements meant nothing, but they made me feel at home with myself. I'd wave him away with my left hand and say,

"Whatever," even though I loved his version of me. I wished I could see myself through his eyes.

When he'd say something romantic, which was pretty much all of the time, I'd get this weird urge to rip my clothes off. By the time we were in the tenth grade, that's exactly what I did, though we never had sex. I was never ready to go there, even though everyone else in my class, except Matt, of course, had. Paul and I got along fine without it . . . or so I thought. He loved me, and I loved him, and just four days ago we were still together. I was happy until he yanked it all away from me on Monday. He had transformed from a warm kitten into a ferocious, rabid tiger; he did this without warning.

So what if we were together almost five years? The breakup was rip-the-Band-Aid-off quick. He told me he was sorry, it was over, and he was with someone else. Our very existence was erased, bombed, excavated. And if breaking up on the phone wasn't cruel and insulting enough, he used the same tone to dump me that he might have used at our favorite Chinese restaurant: "I'm finished with Katie James. Please bring me an order of your latest dish, that Swedish boy climber."

Caught off guard, I said to Paul, "What? Are you serious?"

"Yes, Katie. I'm sorry."

Silence.

"You know how we said this would never happen to us?" he asked me.

"Yes, we promised each other." I was deadpan.

"I guess we didn't know everything."

Silence.

"I wish it didn't have to be like this," he lied.

"It doesn't."

"Katie, it does. It's over."

"How can you be sure? *You love me.*" I was desperate. "You don't mean it. I don't believe it."

"I'm sure. I mean it. Believe me." I heard a female's sinister voice in the background, and I hated her.

"Don't you still love me?"

Paul breathed in sharply, as if I'd finally broken through the deep freeze that had clammed him up. I tingled with hope that maybe I was hallucinating; maybe I had a contact buzz from Vikki J.'s airbrush equipment. Maybe . . .

"How can I answer that question?" he asked.

How could he *not* love me?

"Do you know how stupid you're being? This is mean — and harsh." I willed my voice to stay deadpan — to hide the tidal wave inside.

"It's brutal, but is there any other way to break up?"

"Yeah, in person would've been nice." I'd never heard him speak to me this way. He was colder than sesame noodles. He was bland as chicken broth. His words stung more than hot red peppers. I thought of the Chinese restaurant and how he hadn't tried to rub my knee under the table when we were there last week. He hadn't stopped by my house over the weekend like he usually did. He even forgot to pick me up for school Monday, and I had to wake up Vikki J. to drive me. Breath stopped flowing into my lungs as I realized he . . . truly . . . meant . . . it.

"Okay. Whatever. I won't even miss you," I said. So what if he nearly killed me? I was determined to keep my dignity and act like I didn't care. I nearly broke my finger slamming the phone down on him. Then I bawled and holed up and slept and skipped school and felt sorry for myself and avoided Matt and hung the crucifix and chased away my mother and listened to chanting monks and obsessed about Paul and hated Ho-Hawnnah and stopped eating everything that wasn't high-carb.

By Thursday night, I was tired. My own devastation was wearing me out. In a fit of raging determination, I tore the Muppet Babies off the bed and threw them in the hallway. I cleaned my filthy room. I showered. I took down the religious symbol, and I knew exactly what that meant. I was ready for something — anything — better than torturing myself over Paul, a cruel liar and cheater. For the first time ever, I let Vikki J. be my inspiration. I'd never seen her brood or bawl over anything in her life, not even when Dad died when I was four. She always had a line for any crisis, but her favorite was: "If it don't kill ya, it'll hurt your back." Despite her lunacy, something was working for her. Even if Vikki J. drove me out-of-my-brain bonkers, she was never bitter or unhappy. If she never cried, then I could take a shower.

"Katie James, now that's a whole helluva lot better," she said from the hallway. After I took down the cross, she instantly tore into my room — and into me.

I stared at the pieces of foil attached to her head.

"I'm going lighter, what do you think?"

"That's great, Mom — I mean Vikki J." She hated being called Mom.

"Oh, my hair color is about as important as the father of Avalon's baby." She was dismissing her favorite soap opera, *Babes*, and letting me know that I had priority over her TV show obsession. At that moment, I was grateful for a reminder that she cared about me.

"Hmmm, lighter." If I grabbed my Bible, my mother would run out of the room. I didn't dare; I wanted her to stay.

"You know what I think?"

I reconsidered grabbing the Bible.

"I think you should replace Paul —"

"Don't say his name!" I shouted, actually raising my hands to shelter my ears. "Call him Weedkiller." The P word brought on misery that would lead to crying, and I didn't want to do that anymore, if I could help it.

"I think you should replace *Weedkiller* as soon as possible. There are better, stronger, more attractive Weedkillers out there. Let me give you a makeover, so you can go out there to find a new guy. This new color of mine is going to get me some attention this weekend, just you wait and see."

"No makeovers, no makeovers, no makeovers," I protested. "And Mom, you don't need any more attention — you already have a great boyfriend." She'd been with Bob, a guy ten years younger than her, since I was twelve. After Dad died, she spent one year alone — "down but not broken," as she put it. She bounced back and had several boyfriends all at one time, but she slowed down when she met Bob. If she chose him for good one day, that would be just fine with me. He was my favorite, and he wanted nothing more than to marry her, God help him. My mother refused and said she had her reasons. She didn't fool me, though. Even if she flirted with other men, she loved Bob. I wondered if she ever told him that.

"Listen," she said, "I know you're into whatever you're into, but this is my kind of good book." She handed me a paperback called *The Babes Bible: The Truth Behind the TV Show*. It was the unauthorized story of the stars behind the scenes. It *wasn't* my thing, but Mom was trying, and I certainly didn't have better answers. I looked up, hoped, and tried to keep an open mind.

"Um, thanks. Is this supposed to cheer me up?"

"It'll have you singin' praises. Just wait till you find out who Avalon has slept with in real life. Goddamn! She's nailed every hot actor out there. But that's besides the point. Here's what I'm trying to get to: There is one piece of advice that may get you fixed up right. When Avalon got dumped the dangedest in real life — you know, kind of like you — she got busy. She didn't want to sit around and cry and mope for a week, so she didn't."

I couldn't believe this counted as parental advice. "Busy? You mean she had a lot of sex? Is that what you want me to do? Mom!"

"Who mentioned sex? I thought you had the Lord on your mind, not neckedness. Anyway, this girl decided to go on ten dates in a row if for no other reason than to keep her mind off of her own Weedkiller. I'm telling you, Katie Jay, if you let me give you a makeover and buy you some of them new miniskirts, you'd be a knockout. Not that you ain't already, honey. But you'd have dates linin' up all the way from Shitville to Myrtle Beach. Now, you read this book. I marked some pages you might like best. Thank about it. I've got to get these aluminum antennas out of my head."

Alone and clean with only a bare mattress to cry on, I gave my mother's latest hair-brained scheme some serious thought. I mean, I loved Weedkiller so much that the idea of even kissing another guy turned my intestines into spaghetti. Then it dawned on me: He'd probably been locking lips and other body parts with that boy climber for almost a week . . . or maybe even longer. Meanwhile, what was I doing? I was flopping around on little-girl sheets acting like an overgrown baby. I reached for the remote and turned up the chanting monks to emphasize my ah-ha moment. I knew what I had to do. I had to, as my mother might say, "Get me some." There was no reason for me to be alone while Paul enjoyed PDAs all over Shitville. Why should I live without love and affection and, well, attention? I shouldn't. Besides, prom was coming up in six weeks. Paul and I had planned to go — just to find out what all of the fuss was about. Despite our declared loathing of social activities, I had been secretly excited for it. I sure as hell didn't want to miss it now, and I didn't have to, either.

I knew what I had to do.

Six weeks equaled twelve weekend nights. I decided to go on twelve dates starting the next day, which was Friday. I'd get attention; I'd get action (well, not that much action — but something); and, most important, I'd find a new, better boyfriend in time for prom. Paul was not going to have a good time with his boy climber while I sat at home in mourning, eating French fries. No friggin' way. I was not brought up to be a squished dandelion lost in the mowed grass. I was, like it or not, Vikki Jaymes's daughter, and I vowed that I would be in love again before the dance.

One problem: How would I get that many dates? What if I burst into post-breakup tears on one of them? Going out with new guys sounded hellish, but sitting around feeling sorry for myself sounded worse. I tried to think of it as a challenge to stir up some positive energy. After all, this little project would take my mind off my misery. It would push my limits. I guessed I'd have to go back to school the next day and find a first date if I had any chance of pulling off my plan. God, I needed a miracle — make that plural. Luckily, one of them was waiting for me downstairs tangled up in peroxide and hair dye.

"Mom!!!" I yelled at the highest decibel I could manage. Before I had time to cringe at the thought, I screamed the word she'd been waiting seventeen years to hear: "Makeover!"

The big debut

"For goodness sakes, what in the world has happened to you?"

I was tired and self-conscious after four days of hell topped off by a late night of horror as my mom tweezed, bleached, zipped, painted, pinched, curled, squeezed, buttoned, and did other unpleasant things to my skin, hair, and clothes. For all her attention, there was one thing she neglected to teach me — how to get into a car with a tight skirt on. My blue-jean mini, one of my mother's favorites, kept riding up to show my flowered granny panties as I tried to sit down in Matt's hand-me-down car, Winifred.

"Just drive, okay?"

I'd called him at two-thirty in the morning to be all sweet and ask him to pick me up Friday for school. Even in his slumbering stupor, Matt managed to sound excited about it. He'd been trying to get me to ride with him since his mom had given him her 1994 Camry six months ago. Of course, I'd already had a regular ride with Paul, so at the time, I'd had to turn him down, in the same way I'd turned down his invitations to private pizza parties and study sessions. Really, as unavailable and pre-occupied as I had been for the past four and a half years, it was a wonder he was still such a good friend to me.

"Um, all right, I, well. Oh, for goodness sakes, hi, Katie. What's up?"

The orthopedic shoes had demolished Matt's reputation. His mother made him wear them again freshman year, and they hadn't been a big hit with the ladies or anyone else. Sometimes I overheard people making fun of him, calling him Forrest and Super Feet. I would get upset when they said those things, wishing I was the sort of girl who could go around tying testicles in bows. One of the reasons I never cared about trying to fit in with other kids was because most of them were shallower than mud puddles. They were so concerned with who they were seen with (everyone wants to sit with Cherry), where they shopped, and what brand of cell phone they carried. Being cool trumped being nice. There was a famous story in our school about this guy named Jack, supposedly some cool hot boy who was so caught up in being popular that he boffed a gorgeous girl, then cheated on her with her best friend. I've always been glad that the best friends got together and embarrassed the pants off of him. But the truth is, most kids don't get paybacks. They just go on about their business being snippy, snotty, and mean to great guys like Matt. I hoped people would just get over his geekiness. He desperately wanted them to.

I'd liked Matt's leg braces — he wore those when we were really little, and they made climbing trees easier. We'd take them off his knees and calves and use them as ladders to help us conquer the base and make our way up to the branches. If you asked me, he never really needed them that badly. I mean, who cares if a guy is a little pigeon-toed? I didn't. Matt did because he wanted to be cool and not dorky. I totally blame his mom for that. She was always on him about his manners, speech, and posture, and he became painfully, brutally self-conscious. Mrs. Faulkner wanted him to be a killer criminal lawyer, corporate CEO, or, at the very least, an investigative reporter. She hoped he would stand tall and confident and foreboding in high school, at a good college, and, most important, in his future career. I had no doubt that Matt would be successful one day, but probably not as a lawyer. He was great at being nice to people, especially me, and at playing the flute. He was the kind of sensitive, sweet, straight (I swear to God) guy who'd make a brilliant househusband or kindergarten teacher or pet-shop keeper.

The swim team was Matt's orthopedist's idea. He couldn't run track or play tennis, so swimming seemed like the logical athletic endeavor. As much to Matt's surprise as to everyone else's, he was good at it. Breaststroke, freestyle, relays — they were easier than climbing trees. I knew the truth, though. Matt was never really happy in the water. He would've been better off spending the last three years playing the flute in the Shitville band, but he didn't dare. If he had one shining fault that drove me up a wailing wall, it was his obsession with popularity. If a genie were ever to land on his perfectly developed swimming shoulders, he'd ask for three things: 1) To be crowned Prom King, 2) To win a state title in swimming — but only so our classmates would think he was cool and look up to him, 3) To sleep with the hottest girl at school. Matt was not the kind of guy who would ever admit to the latter, but I knew him well, and I knew he had big dreams now that he didn't think girls had cooties anymore.

"I'll tell you exactly what's up since you won't stop staring," I said to him now. "Vikki J. got a hold of me."

"She sure did something to you. You weren't handling this breakup in a healthy way, you know. I certainly couldn't convince you to get out of bed. I'm glad she did."

"You talk like a girl."

"I don't feel like one."

"Well, I do. Look at me!"

"I did — I couldn't help it." He concentrated on the street ahead, consciously not letting his eyes wander to the passenger's side of Winifred.

"I look like I belong in a music video!"

"Oh, stop it, Katie. No, you don't. You are beautiful." The compliment sounded even weirder when it came from Matt. He didn't flinch when he made the statement — though he said it to the road.

"Well, I refused to wear the red see-through tank top she had me in this morning. But God, a French manicure? And have you ever seen my hair so straight? This is what high-maintenance girls call a blowout. And check out my eyebrows. I have two!"

"Really, Katie, I'm driving," he said. "Goodness. What are you worried about? You've always been pretty. Now you're just prettier."

Why'd he have to go and make me feel funny again? I wasn't used to being self-conscious, and I enjoyed it about as much as I would've liked streaking down a crowded hallway. I took pride in staying out of the way, and threw as much effort into remaining anonymous as others put into their looks. Matt's reaction put me on high alert. I opened and closed the latch on the dashboard, soaking up anxiety any way I could. I mean, for

God's sake, my boobs crested at the V of my T-shirt. My butt had been poured into Vikki J.'s mini. I even dared to wear dangerous girlie sandals instead of Nikes. And by the look of my face, makeup had performed miracles. It seamlessly masked four days of suffering.

My breath was harder to find, and my heart puttered around in my chest like Winifred when she wasn't sure about starting.

"I need a drink," I said. "Matt, maybe you should turn this car around!" Why was I torturing myself when I could've been tucked safely away in the madhouse on Main Street? What possessed me to take cues from the real life of a soap opera star?

"Oh, stop it. Get a hold of yourself." Matt was right. I was freaking like a little kid who just saw a spider. "Everything will be okay. Now, what are you going to do if you run into Paul today?"

Oh, great, I thought. Matt had gone straight to Number One on my panic list. In addition to putting on a show for my classmates, I'd get to run into the guy who'd grilled my heart for lunch. For the first time in my life, I had chosen not to fade into the beige desks and booger-green floor. I'd stick out, making it impossible to fall asleep in glorious privacy like I usually did during class. I wondered what I had done to myself, and why why why had I done it? I didn't want guys at school to size me up. I didn't want girls to notice my manicure. I was never about those things. Now I was putting myself on the line and giving my ex easy aim.

Did I want him to see me? Yes. No. Yes. NO! Crap.

"Call him Weedkiller, for God's sake! From now on, we refer to my ex as Weedkiller." My panic was interrupted by my feet, which were cramping into tight charley horses. Not only

21

did the sandals have a little heel, I'd been tapping my toes so quickly that the muscles were hot and burning. "I'll avoid him at all costs; I cannot stand to see him today."

"Good. And Weedkiller he shall be," Matt said sympathetically. "But the question is, are you really okay?"

"Yeah. I will be. Thanks," I said. "Really, thanks."

Go to school, get through the day, I repeated to myself, mantra-like. So what if kids whispered and speculated? I would probably not die if they gossiped about what had happened to me. I never sought their approval or anything, anyway. I had chosen to take a risk. If necessary, I could always slip back into a pair of worn-perfect overalls. I breathed deeply, which felt good.

"Matt, stay close to me today." I couldn't do it without him.

"No problem."

"Will you walk past my locker in between classes to check on me?"

"Of course."

I closed my eyes when I made my big debut. I imagined I was someone else — a rock star entitled to all-you-can-eat crab legs — and took off down the hall. My only problem? Standing up straight. Strappy sandals with one-inch heels just didn't glide like Nikes. In nice shoes, I embodied a gorilla in a tutu instead of a man-killing Lolita. I pep-talked myself with my mission: *Six weeks, twelve dates, fall in love before prom*. I made my way past the lockers, eyes squinted in concentration, and pretended to be the lead ballerina. I could compete with the Cherries of the world — I knew it. Well, maybe. Just when I thought I'd made it to homeroom intact, I thwacked my sandal into an open door. I hopped around on my right foot, holding my left big toe in my hand. The heel turned on me, and I wound up on the floor. God, I would have been a disaster in toe shoes.

"You okay?" a guy said to me, leaning over to grab my elbow and help me stand back up.

"Huh? I'm fine." I wasn't used to anyone new or unknown speaking to me. We made eye contact, and he stared at me. Well, that was normal because of my Barney eyeballs. Then his eyes lingered long enough to make me really uncomfortable and really aware that I had become someone different.

"You sure? Let me help you, sweetie."

Sweetie? Only Santa Clauses and my crazy mother had ever called me that. Wait. He was cute, too. I gave him the coy penetrating eye glance I'd seen other girls give so many times. It didn't feel as unnatural as I had expected it to.

"What's your name?"

"Katie James."

He seemed to write it down in his memory before we walked away from each other. We glanced back at each other — embarrassed at getting caught — from opposite ends of the hallway.

I tried to propel myself through the rest of the day. I heard guys asking who I was, and girls would roll their eyes and say, "That's just Katie Somebody. You know, Paul Green's ex-girlfriend." Then they'd change the subject and flash the boys their coy penetrating eye glances.

Paul's ex-girlfriend!

Paul's ex-girlfriend!!

Paul's ex-girlfriend!!!

The desert would make a great ice-cream parlor before I would cry in public over the guy who dumped me for a younger blond. That doesn't mean I wasn't melting inside. Me? His ex? That could not be true except that it was.

Every time I heard the words, they ripped through my heart, and the breakup played in my brain again. I hoped that hollow space would fill with something better. I was thankful for my pride; it kept me from getting emotional on the outside. I forced myself to dwell on the positive: I had successfully avoided him, which was pretty easy since I knew his schedule. I didn't want him to catch a glimpse of me until I had perfected myself. After all, I needed more practice to keep from tripping down hallways. Plus, I hoped he'd hear about the new me. That would put him on edge, a place he definitely deserved to be.

"Katie James, is that you?" someone asked in the crowded hallway while I was rushing to science class. I was watching my feet, and had no idea where voices were coming from. I didn't care, either; chatting was not my forte — being invisible was. Luckily, my high school was so huge that it hadn't been terribly difficult to blend in.

"Katie, over here."

"Yeah?" I replied. The girl had home-dyed hair and wore combat boots with her dress.

"I just wanted to tell you how great you look," she said, reaching for my wrist in that warm girlie way. Only she wasn't being plastic. No one besides Paul had ever grabbed me at school, so the touchy-feely stuff from strangers — her and the guy before homeroom — was freaking me out.

"I'm sorry, I didn't mean to offend you. You were pretty before and all," she said, blushing.

"Oh, well, thanks." What was I supposed to say to that? I racked my brain for something intelligent.

Of course, she followed up with the four words I least wanted her to say: "Don't you remember me?"

"Well, um." She was in one of my classes, but I didn't even know which one.

"I'm Frankie. We worked on a science project together in the seventh grade. You know, right before you started dating Paul."

That was weird. I could kind of see the resemblance. But the girl I remembered transferred to another school a long time ago. Plus, those freckles must've been new. I recalled that she was a back-of-the-room loner like me, and she was good at science. Thanks to her, we got a B on that project instead of a C.

"Oh, right. That's so cool." I sounded completely dense. "Didn't you move?"

"Now I'm back. Started here at the beginning of the year. I've seen you around but was afraid to say anything. We have history together this semester."

"Right, right." I had seen her, but I guess I'd forgotten. I was being a moron.

She made small talk and asked for my e-mail address before we rushed away in opposite directions to make our classes. My brain repeated the conversation, and I hoped I hadn't been severely rude. Had I said anything silly or dumb? The encounter, like the whole day, made me wobble. I was an outsider before, but at least I knew myself then.

"Goodness gracious, Katie, you've got to tell me what the heck is going on," Matt said as he walked up to my locker before lunch. "Tell me, tell me, tell me."

I had stood there wide-eyed with cuticles in my mouth waiting for him to come by and get me. All through high school,

Matt and I had maintained permanent seating arrangements at Paul and Company's lunch table. Now we were on our own, and I was a chicken on her way to get defeathered. I grabbed Matt's arm the way people had been grabbing on to me. He had on a red-and-yellow Hawaiian button-down. He'd seen it in a popular TV show and thought it was cool. He didn't understand that Shitvillers made fun of him. He was just ahead of the curve, if anyone had asked me.

He took off like he knew what he was doing, pushing his thick glasses up his nose. He strutted to the swim team table and plopped down like nothing unusual had just happened. His team members scooted down to make room, and they flashed smiles that looked forced. I detected their hesitation when they said "Dude" and "Whatsup?" to Matt. Their just-being-polite vibe gave me another reason to feel weird. I put my hand over the V in my T-shirt. The big toe on my left foot swelled and throbbed.

"Check out that chick," I heard in hushed voices farther down the table. Guys were slapping each other's shoulders while they talked about me. "Dude, she's hot." I looked them dead in their eyes, and the blood in my toe mercifully rushed back into the rest of my body. Their attention overwhelmed and, I admit it, delighted me. Self-consciousness began to drain out for the first time that day. I took my hand away from the V.

"Katie, um, well, I don't know how to say this but," Matt whispered in my ear, "something is going on that you haven't told me about." I couldn't hold it in another second. I spilled everything from the avocado green Kermit to the *Babes Bible* to meeting people in the hallway to what I was feeling right that very second. Matt's mouth hung open as he bent down underneath the table to rub my big toe, ignoring his salami-and-Muenster sandwich.

"Did someone trip you, Katie? Tell me the truth? Because I hate it when they do that to me." The swim team guys chuckled suspiciously, and we ignored them. I may have momentarily lapsed into liking their attention — but that didn't mean I liked *them*.

In another attempt to give myself a pep talk, I reminded Matt that people only picked on the old me. Kids pulled pranks on the former incarnation of Katie James because I'd never tell or make a fuss. But I no longer wanted to remain anonymous, invisible. The only person doing the tripping was going to be me — I couldn't believe my plan myself.

"But I do have one problem," I confided. "I can't start my mission tonight because I don't have a date. Do you think you can bribe someone into asking me out? I have some money I saved from cheerleading tryouts — forty bucks."

"Stop it right now. No one is taking you out," he said, moving in closer to me as if he were proud of something.

"Well, why not?"

His cheeks were cute, lobster red.

"Because I am."

Amaretto ate my brain

Still Friday, April 4

"You shoulda seen that Avalon today, Katie. It's like she's in heat, just a-jumpin' on this one and that one. None of the guys even know they're being played like banjos," my mother said when I walked through the door.

"Great, Vikki J." I was beat; it had been a long day. My brain was turned off, or I wouldn't have said, "I have to take a nap before my date tonight."

She jolted all one-hundred-and-ten pounds of herself right up off the couch, made a big display of turning the TV off, and became a pogo stick in front of my face. Avalon was history; she wanted the scoop from me. The day had earned me more attention than I'd had in the last five years combined. I didn't know if I was thrilled or mortified by this.

"Oh, my God. I can't deal."

"Now you listen here, Kay-Jay — and don't go tellin' me you got to go upstairs and hang yer crucifix and beads and Lord knows what else." She paused to add more drama to her voice.

"I stayed up *half the night* workin' on you, so you owe me some *juicy details.*"

"Okay, okay. You win." My butt was drawn to the couch like a guy to a centerfold. The miniskirt wasn't cooperating, and my granny panties were in full view. I didn't have the energy to care.

"Well, tell me!"

"I think I was a hit today," I said cautiously. "But I can't tell for sure if everyone was shocked and appalled and making fun of me, or if they really thought I was the hot new girl at school. But Mom — I mean, Vikki J. — if I had to guess right now, I'd say they were into me. Especially the guys."

"I knew it! My baby is the bee's knees!" She danced around, shaking her skinny rump. "Wait till I tell Bob. Oh, I knew that a little cut, dye, and pluck would do wonders. Not to mention that great miniskirt you've got on. Now, Katie, you didn't sit like that all day, didja? I didn't raise no goddamned floozy." The dancing stopped.

"I was a little lady, don't you worry." Sometimes it was just easier to speak her language.

"Oh, good, I knew it. Did you see Paul — I mean, Weedkiller? And tell me about yer doggone date. Hot damn!"

"I did not want to see Weedkiller because then I would've lost it right in public."

"You *are* a smart gal," she said wisely, calmly.

"So I went the long way to classes to avoid him. Once, I even had to hide in the restroom because I knew he'd be walking by."

"He's bound to hear all about my hot little ticket, anyway. That's even better."

"Exactly," I said. Then I continued, "So some guys at school were saying I looked nice and stuff in the hallways, during classes and even at lunch." I wasn't worried about bragging to my mother — she expected nothing less. "But I didn't have the nerve to talk to them."

"Oh, well — you and me were so busy last night, I didn't get around to giving you the flirtin' tips."

"Yeah, well, so I asked Matt to set me up with one of his friends and, well, he wanted to take me out himself."

Silence.

"Well, what's the matter?" I asked.

She slumped back into her seat and clicked on the TV. "That ain't a good idea."

"Oh, it's nothing."

"It may be nothing to you, but I bet it's more than that to Matt." She turned up the volume, acting all irritated.

"Stop it, *Mother*." She hated when I used that matronly, maternal term.

"Dang it. I know I'm right. You do what you want with other boys, just don't go breakin' that one's heart."

"I have to go read my prayer book."

She relented, probably seeing that I was in no mood to lose any battle. Besides, my mother was occupied. She had to cook a romantic dinner for Bob, and I hoped that would keep her noise level down for the next few hours so I could nap. He loved her fried chicken and squished potatoes, and she loved getting compliments for her efforts. (I just hoped she wouldn't chip a nail peeling vegetables, because that put her in a feisty mood.) She only fussed with chicken when she was in the doghouse. For the last year straight, Bob had been asking Vikki J. to marry him once a week. She was always concocting ways to ease the blow each time she turned him down.

I wasn't nervous for my date because it was just a trial run, like eating Cheez Whiz before moving on to Monterey. I mean, I could say "Der" to Matt and it would have a secret meaning. (It's our Barbie Alert. I use it when the boy climbers are taking over our haunts, something Matt doesn't really mind.) I could show up with the largest pimple in Shitville history, and he wouldn't stare at it. Still, Vikki J.'s words haunted me. The whole breaking-hearts thing was way off base. We were too close for anything like that to happen. Besides — me breaking hearts? Please. I only knew how to get mine broken.

After some rest, I decided to raid Vikki J.'s closet. We were the same size, which was lucky for me, because I hated to shop. I never wanted to throw myself to the lionesses — i.e., expose my body in dressing rooms surrounded by perky, chic saleswomen. I favored overalls that never needed to be tried on. Skirts and formfitting blouses looked more flattering, sure, but sexier clothes had potential to cause me all kinds of troubles. I found a black-and-white skirt that went down to my knees, which made me feel less rock star and more girl-next-door (or four doors down, to be precise). I grabbed a white tank and a pair of black flip-flops with white fake flowers perched on the toes. I looked more tasteful than I had earlier in the day. I wouldn't have pictured myself in either outfit a week ago, but this was the new Katie, and I had to make sacrifices.

I showered and slathered on lotion that smelled like gardenias — the one I'd saved for special, private nights with Paul. The strange thing was, I felt *guilty* using it now. Even though he was the one who had ripped us apart, I still felt like I was betraying him. I was moving on — or whatever you wanted to call it. But I could still hear and feel him whisper compliments into my ear. As I put on the lotion, I could hear his playful voice purring, saying that he loved me. I got teary thinking about the upcoming evening with Matt. It's not that it was anything special. It was just different. I quickly wiped my eyes and smiled into the mirror. I didn't want to cry. Instead, I vowed to smell my very best. I wanted to look my best, too. Who better to practice in front of than my best friend, someone who'd cared about me even before I started wearing deodorant?

"Vikki J., you've got to get that chicken batter off your hands and do my weary eyes," I said, standing in the kitchen in her outfit, smelling of makeout perfume. She oooed and ahhhed at me and said it was about time we started sharing clothes like Avalon and her mother did on *Babes*. She apologized profusely for being nail-deep in fried chicken, and explained that she couldn't help me because she was two hours behind and Bob was going to be there in one. She was always late, which didn't usually stress her out. Ladies at her salon waited for hours for Vikki J. without complaining — that's probably because she gave them beer and wine, not to mention decent haircuts. Anyway, she was hedging on my makeup just because she didn't approve of my "date" with Matt. She pointed me downstairs to the two-room beauty parlor to do it myself. I didn't grumble — if I could pick out my own skirt and flip-flops, I could manhandle a makeup brush.

I examined her eyelash curler, shadow, blush, foundation, powders, fifty shades of lipstick, and other products that made no sense. I took some brown blush and swiped it over my eyes and cheeks. That was a low-key way to look good, and it suited me well. I found some brownish-pink lip gloss and glazed it on, forcing away sad thoughts about how many times my naked lips had touched Paul's. I wasn't sure I was ready to kiss someone else, even though I was determined to. My eyes watered up, and I examined them in the mirror. They were sleepy, sexy. They sparkled in a way they hadn't for such a long time. My zest for life had drained away when I was twelve and became too cool to climb trees. But it was coming back, and I was almost proud of my violet eyes. I didn't dare brush my curly hair for fear of turning into a Chia Pet. Instead, I applied mousse — it smelled like pineapples — which clashed with the gardenias. Then I threw my head upside down like the girl who orgasms on TV during shampoo commercials. Head back up, I pretended to be so beautiful that I couldn't take my eyes off my bad self. I didn't buy it, but imagining made me feel better.

I *liked* me. I hadn't felt that way since I dressed up like Ivy League Barbie for Halloween in the fifth grade. That day, my mother worked on me for hours and even bought me a brassy blond wig that went down to my butt in beautiful, dramatic waves. I was the princess of the neighborhood and filled my plastic pumpkin with the most chocolate-free goodies of my trick-or-treating career. I was mad when Vikki J. took half the FireBalls, but I kept quiet because she had relented and not worn her matching brassy blond wig. I hadn't wanted her to show me up that night.

Primping wore me out, so I went upstairs to dunk my fingers into Vikki J.'s squished potatoes — that's what she called them — before Matt picked me up in fifteen minutes.

"That's the batch the dawg ate out of." She hated when I sampled the food.

"We don't have a dog. Just me. Woof."

"Oh my, Katie, you look absolutely . . . wow," Bob said, drinking from the bottle of red wine he had brought while my mother sipped Miller Genuine Draft. Bob called himself a carpenter, but his projects appeared to be straight out of art books and not from the back of his company van. He carved beautiful moldings and created sundecks, mostly for rich people, though he fixed up our two-bedroom for free. His rec rooms were far too beautiful for drinking discount beer and watching trash TV. At least all of his hard labor had paid off: He wore the best clothes you could find in Shitville and owned a Corvette despite his preference for the Econoline. He took my mother to steak houses and Thai restaurants in futile attempts to get her hooked on something besides Happy Meals. If I didn't have a dad, Bob was fine with me. His compliment made me blush.

I waited outside for Matt — my cuticles sufficed as teething rings to make minutes move faster. This was not a date, I repeated in my head. So why did our plans make me nervous? We'd gone for pizza a million times. Actually, that's not true — we usually ordered in. Anyway, we'd spent so many Fridays together. Wait, not really — I had long-standing date night with Paul on those evenings. Matt and I talked and hung out as much as we could, but we didn't really go anywhere. I took a deep breath and decided that the makeup was feeding on my brain cells. After all, this was *not* a date.

So why did he get out of Winifred to open the door for me? He'd never done that before, had he? He even had a small bouquet of carnations dyed blue and purple and pink — my favorites. It was sweet but freaked me out. He scared me when he drove to Big John's Pizza because his eyes were always on me instead of the road. I sighed and went back to the cuticles. My new outfits were making the whole world act weird.

"Katie, for goodness sakes," Matt finally said. "You look like you've just seen a mouse." I'm scared of rodents; Matt is, too. When one got into the living room through the front door last year, both of us stood on the couch and screamed. Vikki J. and Bob rescued us, dangled the animal by the tail way too close to our faces, and released it back into the wild.

"Sorry."

"Listen, this is your first date after Weedkiller," Matt said. "It's going to be special. Don't think it's some big deal or anything; it's not. I just want to show you how you're supposed to be treated. I want you to know what it's like to be with one of the good guys tonight."

I had been *with one of the good ones . . . till he fled for the overseas boy climber,* I thought. The first three years with Paul were great — until he started caring more about soccer than food, homework, his friends, and me. I mean, Paul was fine. He remembered birthdays, put up with Vikki J., and watched chick movies. He just turned evil recently for no good reason.

Still, I felt I was the only one who was allowed to put him down. After all, Paul was good enough to put up with boring, overalls-obsessed Katie for almost five years. It was much more complicated than Matt was making it sound.

I flipped the bouquet over in my hands. "But Matt, the flowers? You didn't have to do all of that."

"I wanted to. You deserve it."

Vikki J.'s warnings were on repeat in my brain. I turned up Winifred's scratchy, factory-installed stereo to drown out my mind and lift the heavy awkwardness in the car. I didn't want to feel uncomfortable around Matt. I never had before. Not even when I'd asked him to kiss me in the seventh grade. He'd said no, I'd said cool, and we'd gone swimming.

Matt wasn't going to let the stereo stop him. "Katie," he said. "I don't think you've ever realized that you are the most beautiful girl at school. You are fun, smart, unique, and amazing."

Ugh. Why did he have to say these things? He was earnest, and I wanted to pop him.

He continued, "If I can't get you to believe that tonight, then this whole plan of yours doesn't have a chance. You'll just end up with more Weedkillers."

"Stop. Hush. I mean it."

Beautiful? Me? Whatever. But was I?

"Wait," I said. "Tell me again."

"You are fun, smart, unique, and amazing."

"So are you," I said.

Dressed like I was, I didn't have to be a piece of clear plastic wrap anymore. Instead, I was shiny and interesting, more like a ball of aluminum foil. Matt had always appreciated me, of course, but not on this level. Thanks to him, I was slightly less self-conscious. Besides, the different, new vibe that bounced between us was electric. I could get used to it.

Matt touched my back when we walked into the pizza joint, which was crowded with Shitvillers. Cherry was in one corner holding hands with a guy, moving her body closer to him with each passing second. There were a lot of faces I kind of recognized — a few of the cheerleaders who I'd tried out with, some of Paul's friends (not Paul, thank you, Jesus), a few members of the swim team. For the first time, I wondered who they were and what their stories might be. I'd never bothered to know anything other than their first names. Maybe they felt broken-hearted, even invisible sometimes, too. Through his thick glasses, Matt looked into my eyes and studied them as he pulled me close. He had underappreciated muscular wide shoulders that tapered down into a slim little waist. His body was as firm as Avalon's ex-husband's on *Babes*. He smelled like chlorine and Speed Stick. I always heard Vikki J. call men "fine" with a long emphasis on the "i." Matt was approaching the category, and I couldn't believe I was thinking that. Why couldn't other people see past his limp and genuine sweetness and forgive him for being a geek? What did *geek* mean, anyway?

"Stop it, stop it, stop it!" I warned myself out loud.

"What? I love to hug you."

"No, not that — just talking to myself," I said.

Over mozzarella sticks, we joked about our past filled with Barbies and leg braces and crazy mothers. I loved Matt; I loved Matt; I loved him. But did I love him *that* way? Did he love me *that* way?

Nah, he was just acting cuddly in public to up his cool status at school, a cause I could tolerate if it made him happy. I mean, he wanted to be seen with a chick, any chick, not necessarily me. His last girlfriend, a pimply-faced, giggly band member named Juliana, had dumped him very publicly. Though she was hardly a popularity magnet, Matt cared about her. At the lunch table, she told him she was seeing a tuba player, right before Matt could eat his Twinkie. He was so upset that he got up and left the treat unwrapped and untouched. He limped out of the cafeteria while the jocks laughed at him.

So if I could help him out — well, I considered it my duty. I just didn't want to get hurt in the process. I even held his hand

and touched his face whenever I could tell people were watching us. When he beamed, his glasses slid farther down his nose.

I went up to the counter to order more banana peppers and some pepperoni. The accidental soft brush against my right boob shocked me.

"Excuse me, I just want the parmesan. Really, sorry." It was the guy who'd helped me to my feet after I had crashed in the hallway before homeroom. "So, sweetie, how's the big toe?"

"Oh, um, hi. Fine," I said, head down, heart beating, blushing and embarrassed because my nipples were suddenly poking through my shirt.

"I don't know you very well, Katie, so this is kind of awkward," he said.

"You don't know me at all," I pointed out, walking away with my head down, pepper plate hiding one breast and pepperoni bowl over the other.

"But wait, can I get your phone number? If you're not busy tomorrow night, I can get you in to the Little Mr. Shitville contest."

"The what?"

"It's this thing where elementary schoolboys have a weight-lifting competition. You know, like Mr. Universe or something. It's really cute, not beefy at all. I'm their instructor at the YMCA. You know, studies show that playing sports builds self-esteem and confidence, so we like to start our kids at an early age."

I remembered my mission — to fall in love before prom — and I answered: "Um, sure, I'll go." I smiled and tried to remember what he'd just said. I made the decision to look pleasant and stay silent for fear of uttering phrases that made absolutely no sense. I asked the cashier for a pen, wrote my number on a napkin, and hoped Matt hadn't seen a thing. I wasn't improving his slick-with-the-women reputation if I was flirting with other guys. I wasn't going to make Matt fall for me, either. Wait, I wasn't trying to do that! Why was this whole episode making me feel odd and guilty, too? We were not on that kind of date.

"What was that all about?"

I couldn't bear to lie to Matt, nor could I look him in the eyes.

"That guy just asked me out for tomorrow night," I told him, trying to make things sound one-hundred-percent ordinary.

"That was Kevin Ebernackey. Sheesh." He rushed to the restroom. I got all antsy. Was Matt jealous? Mad? Was Kevin the guy on student council? My cuticles were already too sore, so I chewed on my food. While eating, I let Cherry and her prey entertain me. They'd been making out for five minutes. Everyone in the pizza joint watched them except Kevin, who had left. I couldn't take my eyes off them — Paul and I never did stuff like that in public. Was it pervy to get totally turned on by their mini porn show? Despite myself, I did.

"Come on," Matt said. I didn't even know he was back until he was guiding me up out of my chair. At least he didn't seem irritated anymore, just hurried. He held my hand and took me to the car. Once there, he pulled out a little bottle of Amaretto he'd stolen from his parents' liquor cabinet. I knew he'd drunk with Juliana once or twice, but he'd never had any alcohol with me.

"Just a swig," he suggested, driving toward the romantic riverfront. Going to the makeout spot with Matt was weirder than the silence that hung in the air between us.

"Okay," I said to the Amaretto. My head and heart hurt, and

I was tired of thinking. A sip of something was a simply brilliant idea. So what if I'd never drunk anything stronger than Yoo-hoo? I was a new woman.

Two hours and a gulp or two — hell, I lost count — later, he stroked my head. Which was in his lap.

"You know what my biggest regret is ever?" Matt asked.

"What?"

"That I didn't kiss you when you asked me to."

I had been terrified that he might say something warm and fuzzy. We were not on that kind of date, so I wasn't comfortable with how romantic it all felt. Yet I craved his sweet words even more than I craved the last few sips left in the bottle. I looked up at him, half freaking, half wanting.

"Oh, that. I just wanted to know what it felt like."

"Me, too." He planted a big one on me with stealth speed. I had no time to consider objecting, though I'm not sure if I would have. My insides tingled, so I guessed that meant he was a Casanova kisser. He stopped to take off his glasses and resumed. His lips were soft and gentle as they opened and closed on cue with mine. His tongue gently teased me in welcome ways. Paul had always kissed me hard, but I'd thought that's what it was supposed to be like. Matt's kisses were soft and thoughtful . . . like him.

Dread, lust, and warmth formed a dangerous cocktail inside of me. I didn't understand what I was feeling for him. I kissed him for at least an hour because, after all, there was no other way to figure it out. I did know one thing: Being this close to someone besides Paul felt so great that I just couldn't get enough of it. When Matt finally stopped, I forced myself to lift

40

up, and he held my hand. I was hot inside and — ohmygod — woozy, too.

"Oh, man, that was awesome."

"Umpth. Yes. Why'd you stopth?"

"I have to go. My mom will kill me if I'm not home by curfew."

What senior guy has to be home at 11:30 p.m.? Matt's problem with social climbing definitely had a lot to do with his backward parents.

"Can you drithe okay?"

"Yes, I'm fine. *You* drank all of the Amaretto. I hardly got a drop, for goodness sakes."

"What just hapthened, Matt?"

"I don't know. Goodness, that's a good question. Maybe after all this time, we just had to see what we've been missing."

Before I could analyze his comment, we were in my driveway, and he kissed me again despite my tangy post-liquor breath. He rubbed my back so hard and even let his hands brush over my butt. I kept my arms around his neck, afraid to let go. I was thankful I had chosen the flip-flops over the heels when I tried to walk a straight line into my house. Bob's Econoline was still in the driveway, so I thought Vikki J. would be occupied. I had no such luck; she was standing by the door with a front-row view of the whole steamy scene. She had turned her TV off — a sure sign that I was providing far more titillating entertainment.

"You've had a nip, gal. Jumpin' Jehoshaphat, I didn't raise no goddamned drunk."

"Oh, Mothver, it was nothing. Just a few ships of Amaretto. I'm almost butter now."

"I can sure as hell tell."

I peered up at her to flash pleading, puppy dog eyes.

"You shouldn't be tipsy much longer, darlin'. Looked like Matt was busy sucking all of the liquor right outta yer face."

"Oh, my Dog," I said as I lifted my heavy body up the stairs. I lay down to watch the world spin and wondered what — besides the spirits — had gotten into me.

As the world spins counterclockwise

Saturday, April 5

"Hi, is Katie James there?"

I was half disappointed that it wasn't Matt on the phone the next morning, but also partly relieved. Anyway, whoever was calling, I didn't want any part of him. I considered telling whoever it was that Katie James had died in a freak accident involving tongues and too much Amaretto. But that would've made me weird.

"This is she," I said.

"Hey, this is Kevin Ebernackey, the guy from the pizza place last night. How is your toe? It usually takes two to three days for minor injuries like that one to heal."

He'd already asked me about my feet at least twice. Annoying. But then again, I could've been looking for any excuse not to like him. After all, I loved Matt, at least kinda sorta and especially when I was drunk. And I loved Paul, too — the ding-dong freshman-loving lying-piece-of-stinking-cheese jerk. What was this guy's name again?

"Are you there?" he asked. "You know, this is Kevin from the hallway."

"I'm here." I rubbed my temples and noticed that my hair was sticky and smelled like sugar.

"Still want to go to Little Mr. Shitville, sweetie? I'm getting an award."

"Oh, really?"

"Totally. I'll pick you up at six if that sounds good to you."

Prom. Six weeks. Get over Paul. Date. Fall in love. "Okay," I answered.

"Cool, man. I'll see you then!"

"Wait — "

"Yeah."

"Aren't you the guy who's on student council?"

"Um, yeah. Actually, I'm class president this year. Did you vote for me?"

"I honestly don't remember. I'm sure I did, though. See you soon." My life was bizarre and every scene in it was becoming more awkward.

Plus, Matt's lips were still warm on my mouth, and there I was saying yes to a date with a guy who liked to watch little boys lift phallic objects. *That was a mean thought*, I decided. Kevin seemed nice enough, but my date with him still made no sense. What was I doing? I reminded myself that I had made a pact. No matter who came along or what I did, I had to move forward. It would be difficult, but I would have to date boys, many boys — one boy each weekend evening for six weeks straight. I had it rough. Really, I did. My post-alcohol state made my thoughts choppy, incoherent. So I decided to think about Matt later.

After all, I had a brain-rattling hangover, a dangerous best-friend liaison, a date with a class-president weight lifter, a mother who'd watched me make out drunk in the driveway, and, to top off my stressful Saturday morning, I also had an unexpected e-mail. This was sensory overload. It was like seeing too many abstract paintings on a museum wall all at once. I simply couldn't process.

But I couldn't ignore the e-mail, either:

Hey Katie, this is Frankie from school. Are you busy this afternoon? I need some company at Ear Bangers, you know, the CD store. Peace, Frankie.

I didn't want to be free to hang out, but I was. I could either spend the afternoon on trial by my mother or go pick out some music . . . which would potentially make me miss Matt's phone call. I decided it would be best to avoid all people with Main Street addresses. I was one-hundred-percent sure that he'd say last night was a mistake. I mean, Matt was very sensible. He was the one who'd talked to Vikki J. about the importance of taking vitamins when we were in the second grade, and I'd been on Flintstones ever since. Oh, God, he was my best friend! I couldn't decipher if I was having feelings or a freak-out.

I preferred to browse CDs by myself, but that was difficult since I didn't have a car. Calling Matt was unwise, and Vikki J. would want to go with me if I asked to borrow hers. My choice was made — I would go with this girl Frankie even though I had reservations. First off, why was she e-mailing me, anyway? The truth was, I gave up on making friends with females when I was seven. In the first grade, I was traumatized when a group of them refused to let Matt play hopscotch during recess. He and I had to play in the dark, shady corner of the blacktop because the sunny spots were all taken by the giggling rosy-cheekers. As a last-ditch effort, I asked a few of them to climb trees with Matt and me — we even told them they could use his leg braces. The prissy little things laughed not-so-politely, rolled their eyes, and told me no. After that, they never asked me to be in their sticker clubs, and I gave up for good. I pretended not to care, but it still hurt when birthday party invitations would get "secretly" handed out at lunch — skipping me.

My mother forever wanted me to be popular, but not because she was more socially obsessed than anyone else. It was because she hated being a childhood nobody and had higher hopes for me. She always said, "Blonds have fun. But screw 'em. Popular people have even more." At least she understood how I felt when they dissed me. In the second grade, I cried when I didn't get invited to a classmate's Barbie-themed birthday at McDonald's. My mother conspired with Matt's to make me feel better. We were up in Matt's backyard maple tree when Vikki J. brought two kids' meals and used a broom handle to deliver them up into the branches. Later that day, Mrs. Faulkner put the sprinkler below our butts to cool us down. Since then, I kept expectations for girls at school really low; that way, they couldn't disappoint me. Besides, once I had a boyfriend, I really didn't care. I didn't think I needed much else until he went and quit me cold turkey.

I did recall how Frankie had toiled away with the dandelions, glue stick, and research during our middle-school science project. Paul and I were flirting too much to be bothered with actual work. Meanwhile, she barely let out a squeak, not even when we found spiders and worms and garter snakes among the plant life. Frankie would keep at it when we stopped for pizza breaks, and her cheeks flushed pink when we finally convinced her to join us. Paul, Matt, and I were hardly cool, but I do remember thinking she was even more of an outsider than we were. Matt and I didn't try to make her one of us if she didn't want to be. We understood.

I typed back:

Cool to hear from you. I have to be back home by five, but I can hang out anytime before that. Can you pick me up?

She wrote back that she'd see me in two hours. I went back to bed for as long as I could.

The second I barreled down the steps, purse in hand, Vikki J. put the TV on mute and set down her beer. She was wide-eyed, clearly full of questions and warnings about Matt. I told her I'd talk to her when I returned. I had plans with Frankie.

"Who's he? You are just dead set on sandblastin' hearts all over Shitville."

"Frankie is a she, and we're going to Ear Bangers. I *do* have a date tonight — not with Matt — so don't worry. Some guy's taking me to the Little Mr. Shitville contest." I grabbed my jacket off the couch and headed for the driveway.

"Little Mr. Shitville! I've been to that. It's a hoot. Now what about this Frankie? Are you dating girls now, too? Oh my,

47

sounds like there's lots of stuff we need to talk about. Although at least I don't have to worry 'bout you getting knocked up by this one. Do ya have to run now?"

"I'm not dating girls, Mother," I said, standing in the doorway. "Is it too hard to conceive that I might just make a friend who's a girl?"

"During your senior year? I'd think hell would start an ice-pop factory first, sugar."

She was infuriating. "I'll see you later," I said, ending the non-conversation.

I fished two Tylenol out of my purse, swallowed them dry, and hoped for the best when Frankie arrived. If I could survive a date with my so-called platonic best friend, I could handle this girl outing, the first I'd had since my cousin came to town last year.

Frankie was easy, since she didn't talk that much. Hanging with her at the record shop was the same as spending time with Matt, pre-makeout. Though we were both pretty quiet, there were no uncomfortable silences. When we did feel like talking, she said amusing things using her favorite mother-of-all-expletives cuss word.

When she mentioned her ballet classes, her freckles doubled in size. She said she'd never had time for friends and parties and could hardly squeeze in school stuff like science projects. Every day until last month, she went to the dance studio in the larger town nearby. She attended some private school over there, too. She insisted that ballet hurt her social life, but I think she wanted it that way. I envied her because I'd never been busy with anything but Paul. He'd been my only after-school activity.

48

"They don't teach you how to be social in ballet class," Frankie said when I mentioned this to her.

"Still, why did you stop dancing?" I had to ask.

"I ripped the tendons in my [cussin'] shins. The doctor said I had to take a few months off. I decided it was a good time to actually make friends. So [cuss] me, here I am."

I didn't understand why she wanted to point her toes and jump like a fairy with no regard to gravity, but I enjoyed hearing about it. She truly loved ballet, and she wasn't bragging or trying to show me up the way other girls did. I longed for a hobby, talent, or skill. I wanted to live to do something. Vikki J. had her nails and hair; Matt had the flute and even swimming; Paul the Wanker had soccer. The only thing I'd been passionate about was dating my ex and now dating future boys who could become my exes. I wondered if senior year would be too late to get a life.

I picked out more electronic music — this new CD was by a guy who plays buckets that plug into the wall instead of drums. I also bought some new singer who belts out sweet, cheesy love songs that would be perfect for soap operas. When I offered to copy the CD for Frankie, her brown eyes sparkled and the freckles doubled again.

"So, are you and Paul totally through? Or . . . I'm sorry . . . is that a sore subject?"

"I've moved on; I'm totally over it. By the way, the sound of his name makes me want to break things. I only refer to him out loud as Weedkiller."

"Good." I don't think I ever smiled as much as she did during mundane tasks like flipping through CDs. "Do you want to come over to my house and burn that one on my new computer? Maybe you could even spend the night." When she asked, she grabbed my hand. I wondered if other girlfriends held on to each other like that. If so, I hadn't seen them do it in the school hallways.

"Um, sure."

"Maybe we could go listen right now." Frankie rubbed her thumb up and down my palm in that soothing, warm way Paul used on me when he wanted to make out. When he did it, I'd get frisky. Now that Frankie was putting on the smooth moves, I just felt jittery. At that moment, I was positive that friends did not touch like that — not straight ones, anyway.

"Listen, Frankie, I'm not *that way*." I was sweating, and she knew it because she was holding my greasy paw. How was she staying so calm? The whole store could surely hear my heart beating like the bass on the overhead music. The store clerk, a suburbanite who tried desperately to look urban, was frothing at the mouth (and other places) over the possibilities implied in our painfully embarrassing conversation. In the last 43,800 hours or so, I hadn't had one new person interested in me, male or female, for friendship or otherwise. And within the span of twenty-four hours, three people had come on to me. Frozen cherry-flavored push pops were surely being mass-produced in devil country.

"But you usually wear overalls! You're so beautiful — yet . . . so . . . so . . . [cussin'] butch." She dropped my hand and looked at me. She had scarlet-colored cheeks; she was wounded. Meanwhile, I had enough embarrassment for both of us and the whole rest of the world. And, boy, did I understand wounded. I could handle this situation gently, I decided.

I shot the salesclerk my meanest stare — my eyes could turn

50

fierce when I seriously needed them to. "Do you mind?" I said. He hung his head but didn't stop peeking. I knew because I caught his mischievous bright blue eyes under his mess of jet-black hair. I think I'd seen him at school before, but I paid so little attention in the hallways that I could never be sure about those things.

"[Cuss], Katie," Frankie said. "Man."

"Look, this is nothing to be embarrassed about. I mean, you want to talk about embarrassing, last night I —"

She shook her head either at me or herself, whispered "Oh, goddamnit," and took off toward her car. I caught up with her and offered to have my mother pick me up. I was shocked when Frankie actually took me up on it and left. I borrowed the phone from the hipster with blue eyes. I noticed that underneath his Cousin It hairdo, lip piercings, and black eyeliner, he was ice-meltingly hot. He kept his focus on me much longer than was polite. I decided I'd had enough Ear Bangers for the day and hightailed it out to the parking lot.

Vikki J.'s speeding ticket was tucked under the sun visor on the passenger side of her car; that was her signal to let me know that she planned to get some gossip in return. I don't like to let it all out, but I couldn't stand the way my new secrets simmered inside me. I reluctantly unleashed everything. We covered the subjects of Frankie and Little Mr. Shitville, and I knew exactly what would come next.

"So, whatcha gonna do about suckin' face with Matt?"

"I'll have to pray about it, I'm sure."

"Prayin'? Good Lord, I don't know where you get all of that Bible thumpin'. You pray all you want, but kissin' your best friend is gonna turn out to be like kissin' your own flesh-and-blood

51

brother. You can kiss your friends, you can kiss your friends' friends, but you cain't kiss your brother or your goldfish. Not unless you're weird, anyway."

"It's something I have to figure out. I can't tell you what I think about it because I don't know. I'll ask the Lord."

"You better ask somebody besides me, because you already know what I think."

She heeded my cues for silence at that moment. I changed the subject and talked about her hair and her clients (who were home waiting for her), and she had lots to say. Once I was home, I borrowed her clothes for my date with Mr. President, and the ones she helped me pick out didn't even look like they came from Wal-Mart. The white skirt with eyelets was tasteful, and I was sure I hadn't seen her wear it before. Bob wouldn't be at our house for a few hours, and she said Soap TV was too exasperating to watch. She displayed a full spread of makeup that covered the bathroom counter. The way she took to my face, you'd think she was sculpting crystal. She worked with such concentration and precision that I decided to make myself wait until later to wipe some of it off. She did my nails, too, begging me to let her airbrush little barbells onto them. I wasn't going for that, so she gave me a French manicure instead. Somehow, she even whipped my curly hair into shape, blowing it out perfectly shiny straight and adding a sexy little braid on the left side. My hair and makeup were much more Shitville cheerleader than Katie James. But the truth was, I felt pretty.

Kevin arrived early. I was waiting outside at the driveway, patting at the blush with the inside part of my sleeve. He pulled up in a wood-paneled SUV, killed the engine, and hopped out of the car before I had time to lift my purse up off the blacktop. He insisted on picking me up properly and wanted to ring the door-bell and everything. His whole body twitched when he spoke.

"Are you kidding?" I asked, knowing my mother would turn the standard meet-and-greet into an embarrassing mill-and-grill.

"No, I would never take a girl out without meeting her parents."

"I just have a mother, and believe me, you don't want to meet her." Who knew what Vikki J. would do? Surely, she'd try to decorate *his* fingernails with barbells, too. Or worse, she'd start telling him which of Avalon's boyfriends he most resembled. Another look at Kevin, though, with his determined gray eyes, and I knew if I argued with him I'd lose. I rolled my eyes, and my mascara-caked eyelashes chafed my skin just underneath my eyebrows. Before he had a chance to ring the bell, Vikki J. "magically" appeared and started to open the door.

My mother smiled. "Well, lah-tee-dah. Do tell. Now, how do you do?"

With a mother like Vikki J., I often took a few steps backward and hoped to camouflage myself as part of our wallpaper. The two of them hit it off, talking over each other about me, the contest, and even *Babes*. Kevin liked the show, too, for heaven's sake. Boredom caused me to rub my eyes. When my patience wore out, I pinched Vikki J.'s behind, and she took the hint. She looked at her wrist even though she never wears a watch and ran off while babbling about missing a special investigation about the beauty industry on E!.

Kevin didn't open the door for me, nor did he bring me flowers. I didn't mind because who did that, anyway? Matt's chivalry had been so over the top — guys didn't do that stuff for girls anymore except in straight-to-video movies.

"She's great. I love her."

"Yeah. Me, too." I rolled my eyes so hard they hurt.

"I teach gymnastics to fourth- and fifth-grade boys every Monday and Wednesday night," Kevin said, further signifying that his mind went off on more than one track at a time.

"That's cool."

"You may think it's odd to have a weight-lifting contest for gymnasts."

"Actually, I hadn't thought of it." It was more than odd!

"Especially little boys so young."

"Well, I wouldn't think they could lift much more than an oversized cat."

"That's about right — it's not even safe for them to lift weights yet. Their bones are still growing, which makes them prone to breakage. They also experience a lot more muscle strain than older boys do. Anyway, this is just a fun event we put on for them. They lift fake barbells and weights, and they all win prizes. We designed the program to build their self-esteem, because they get more confidence —"

"I know. You told me."

"Sorry, I do that. Anyway, to be honest, it's a funny show for their parents, who pay tanks of money for these kids to attend our award-winning school."

I tried to bat my eyelashes and look interested. Then my contact almost popped out. The visor mirror alerted me to the smeared mascara on the pouch of skin just under both eyeballs. I looked like I was wearing a Halloween mask, and I couldn't find my Kleenex. I instinctively opened his glove box to search for a tissue, because that's where my mother kept them. Unopened condoms fell out, and I didn't think I should wipe my eyes with those. I examined one of the prophylactics, bringing it four inches from my face to read the expiration date . . . which wasn't for six years.

Kevin started twitching so badly that I worried he'd lose control of the car. "What are you doing? That's so embarrassing."

"I'm not embarrassed." If they'd been open — *then* I'd have been embarrassed.

"Just so you know, I didn't buy those because of you."

"I was just looking for a tissue," I explained. Then what he said hit me the wrong way. "Wait — are you saying I'm not doable?"

"Um, well, you're totally doable. I love your nails. I love it when girls run their fingers down my —"

"So you're saying you think I'll give it up just like that?" I acted offended just for fun, just to distract myself. Even last night when I was having way too good of a time with Matt, I still felt like a misfit because I wasn't with Paul. Why and how did he and I fit so well for so long? Why and how did Kevin continue to talk and talk and talk? He was saying too much, and I wasn't saying enough. Paul and I had the perfect balance.

Oh, well. Kevin was cute, I guessed, but he just didn't turn me on. So what if he was a gymnast with nice biceps? I missed Matt's shoulders and awkward walk and falling glasses. I longed for Paul's — well, Paul's everything.

"No. I mean. Look. Those are there because of my really horny ex-girlfriend."

"That's even more reassuring." It was fun to watch him squirm. Well, fun for me.

"Let's just not talk about it. I was seeing someone for a long time. I just couldn't get her to commit, and I'm really embarrassed about the whole thing now. It's funny how being crazy about a girl can get to you, you know?"

Now I was curious. "You're still crazy about her?"

"No way. She hurt me too badly. She put my heart into a food processor and hit pulse too many times. She messed up my life for a while — I couldn't even concentrate on teaching gymnastics classes. I was sleeping less and less every night, which is totally bad for my complexion. You can tell a lot about a guy by his skin, you know. If it's full of scabs, he's anxious as hell and picks his face all the time."

I was surprised Kevin's face was so clear. I replied, "Yeah."

"Yeah, totally. I think you get what I'm talking about. Sometimes that happens; two people just get on the same wavelength. Hey, I know the guy you used to date. You okay? Do you want to talk about that?"

"No, I'm totally over him, too." Lying became my policy. If I had been honest, I would've told Kevin the mere thought of Paul made my chest collapse. I would have admitted that, at that very moment, I wondered what Paul was doing with his boy climber. Besides, did I really want to open up to a guy who kept so many fresh condoms in his car?

Once we arrived at the packed YMCA, little boys and beaming parents seemed to bum-rush him, successfully diverting his attention. My mother had been to the contest a few years in a row, and she assured me that it would be entertaining. Of course, she's also impressed by discounts on double cheeseburgers. I sighed when I saw the blowup barbells and three-foot plastic first-place trophies for each little boy. I wondered what kind of events they had for the girls. Bring your doll-baby to cartwheel class? The whole ordeal was too juvenile even for five-year-olds.

Ten boys followed Kevin around everywhere we went. "Who's your girlfriend? Where's the one you brought to our class?" they asked. In unison, the pack of high-voiced preteens asked him to watch their forward rolls and backward bends. They clamored to jump on the trampoline. The contest, attended by way too many parents, YMCA employees, and bored Shitvillers, ended with Kevin's ooh-ahhh award: Most Valuable Teen Employee.

From what I could tell, he was their only teen employee. The sparkle did come into his eyes when he sprinted down to the small, homemade stage to accept his gift certificates to a local steak house. He said thank you for ten minutes straight and mentioned each of his students' names and best characteristics. The ordeal had its charm but was about as exciting as four hours of live congressional coverage.

Was this what dating was really like? Was this what I'd been missing all those years when I was with Paul?

It only made me miss him more.

Crap.

"What did you think, Katie?" Kevin asked once his speech was over.

"It was pretty cool. Those boys are adorable!" If I wasn't getting anything out of the date, I figured I might as well practice my flirting technique. I tossed my blown-out hair to the left side, exposing my neck. I laughed even when comments weren't funny.

I felt like a fake. Sure, there were times with Paul when I'd had to play along, too — I sat through way too many soccer games, for one. But that faking didn't feel like this kind. That faking had a purpose. It made him happy, and that made me happy even when I was pretending. But this — this? It was just plain old pretending.

When I finally thought of something interesting to say, we were leaving, with ten boys cheering Kevin on.

"Want to grab some steak?" he asked. "It's on me."

He ate ferociously, talked energetically, and at the end of it all, ran me to my door instead of walking me there. When he kissed me, he must've been on a mission to reach down and clean my esophagus. We made out on my blacktop for about five minutes. After that, he pulled away from me respectfully without even trying to go up my shirt. As I lay down to sleep, I was overwhelmed with disappointment. When he kissed me, nothing had happened to my insides the way it had with Paul. Nothing felt warm or sweet like it had with Matt.

The Phone: Part enemy, Part friend

Sunday, April 6

"Katie, hey, how are you?"

According to the note on the table, Matt had called at six-thirty — right after I'd left with Kevin. I vowed to phone him back the second I woke up, but he beat me to it. I still hadn't sorted through the fifty-million feelings I was having about him and everything else. I wanted to cry when he called, but I didn't because things between us had changed. He was no longer the friend I could talk to when I was down. He was just another guy I had to be careful around. I wondered if he thought about me, what he did last night when I wasn't around, and if he liked me (and in what way).

I did like him. I mean, I loved him. Maybe we could have a relationship that was much more meaningful than our prior arrangement as best friends. I half hoped, but the thought also terrified me. Would we be gaining enough to justify what we'd lose? Why didn't he sound nervous or weird on the phone?

"I'm fine," I said. "I'm not hung over anymore."

"You're not? You didn't get drunk on your date last night?"

Of course, Matt knew I had a date — and that I would keep having dates every weekend night for the next five weekends, if everything went according to my grand plan. I wished I hadn't told him all about it. Besides, the date with Kevin was made before the Amaretto, before I threw my head into Matt's lap, hugging and kissing him for hours.

"Matt, you know I don't drink."

"You don't drink *or* date, do you?" He didn't sound snarky; he was teasing. I wasn't happy. If he liked me, he shouldn't be so flip.

"Stop it."

"Well, goodness. Did you at least have a good time with Kevin from the flying trapeze? I mean, the YMCA?"

"Actually, it wasn't that great. It was okay, I guess."

"So do you always kiss guys who it's just okay with?" Could he have seen us from his house?

"Oh, my God, Matt. What's going on? What happened between us? Please tell me, because I have no idea." I didn't like the bratty, "whatever" tone he was using with me. I hadn't heard it since I figured out his e-mail password freshman year. (I thought it was funny to send him love notes from himself.)

"For goodness sakes, let's just forget about it."

Disappointment overwhelmed me. I might have been happy going on the next ten dates with Matt. At the same time, the nerves in my stomach immediately stopped shimmying. Maybe the feeling was called relief, even though that didn't make much sense. The only thing that was clear was that my breakup with Paul was turning me into an emotional schizo-phrenic.

"Okay."

"I'll still pick you up for school if you want."

"Okay."

"Let's act like we always did," he said, sounding a little more comfortable now. Relieved, too, maybe? "This will all blow over. Anyway, Katie, you have dates to go on. I haven't forgotten that you're on a mission, that you have a grand-shazam plan."

I did have a goal. Why did Matt have to be my first date? Why why why?

"We're still best friends, aren't we?" he asked. He was not only relieved, but also concerned. Damn him for being such a great guy.

"Okay."

"Goodness, just *okay*?"

"Of course we are. Of course." It didn't feel like enough, but it was all I could say. I would've cried my eyes out. Or pulled out my hair. Or something. But the friggin' phone rang again.

Kevin.

"Hey, baby. What's up?"

I hate being called baby, babe, cutie, sweetie, and/or hot stuff. Those terms are for stuffed toys and hookers. But it would have been mean to say that to Kevin. So instead, I tried to sound un-annoyed when I answered, "Not much. Just doing some homework."

"I had a great time with you last night. You're a special girl. . . ."

"Thanks, Kevin." The sweet sentiments were getting on my

61

nerves. "Look, I had a nice time, too. And I really appreciate you using your gift certificate on me and all but —"

"You don't want to see me anymore."

"Well, I like you. I think you're a really cool guy. But just as friends. Really, you don't know how badly I need friends."

"Then friends it is." He said this as if it made perfect sense.

"It's not that easy, though," I warned him. I didn't want another Matt situation on my hands.

"Well, why not? It is for me. The truth is, if I dated you, I'd probably wind up freaking out and ruining everything."

"Am I that bad?" I had to ask.

"God, no, sweetie. It's just that I'm not ready for a relationship, anyway. My ex really did a number on me. You know what they say — it takes twice as long as you were with someone to actually get over them."

For me that meant almost ten years. "God, I hope not that long," I said. But what about the time when Paul first got his license, and we drove around town putting Valentine's Day cards in everyone's mailbox (in March — his goofy idea)? My mind raced through romantic recollections in a rapid sequence. The most painful haunting memory was of last year's prom — we decided to skip it, regretted doing so, then danced close at the lake all night long.

Getting over Paul? Ten years — definitely.

i'll never have
two-headed babies

Monday, April 7

You know the scene in a movie where the main character struts down a tree-lined street or into a dreamlike teen party with a disco ball? The good guy or girl — the one you've been cheering on for almost two hours — walks to the beat of hip music, looking so cool you're tempted to go out and buy the sound-track that day. I wished I could re-create those scenes of confidence and triumph in real life. I longed to be the princess of something, complete with my own theme music.

I would hardly say I was princess of Shitville High School when I returned Monday, but I did command a new, higher level of respect than I'd ever received before. I was made up, curly hair straightened, and wearing a pair of jeans so low that I had to be careful to pull them up in the back whenever I sat down. (I knew this because a guy in first period yelled "Buttcrack Alert" in the middle of a pop quiz.) My posture was pretty good as I walked down the hall in a pair of red two-inch ministilettos, compliments of Vikki J.'s crammed closets. My favorite chanting-monks songs were making themselves at home in my brain, so I walked to their beat the best I could. I was not invisible anymore.

Confused, the guys and girls asked my name and got all wide-eyed when they realized that I was the same Katie James who was recently obsessed with Paul Green and overalls. Talk was circulating about my date with Kevin. (I didn't hear any gossip about Matt and me.) Word got around after the Little Mr. Shitville contest, I guessed. When I met him in the hall that day, I hadn't known that twitchy Kevin was a member of the popular crowd, a much cooler group than Paul's soccer buddies. Not that it mattered — I couldn't keep social strata straight, anyway.

I was starting to see how the rest of the world found Kevin's tics charming. He went out of his way to find me twice. We talked about music — he loved chanting monks, too — and movies. He was far more interesting than he'd been on our date. He was more focused, now that he didn't have to focus on impressing me.

"I was really nervous to take you out," he admitted to me during lunch. He stopped by the swimmers' table right before the period was over. As soon as Kevin showed up, Matt rushed out. At least Kevin kept me from sitting there alone with a bunch of people I didn't know.

"God. Why?"

"Because you're beautiful."

"Kevin!"

"Don't think I'm hitting on you — I'm not. I think you're right. We didn't have any chemistry when we kissed."

Well, that's because he was terrible at it. But this time (as opposed to when we were locking lips), I kept my mouth shut.

"I don't mean to offend you or anything. It's just that some people aren't meant to be together. When you don't have chemistry with someone, it's your body telling you that person isn't a good DNA match. It means that you might have two-headed babies if you were to go off and marry that person."

I laughed. "You're weird."

"You are, too. I really hope we can become friends. Most people say that all of the time, but I don't. I mean it." Kevin, despite popularity, was not shallow. I admired him for that.

I wouldn't say I chatted with people other than Kevin and Matt that day, but I did make eye contact and say hello before they went off to whisper about me in their little groups. At the very least, I could feel myself becoming a player in the social game. And I wasn't even freaking out about that. I hoped I wouldn't have to sit alone at pep rallies or during downtime in gym class ever again unless I wanted to (which I might). I discovered there was safety in friendship. I liked that thought so much that I decided to seek someone else out. If Kevin and I could do it, so could Frankie and I.

During history class, I passed her a note:

Hey, I had a great time with you Saturday before, well, you know. I hope you don't hate me or anything. ☺KJ

She wrote back:

I guess you're really and truly not gay. I heard you kissed Kevin Ebernackey over the weekend. That lucky dawg. Anyway, I had a great time with you, too. It's hard being queer old me, because I can never tell who is fair game and who isn't. (Just ask the girls from my ballet classes.) I can't wait to go to college next year.

Ignoring the lecture on D Day, I slipped her another note:

If you want to hang out again, you know, as friends, we could. I'd love to go back to Ear Bangers. ☺KJ

Frankie and I talked after school before Matt ushered me into Winifred and sped me home. I wondered if it had always been this easy to make friends. I was seventeen years old and had been hiding out in a beauty parlor my whole life. Not anymore!

He turned my day into a dirty cheez Ball

Tuesday, April 8

The smell of Zest and fresh grass wafted through my living room Tuesday after school. I inhaled the warm familiarity. I'd been waiting and hoping and dreading and expecting. Paul was sitting on my couch, eating from Bob's can of Cheez Balls. He stood up; the last time he'd really seen me was several days before our breakup. While I couldn't hide from him at school completely, I tried my hardest. Of course, there was no missing him at lunch, though I hadn't looked toward his table once. If he had looked at me — well, that was his problem. Only now, the problem of Paul was two feet away from my face.

"Hey," he said.

"Hey."

"Can we go up to your room and talk?"

Vikki J. ignored her soap opera to watch some real drama. I was surprised she hadn't thrown Paul out the door yet. Her eyes were so wide that her fake eyelashes were about to pop off. She spazzed her head back and forth in small, jerky movements while Bob patted her knee to calm her down. Being as subtle as a woman who wears fuchsia nail polish could be, she gave me signals that I'd be crazy to let Paul go upstairs with me. My bedroom had always been our primo makeout spot.

"Let's talk outside," I said and headed out the front door, my theme music bumping in my head. Paul's eyes were taking in every inch of my body as he followed me. He furrowed his eyebrows together and pursed his lips into a neutral, unsmiling expression. He was struggling to process the changes in me: my makeup, straight hair, skirt, and sandals. I wanted to tell him the Nikes he'd given me were long gone — I'd donated those clunky clodhoppers to the Goodwill, along with most of my overalls and all of those single-color pocket tees. So what made him look so relaxed, so cocky? Why did he smell so sexy?

Paul bit his bottom lip while he surveyed me, starting at my sparkle-dusted eyelids down to my pink toenails. His gaze softened and became mischievous. He wanted me, and I was shamefully proud of it. But seeing him caused me so much pain that I stopped glowing soon enough. I still cried in private when his after-school phone calls didn't come. I still missed the way his scent took over my room and lingered there long after he was gone. Sometimes before I'd go to sleep, I could still feel his fingers stroking the back of my hand.

"So," he finally spoke. His tone suggested that nothing bad had ever happened between us. He was soft, concerned, and way too sure that he still had me.

"So, why are you here?" I tried to sound annoyed; he heard right through it.

"I need to talk to you."

"Obviously." I *was* annoyed — and torn up.

He surprised me, diving into the subject instead of dodging it. "I know what I did to you was brutal."

"You did me a favor. I'm so much happier now," I lied. "I mean, I've made friends, good ones, for the first time in my life." At least that was the truth.

"And you've gone on dates."

"Yes, maybe I have. But I wasn't going to mention that. So, how is Johanna?"

"I wasn't going to mention *that*." The thought of them together crushed me over and over again, especially with him standing right in front of me. I refused to show it, which was difficult because Paul was Paul — the one I'd loved for almost five years. His golden hair was longer than it had been, and his bangs kept falling down into his eyes. He'd reach up and brush them back with the confident manner of a surfer god. I reminded myself what an ass he was so I'd forget about the cute ass he had.

"Anyway, here's the deal: I know you were kissing random guys all weekend."

"They weren't random! I kissed Kevin and — wait, I can't believe you. Who are you to tell me who I should and shouldn't kiss?"

"I was with you for five years. I think I have some say on where you put your lips."

"My lips are no longer your property, and — wait — *they never were*. I choose what to do with my lips, and I shouldn't have used them on you for so long. What I'm trying to say, anyway, is that you have no say whatsoever." My speech never reached the level of eloquence I was aiming for. "It was only four and a half years, anyway."

He backed away from me a little, the sparkle draining from his huge eyes. I could've sworn they were watery, but maybe he was just allergic to my gardenia perfume. "I came here to be nice to you, Katie."

"You call this nice? I'd call it conceited."

"How can it be conceited to tell you that I don't want you to be with other guys?" he said, his voice rising and breaking and losing all cool. "It's bad enough that I have to listen to people call you this big hottie now. I don't want to hear rumors that you've kissed this guy and who-knows-who-else, too. Do you know what that feels like for me?"

I swear I could feel anger shooting out of my toenails. What about what he'd done to me? What about running around school PDA-ing with Ho-Hawnnah? Oh, my God, I was fuming, but I wasn't surprised. Paul had run my life the entire time we were together. He'd planned our romantic outings, our study sessions, even when I could and couldn't watch him play soccer. I never minded because I had nothing else to do besides my homework, which never took that long. I let him map out my social schedule, what little of it there was, because I loved him, and I was weak. He was naturally more outgoing — make that bossy — and I never saw any reason to complain. With or without him, I was never a leader; I preferred to be led. But I only followed people who were worth following, and Paul had failed me. I still loved him, but I didn't need him to fill my calendar anymore.

"I can do what I want with — I don't know — anyone I want," I told him. "You hear that? *Whenever* I want, too."

"But you're making out with Kevin? That's so cliché, Katie. You're making out with the class president to make me jealous — that or you want to be First Lady. Hanging out with that crowd now? Barf."

"Whatever. I'm not listening to any of this." And I thought it would be hard to be genuinely turned off by him. Luckily, he was making it easier. Paul was stooping low. I mean, his friends Wren, Mike, and Keith were hardly upstanding superstars at school — they were famous for streaking at parties. And I never once complained about any of them. He was just being a jack-ass. I saw the opportunity to gain control of our fight, something I had rarely ever done, and knew I had the power to end it before he stooped any lower.

"This conversation is over," I said, turning toward the living room as he tried to grab my hand. His fingertips were rough, like the pad of a dog's paw, and warm. I missed them, but there was no way I'd stay out there . . . even though a small part of me wanted to. I hated and loved Paul at the same time — a state in which there could be no happy ending, not to mention dignity.

"Please don't do this, Katie," he begged. "I shouldn't have said that. Please, beautiful."

I slammed the door in his face and struggled to get my breath. I secretly hoped he'd knock again and clamor some more for forgiveness. Instead, after a moment of stunned silence, I heard his footsteps walking away. The car engine started and his tires made loud screech marks on our blacktop. He sped away, probably to Johanna's, leaving me a total wreck. He cared enough about me to act like a jealous freak, but not enough to figure out the right way to make things better.

I forced myself to smile at Bob and my mother, hoping they'd see me as strong and self-assured instead of the baffled weakling that I was.

Bob draped his heavy left arm over my shoulder. He squeezed me close, making the heartache a little easier to bear. "Damn that boy," he said. "Why did he have to make a mess in the driveway?" Bob had laid our blacktop, but I know he wasn't worried about the tire marks. I looked into his big brown eyes. "I know where you got that feistiness, Kay-Jay," he added. "You aren't so different from your mother." Bob meant that as the highest of compliments, so I didn't dare get mad at him.

Vikki J. jumped up and high-fived him and me, knocking over his bottle of wine. She didn't care that it was dripping all over; our carpet had a lot of stains. He held her hand and smiled at us both. Only I noticed when he slyly snatched the remote control and switched the TV to the food channel.

"Yeehaw! You sure sent that fish back to the fryer. You'll be lickin' your chops of that one soon enough. Now, Katie, you just remember one thang: Nothing mends a broken heart faster than a can of Cheez Balls." She nearly knocked those over, too, when she tried to pass them to me. I forced down a few of the glow-in-the-dark puffs. They tasted like plastic.

I licked the fake cheese from my lips and fingers, unable to control the tears rolling down my cheeks.

i have to flitter away

Tuesday, April 8, through Thursday, April 10

The return of Paul meant one thing: I had to talk to Matt immediately. I rushed to his house shortly after Paul left, as soon as Vikki J. and Bob stopped fussing over me, and I pulled myself back together. Matt and I weren't on the best of terms. We'd only had meaningless, polite conversations on the way to school and during lunch. I just figured I'd leave it alone. It would take a few days for the memories of our Amaretto-laced love to fade away. Regardless of our complicated feelings for each other — I was harboring them, and he wasn't — there was no one on the planet I wanted to talk to more. I was hurting, and I needed my best friend. In my frantic state, I almost forgot to knock, which would have annoyed his mother to no end.

Mrs. Faulkner pointed me to the basement, leaving the door open and watching me walk down. Even though I'd been hanging out at their house for more than fifteen years, she still wouldn't let us go up to his bedroom. In fact, wherever we were in her house, the door had to remain open. She was worried that we might make out or something, God forbid.

Matt was still wet from a late swimming practice; his broad, bare chest was covered in a white towel. The season was long over, but Matt hoped to be a walk-on for his college team next year. He was good at a sport he didn't like. He only stuck with it because he was addicted to the little bit of confidence it gave him. In his mind, swimmers were popular, and he ignored all of the times when bullies chanted Super Legs and Pool Boy right in front of his face. I just went along and supported him whenever he wanted me to. As for which college he would attend, he was on the wait list for Georgetown, but I knew he really wanted to go to Franklin, a small liberal arts school filled with would-be teachers just an hour north of Shitville. (I hadn't even applied to the local colleges yet.) He kept his fingers crossed that Georgetown, his father's alma mater, would can him. His flute sat next to him on the floor, his cranberry juice was nearby.

"Hey, you won't believe what just happened."

He didn't even look up at me when he said, "Paul was there. I saw him speeding down the street when I got home."

I expected Matt to jump up and down, his towel falling off, screaming, "Goodness gracious, oh, my goodness." Instead, he was lifeless. He seemed really tired. Maybe he'd had a killer practice.

"Matt, are you okay?"

He wouldn't look me in the eye. "I knew you two would get back together."

"Oh, my God, we totally didn't. He was just jealous."

Matt perked up, even fiddling with his flute. "Wow. He was? Ooooh, man oh man."

"I told him to leave and slammed the door in his face." I was proud — and surprised — that I had done that.

Matt jumped up, stumbled over his poor instrument, and the towel wound up on the shag carpet, exposing his shoulders and Speedos, which more than made up for the knobby knees, if anyone ever asked me. "Goodness gracious. You did? You go." He wasn't as enthused as usual, but he hugged me. It felt a little different from our pre-Amaretto days, but not too weird. Together, we overanalyzed (i.e., ripped to pieces) Paul and the boy climber and stupid soccer fetishes. I had gone to Matt's because I didn't want to cry anymore over Paul. It worked. I started feeling more positive and less confused.

But then when I left, I wondered what it would be like to kiss Matt again.

Things seemed okay as we schlepped back and forth to school over the next couple of days. I'd say they were almost normal even. I had feelings for him, but I was becoming more convinced that we'd made the right decision — or at least he had — to just remain buddies. He and I rode around in Winifred and wasted away the forty-five minutes we had for lunch. Kevin and Frankie had been sitting with us all week, so we'd claimed our own table. I liked it better that way. The swimmers weren't as nice to Matt as they should have been, yet he always took their jabs with a goofy smile and a thumbs-up sign. He thought they were teasing him because they liked him. I thought they just let him sit at their table so they'd have someone to pick on.

"Kevin, here's a question for you. Why do you want to eat lunch with us?" I asked him one afternoon when Matt and Frankie left to raid the gymnasium vending machines.

"According to recent studies" — he often started his explanations with this line, and he always looked confused when the rest of us cracked up — "the more friends you have, the longer you'll live. People who are isolated die up to ten years sooner than people who are not." He didn't even look up; he was fully absorbed in folding his empty chip bag into one tiny perfect square.

"They say the same thing about humans who have pets, you know," I added.

"Well, then, you all are my pets." He smiled. "You can be the kitten. Meow." He dodged the subject every time I asked him, signaling that something was up. From what I'd heard from Matt, Kevin Ebernackey could turn out to be the king of the Shitville prom this year if he wanted to be. I hated myself for thinking this, but Matt was a wannabe who secretly played the flute; Frankie was the New Lesbian in Town; and I was the ugly invisible girl who turned pretty overnight. I liked that Kevin wanted to hang out with us, but why?

Maybe we were cooler than I gave us credit for, because another member of prom royalty made her move on our ground. I was sitting alone at the table finishing Vikki J.'s fried chicken wrap; Matt, Frankie, and Kevin had already taken off. (I was always last!) I was wiping ranch dressing off my lips and checking my teeth in the compact makeup mirror I had stolen from my mother, when the most unexpected visitor popped by.

"Hey, baby cakes, can I borrow your mirror?" Cherry the Cheerleader plopped her popular butt right down next to me.

"Um, sure." I hadn't finished getting the lettuce out of my eyeteeth, but I didn't want to tell her that.

"So, Katie, how have you been? I haven't seen you around since tryouts."

I was surprised Cherry even knew my name. I put my head

down when she spoke to me, and I pulled my shoulders inward. I wanted to be smaller because I didn't know what to say to the captain of the squad who had rejected me nine times straight, starting in the fourth grade. Boys had been approaching me all week, and I could play silly eye games and smile shyly. My vocabulary was the last thing on guys' minds. With girls, interactions were about wittiness and chattiness. Frankie was the down-to-earth exception, while Cherry was high pressure. I couldn't flirt my way out of an awkward conversation, so I reduced myself to fidgeting.

If I acted duller than a tool in wood shop, she didn't notice. Cherry looked in my mirror and put some shiny red goo on her plump lips. Then she lifted the applicator pad from the compact and applied my mother's translucent powder to her perfect skin without asking me. We hadn't even made eye contact yet.

"This is great stuff," she said in a voice that sounded, well, *Cherry*. "Can I have it? The shade goes so well with my tan. I go to the beds, you know."

"Yeah, um, I guess." What was I supposed to say to a question like that? I was glad she didn't ask for my skirt and shoes, too.

"We should totally hang out sometime."

Huh? "Are you kidding?" I asked.

"I don't kid." She set the compact on the fake-wood-paneled tabletop, leaving the mirror open. "I'm a totally serious person. Do you think this lip gloss looks good on me?"

"It's fine." The lipstick was way too bright — it was a shade that would only look good on a drag queen. My inability to shell out compliments shook her visibly. I quickly realized that talking to her would not be difficult. "Do you even know who I am?"

77

"Of course. You're Katie James from tryouts. I've known who you are for, like, ever. You got a lot better at cheerleading, you know." She was lying. I couldn't remember a routine any better than I could recall which guy she was kissing at the pizza place last Friday night.

"Come on. I did not."

"You're right, you didn't. But you have to love a girl who tries as hard as you did, baby. Every year, we'd take bets on whether or not you'd show up."

"Did you win?"

"Yes, always. I knew you'd be back."

I felt a need to explain. "I wasn't trying very hard, though. I didn't care about cheerleading. My mother paid me to go. I'll be sure to tell her that I was providing gambling opportunities for young girls. She'll like that."

Cherry thought I was being sarcastic, and I wasn't. "Oh, that's so freakin' funny. I can't believe it. That's the best story I've heard all year. It's almost as good as the one some guy told me last night." Her laugh was as phony as Vikki J.'s beauty marks, but there was warmth in her voice that made me smile even though I didn't want to. She slapped her knees while she glanced at herself in the compact mirror. I'd never seen some-one put so much effort into being cool except for Matt. Matt was lousy at it, so how did Cherry pull it off? Then I thought: Cherry was so perfect-bodied that she could moonwalk in the lunch line and everyone would go home and practice. If Matt did it, they'd fall on the floor laughing. Cherry was pretty and always had been. She had it easy.

"What was it like being with Paul Green for such a long time?" she asked me. "I can't keep a guy around for more than a date or two." Matt had made the same inquiry of me at least a hundred times (minus the second part, of course). I was shocked to hear it from her, though. Cherry seemed like the least lonely girl in the whole state — the most self-confident, too. Yet, her conversation made her sound self-conscious; maybe she was searching for something just like I was. I sat up straight, broadened my shoulders, and looked at her. She was already staring at me.

"I call him Weedkiller," I told her.

"What did you say, girlfriend? I know what you mean, love is a killer."

"No, no. It's just that I can't stand the sound of his name. So if you don't mind, let's refer to my ex as Weedkiller from now on. Do I have to answer your question?"

"Not if you don't want to, but I would like to know."

"Here's what I always tell my friend Matt: It was comfortable and predictable to be with one guy for so long — you wind up loving and relying on each other like your oldest worn-out stuffed animal that you can't bear to throw away. But now I don't know if the heartache was worth it. The good times don't seem so great anymore. The breakup screwed me up too badly."

"Wow. I love my teddy bear. I never go to a sleepover without it," she said as she put a layer of clear gloss over her burstingly plump red lips. "I know all about getting your heart broken. It totally sucks. Guys don't feel it the way we do. They just get on with everything — like school, making friends, and asking other girls out."

"It's awful."

"Totally sucks. I hear ya. Now, tell me about the good stuff. What about the sex? I bet it was great."

"Um, well, yeah. I guess." My virginity was my business. I wasn't lying, anyway; we had an amazing sexual relationship even if we never actually did it.

"I definitely want to hear more about that. But I have to flitter away now. Like I said, girlfriend, we should totally do something sometime." She fished around in her purse for a paper and pen. "Can I have your e-mail address?"

Was this really happening? "Sure." Did I really want it to?

"Here's mine. But, like, don't send me any of those silly jokes and stuff. I only use e-mail for communication."

"Yeah." I rubbed my temples before I was able to write. "Here you go."

"I'll catch up with you soon, then." She took one last look in the mirror, threw it in her purse, and was gone. I saw her in the hallways and after lunch the next day, too. She cornered me at my locker, asking for my e-mail address again because she'd lost it. Matt was there with me, and he flirted like he had a chance. I wasn't jealous until she started flirting back. I stared at them both with my mouth open, and so did others in the hallway. The thought of Cherry coming on to Matt was Ripley's material. I would've been happy for him if he hadn't put his tongue in my mouth less than a week ago. Maybe.

I knew it was childish, but just to make things even between us, I told him my own news on the way home from school in Winifred.

"So, I have a date tomorrow night," I said.

He didn't have a reply, and I was glad. If he had perked up and said, "Oh, my goodness gracious," I would've known for sure that he wasn't holding tight to any secret romantic feelings. His silence told me exactly what I wanted to hear.

"So I met this hot guy at the record store with Frankie last Saturday. He had the bluest eyes I've ever seen in my life. He got on my nerves at first, but then I couldn't stop thinking about him this week."

Matt was quiet for a few minutes. "No one has eyes as cool as yours," was all he could say. His attention stayed on the road, and his voice went dead. He hadn't been that void of emotion since I showed up in his basement all worked up over my Paul sighting. It wasn't like it was cruel to talk to Matt about a new guy. *He* was the one who'd insisted that being friends was best. But if he was taking my jab to heart, I wished he would've understood that I was just doing it out of jealousy. I couldn't tell him any of that, of course.

Why did so many things have to be left unsaid?

Something about the guy from the CD store *had* stayed with me in spite of various dramas with Paul and Matt and Kevin. I thought I was dreaming when he found me outside of the girls' bathroom on Thursday. We were both supposed to be in class. To keep myself from falling asleep — drooling was hardly sexy — I'd asked for the hall pass. I was just goofing around because I didn't want to go back.

"Psssst. Katie James."

I thought it would turn out to be Kevin or Frankie. When I saw who it was, though, I pulled the hairs on my left arm hard. I didn't want to squeal or do anything to embarrass myself. The pain helped me get myself together and prepare to bat my eyelashes.

He jumped in front of me, nearly pushing me over as he opened the door to the girls' room. He didn't have time for glazed-over looks or flirting. "Is anyone in there?" he asked, though he was already inside. His hair had been trimmed. The black mop was shorter but still curly and soft and wavy. His eyes weren't hidden anymore, and he wasn't wearing his piercing or black eyeliner. He was hotter than ever in his plaid pants and button-down bowling shirt.

"No."

"Come on in."

I followed instructions, thinking this would be a funny story to tell my mother and maybe even my new friends. I was nervous, but not because of the guy. Instead, I was more concerned that we would get caught.

"What on earth are you doing?" I asked.

He pulled me into the stall, stood up on the toilet to hide his feet, and squatted back down. "I want you to go out with me tomorrow, this Friday. I can't stop thinking about you. Give me your phone number now. I need it."

"I don't have any paper."

"Get some."

"Look in the phone book under Vikki Jaymes, J-A-Y-M-E-S."

He smiled and flopped his hair over in a way that said *Dude, I got her.* I was getting excited. "Cool. You're going." He was magnetic, charismatic, irresistible. His hair, his eyes, the way his left shoulder moved so slightly while he talked.

"I don't even know you." I had to say that to save face. I didn't want him to think I'd go out with any guy just like that.

"I'm a junior. I love music. I don't kick puppies or harm humans. I stopped picking my nose three years ago. I hate cigarettes, and I love old movies. I'll take you to one this weekend. I'm thinking *Casablanca.*"

"I've seen it." I didn't feel nervous around this guy. I loved the way his eyes surveyed me.

"*Vertigo*, then."

His face was so close to mine that I thought we might accidentally kiss. I closed my eyes in preparation, but all he was doing was leaning forward to hop down. His attention was not on me. In less than a second, he was off the toilet and peeking out of the girls' bathroom door.

"The coast is clear," he said. "I'll see you Friday."

"Um, okay. Wait. What's your name?"

"Just call me Blue."

He was gone, and I was in love. But I'd been in and out of love a lot lately. I definitely didn't trust my instincts and figured that maybe I was just horny. Or maybe I'd been watching too many romantic comedies. Or maybe I just wanted to see the whole world — meaning Matt and Paul — eaten up with jealousy. Wishing jealousy wasn't really my style, but what was? The sandals I had on?

My mind came back to the uncomfortable silence in the car with Matt. He hadn't uttered a word since I'd mentioned Blue.

"I may have a date, too," he said at last.

"With who?" What, were we one-upping each other?

"I can't tell you yet. I'll tell you soon."

I was irritated. For starters, Matt always told me everything. Then he dropped me off without a good-bye. Matt and I had never fought in our lives, and we weren't really fighting then. Somehow, though, we had managed to lock ourselves into a silent stalemate.

"So, are you going to pick me up tomorrow?" I yelled back into Winifred.

"Oh, for crying out loud. Goodness gracious, Katie. Really." He was annoyed with me — another rare occurrence.

"Well, are you?"

"Yes, of course I am. You're so weird lately."

"You're weird, too," I said.

"I don't quite feel like myself. I think I've got a lot on my mind."

That made two of us.

After our car ride, I decided that I could no longer tell the difference between discussions with Matt and intentionally inflicting myself with wounds. Two weeks ago, I had Paul and Matt to confide in. And I suddenly felt like I had no one. More than once, Kevin had said I could talk to him anytime as long as he wasn't teaching at the YMCA or romancing a new chick. He sounded busy, but since I didn't have anyone else, I gave him a try. He told me to forget about Matt and explained a newly discovered phenomenon called male PMS. "Guys' testosterone levels go up and down on a twenty-eight-day cycle," he said. "Clearly, Matt is going through the male version of starting his period."

I was impressed that Kevin used the P word. Our friendship was cemented. He listened to my gripes patiently before revealing that he was not having a good day. He said it was because he hadn't broken his own one-hundred-and-twenty-one-sit-ups-per-minute record, but I wondered if it was something else. Kevin asked me to tell him a happy story, his polite way of letting me know he had burnt out on the Matt topic, a straightforward tactic I could appreciate. I complied. I rattled on about Blue hopping on the toilet in the girls' restroom to ask me out, and as I did it, I realized that was the one story I really wanted to tell.

"I am totally stealing that move," Kevin said. "Quirky guys always get the girls before the conventional ones do. Ask a girl out by passing her a note, and she's sure to say no. Write her name on your underwear, and she'll say yes. I think I'm figuring you people out."

indiana farm animals

"Tonight you're going out with *Blue*?" Frankie screamed at me when we met outside after school. Matt said he had swim practice, which I didn't actually believe, and thankfully Frankie offered to drive me home. Or maybe not so thankfully, because she was clearly in a bad mood. So far in our nascent friendship, we were two peas in a pod (albeit an odd pod). She'd do things like slip me a piece of her mom's pecan pie at lunch while the others weren't looking. We'd look at her music magazines in between classes — she was so much cooler about that stuff. She passed me smiley faces during class with notes that read, *How ya holding up? Weedkillers suck!*

I hadn't seen her fiery, actually quite bossy, side until that moment. "Who told you?" I asked. "I wanted to talk to you about it on our way home."

"Kevin asked me if I'd heard of Blue today while you were hiding out during lunch."

I'd heard Paul was getting X-rated with Ho-Hawnnah again, so I had dined in the gymnasium to spare myself. For a few days

86

after I'd slammed the door in his face, he'd lain low, then he decided to put on a show in my honor. He taunted me with her at first, going out of his way to make sure they crossed my path in the halls before first period — and then again before second, and third. It bothered me a little less as the day went on. I just hung out in the restroom more between classes — that place had happy memories, though I hadn't run into Blue again. So what if I ate alone for one day? I needed some time to study for the fifth-period exam I'd forgotten, anyway.

"You know him?" I asked Frankie cautiously.

"Do I know him? Do *I* know him? [Cuss.] Does a hydrant know a dog?"

Frankie was usually such a soft-spoken gal. I always moved in closer to her just to hear her speak. Her loud, angry tone alarmed me. Frankie's brown eyes became feral-cat fierce. We had only been friends for less than a week. Clearly, there was a lot more to learn.

"I guess that means you do." I spoke carefully.

"He's only the most disgusting, despicable excuse for a human being on this entire planet. He keeps to himself because no one likes him. He's a total [cussin'] freak, which is fine, but he's mean on top of it."

"Calm down, Frankie." I took a few breaths while she held a death grip on her poor, suffocating steering wheel. My heart raced faster than Frankie's speedometer. I'd had one too many confrontations in the last few days, and I was getting tired of them. I decided to put this fire out fast. "I'm more than happy to listen to whatever you have to say. As long as you stop yelling. I feel like I did something wrong."

I silently cursed my luck. Why did Frankie have to go

bonkers on me? And why did she have to know — and clearly dislike — Blue? Why why why?

"He's a total complete loser boyfriend. I mean it, Katie. You cannot go out with him. You won't even want to when I tell you this story."

"Tell me." I chewed cuticles to absorb my anger and keep my insides calm. I cussed to myself.

"His mother is one of the ballet teachers, so he's been in and out of the studio as long as I've been going there. I mean, I've known him since I was six."

She didn't know anyone — like me! But the one guy with potential? Crap.

"Does he dance?" I thought it would be really cool if he did. Then it dawned on me . . . I probably shouldn't think well of anyone who could inspire the fury of Frankie.

"No, he just cleaned the floors and mirrors for extra money. He liked hitting on the ballet girls."

What was so bad about that? I wondered.

"But that's not all he did," Frankie explained. "We liked him a lot for a long time. Everyone flirted with him, I mean, not me. We loved his music collection — he always brought the coolest CDs. But then he became a big fat [cuss]."

She flipped her short hair violently, her body language saying, *No no no!* She turned off her car stereo and increased her volume again.

"He spent three years wooing a friend of mine named Heather. He was so charming, so believable. Finally, she gave in to him, and they were together for two months. She fell hard. I mean *hard*. Lost her virginity and everything. Meanwhile, he was doing two other girls in the class at the same time. He lied to all of them. It was beyond disgusting."

"Oh, my God." I wanted to cry.

"I'm not [cussin'] kidding about any of this. He makes Weedkiller look like a sweet little girl in pigtails. Blue didn't break one heart. He broke three!"

"I'm sick to my stomach," I said.

"Don't be. He's not worth it."

I couldn't lie. I still wanted to be with him, but I also knew that was stupid. Frankie was only being my friend. She was being a good friend. She was right; I was sure of it.

"Thanks," I said, patting her tight shoulder attached to her tight fists. She relaxed slowly, one muscle twitch at a time. Why had she become so worked up?

"I just get upset about these things. I can't stand when people do each other wrong. I'm not going to watch it happen to you," she said, reaching in her glove box for a tissue.

"Really, thanks. I hate guys like that." No more lying, cheating, snakelike boys for me. I was with Frankie; I hated Blue, too. For a lot of reasons, the main one being that all guys were big disappointments.

Finally she turned the radio back on, and she gave the tensed skin on her face a break. "I usually check to see if his car is there before I even go into Ear Bangers, Katie. He knows I hate him, and he hates me. Maybe somebody dropped him off last weekend. I was so embarrassed that he saw us there together. Then he heard everything that happened. He must've had so much fun telling the girls at ballet class. It was bad enough that you were turning me down — but he got entertainment out of it, too."

"That's so terrible. I'm sorry. I really am. But are things fine with us now? I mean, we are totally over last Saturday, right?"

"Oh, yes, things are fine, Katie. I mean, as long as you don't go out with him."

"I won't." Guys sucked!

Her words became softer, harder to hear again. "Things are fine, I mean it," Frankie said. "I just can't stand him because of what he did with — I mean to Heather. Blue is a [cussin'] dog. Sorry I got so worked up."

"Maybe we should go to the CD store together so I can turn him down while you're standing there." I was surprised I suggested such a thing. That was confrontational and mean and sort of unlike me.

"Are you kidding?!!! Katie, no way! What he did . . . it was . . . it was mortifying for . . . my friend."

"Okay, okay. That was a bad idea. Let's just forget I mentioned it." I did need to cancel on him, though. Even if he was Indiana's biggest canine, I didn't want to stand him up. I didn't need any more negative karma. "You okay?"

"I'm fine, I swear."

"Don't get mad, Frankie. But there's just one thing," I said. "I *need* a date tonight. It's part of my whole plan, you know. The one I told you about that's going to help me get over Weedkiller." I hadn't dared tell her about Matt, nor did I ever plan to.

"I have an idea. I'll be your date."

Silence. I'd heard that one last Friday from Matt. Thankfully, she added, "Just as friends, I swear. We're over that, remember?"

"Oh, of course. I know." Was I a good fibber? "Where will we go? What's your idea?" She'd better have a good, nonromantic one, or I was going to have to use the sorry-I-gotta-get-with-God lines.

"There's this huge party tonight somewhere in the state park."
Good answer!

"I heard about that from some guy in math class," Frankie continued, "but you know I'm never invited to those things. Are you?"

"Hell, no."

"What about Kevin? You *know* he's invited." Frankie may have been hotheaded, but at least she was brilliant.

Back at my house, we called his cell phone, and he was enthusiastic, even cheerleaderlike, about the idea of taking us. When we admitted that we'd never been to any Shitville parties, he responded, "News flash! I know that because I've never seen either of you there. Not till tonight, anyway."

I could've gone to parties, I supposed. When Paul wasn't skipping them to hang out with me, he went to a few with his friends Wren, Mike, and Keith. (He swore he never streaked like they did.) He asked me to go, but I never felt like putting out the effort to be around a crowd I didn't care to know. I was happier catching up with Matt or doing homework. Was that pathetic? The other truth was that I never felt welcome or, therefore, very comfortable in those situations. The new Katie, the one who woke up thirty minutes earlier for five days straight to blow out her hair, had a different attitude. I was kind of starting to chat with people, like the ones who would be at the party. Besides that, I had a crucial mission: I needed dates. I certainly wasn't going to get them at home watching the reptile channel. I figured if I couldn't go out on a real date with Blue, I could try to snag a boy at a party. That was a perfectly good substitute — maybe even a better one — than a full-on date.

I did wonder what Kevin's more popular friends would think when he introduced us — two no-names, one recovering gay recluse, and one recovering straight geek. I didn't care, though. For the first time ever, I was curious about what happened on the weekends. Frankie was clearly itching to experience a Shitville party, too.

She went home to get ready. What that meant, I didn't know. She always wore similar flowered dresses, properly described as button-down-the-front frocks, and combat boots in either brown or black. Her hair was short and blond, always parted sort of on the left and free to do what it wanted. When I was finally alone for a few minutes, I decided I'd better cancel the date with Blue. I really did say a prayer, to what god I don't know, hoping to get his voice mail. I wasn't so lucky.

He answered without saying hello: "*Vertigo*, nine p.m. Indian food beforehand. They may not sound like they go together, but they do."

"You are such a butthole."

"My preference for old movies and Eastern Asian fare hardly makes me a rear end. Wait till you know me better, then you can call me names."

"Frankie Smith is my good friend. She told me about what you did to her friend Heather — and to those other girls. Or maybe you didn't think I'd hear about that?" I paused for effect and was put off to hear him laughing. "What?" He was still chuckling, and I think I got too emotional. "What is your problem, anyway?"

"She did *not* tell you that," he said. I could tell he was smiling, even over the phone.

"She did, and you're even more of an ass for laughing about it."

"I've been upgraded to a farm animal. Really, let me explain."

Frankie said he was charming, convincing, and, most despicably, conniving. I was no ding-dong. I wasn't falling for a guy's line of crap again.

"How can you give an explanation for cheating on your girlfriend? I've been there, believe me. I don't think you should call me again." Afraid that he'd woo me, too, I hung up the phone. And just like that, the matter was settled. I was proud of my boldness, my conviction, and my loyalty to my new friend. I thought I just might master this standing-up-for-myself thing with a little more practice.

If I had to come clean, though, this Blue news still disappointed me. If he had been the *honest* charming guy I expected, he could've had me, I thought. You'd think a guy who owned eyeliner, especially in Shitville, would at least be a little more sensitive and a little less of a player. Well, I would be the last person to make assumptions again; everything that I'd thought was true had turned out to be something else entirely.

The phone rang, and I knew it was him. It took some willpower, but I didn't answer. I'd let him make his excuses to our voice mail.

My nerves were rattled wrong side out. Then Vikki J. held me prisoner for thirty full minutes. She got it in her head that I was going on a second date with Little Mr. Shitville, and she didn't want to believe me when I told her I wasn't. On top of her apparent crush on Kevin Ebernackey, my mother also coughed up a hairball over my attendance at a keg party. My seedling social life caused mildly out-of-control gleefulness, and she was sure that those endless years of cheerleading tryouts were finally paying off. Her interest didn't go without warnings:

"Last weekend shoulda taught you that you cain't hold yer liquor. Them lips of yers ups and gets a mind of their own after a few sips." My mother elaborated on the dangers of alcohol, telling me that it used to make her take her top off when she was underage. She begged me to wear a bikini instead of my bra in case nudist tendencies were genetic.

She was so wound up that she couldn't finish her serious project of the night: application of new fingernails. My mother was such a wreck, in fact, that Bob had to affix her tips while she watched *Babes* and took Lamaze breaths. This was not a task for the fainthearted. Bob was performing a godly, selfless gesture, even for a great man like himself. I knew he was gearing up for his weekly marriage proposal, and I definitely didn't want to be around when she told him no for the twenty-thousandth time. He was finding her dismissals less and less amusing. So was I.

I excused myself to go upstairs and "pray" until Kevin finally rescued me. I was buckling under the pressure I put on myself: I had to meet up with a new guy because I needed this night to somehow count as a date. I would not fall behind in my plan, and I still believed that it was possible to be in love again soon.

To hell with previous setbacks, I told myself. *Maybe tonight is the night.*

"i want to chill wichoo"

Frankie was already in Kevin's car, much calmer than she had been earlier. She sensed how nervous I was and patted my leg right above my knee, but not in a sexual way this time. She read my anxiety and gave me soft, understanding looks, her human Xanax. Meanwhile, Kevin had the chanting-monk music turned up so high that I couldn't hear myself think. That was fine since I was driving myself crazy.

I didn't know what to expect at a party that took place way out in the middle of a field surrounded by snoring cows. I pictured beautifully dressed teenagers with flawless faces frolicking about a bonfire, a glamorous band playing under a small tent, and a cute college guy standing next to a keg to pour perfect pints of beer without all of that froth. I'd seen too many shows on cable where the party scenes were perfect: tiki torches everywhere, Astroturf instead of grass, streamers hanging from trees. I hoped everyone would throw their keys in a bucket, start out shyly, dance more aggressively, get trashed incrementally, hook up randomly, and then bond sloppily.

I was shocked when we arrived. No one gave a cow patty about the car keys or who would stay sober enough to drive. I saw no grass, only mud, and the bonfire didn't exist. In its place was a pile of forty glow sticks that hadn't been snapped in half yet. Scattered around were cases of beer so cheap that I didn't even recognize the brands. No one frolicked, either; they sat on black trash bags to keep their butts dry. Everyone was transfixed by a group of cheerleaders who took turns around a four-foot bong that was so big it had to stay put. The girls wore bandannas on their heads, and ratty clothes on the rest of their bodies. Everyone was mud-splattered, and I hoped Vikki J. wouldn't mind the dirt specks that were already on her white jeans. (She wouldn't.) One fancy truck, a shiny black low-rider, blasted tunes. Maybe we were cool. I mean, who cared about tiki torches? We had our own private deejay. The crowd was loud, voices rising above the bass, even though it was early. Some people laughed, sincerely and otherwise. Others played serious drinking games and bickered.

"Mr. Teeter is so much cuter than Mr. Henry."

"You need to stop smokin' so much crack."

"No, you need your head examined by a podiatrist."

The boy climbers were having loud discussions, and I was thankful not to hear a Swedish accent coming from the bunch.

We were welcome to drink, smoke, and fornicate till our bodies went numb out in that remote area, twenty-five miles out of Shitville. Only the owner of the property would know about our hidden location, and I'd heard that he was out of town. I didn't feel uncomfortable because we were with Kevin, who everyone liked. And, more important, most people were already drunk as donkeys or higher than treetops, so they couldn't have

96

known or cared who was actually invited and who wasn't. Frankie and I kept each other company while Kevin made the rounds. The hormone count kept increasing as more kids arrived in small, ganglike mobs.

Frankie and Kevin found a cooler lined with a trash bag. At their trough, they filled wax-paper cups with something called a Kool-Aid Surprise. Unrecognizable fruits floated in their drinks. They didn't bring me a cup.

"According to statistics," Kevin said, "eight teenagers die every day due to drunk driving." He took a gulp. "If Katie doesn't stay sober enough to drive, I'll just sleep out here with the chiggers, and you hot chicks are welcome to join me." His cup was already empty, and he ran back for a refill. Kevin naturally went through life on his own personal trampoline. Add a few chemical substances, and he was a walking pogo stick. At least he'd mentioned our car situation — I was relieved that he was conscientious enough to care. Maybe other kids would get DWIs, but we certainly wouldn't. After last Friday night, I knew liquor turned me into a kissing bandit.

"Believe me, I'll drive," I said.

"Woo-hoo."

"[Cuss] yeah."

They made their way back to the Kool-Aid Surprise, as if this arrangement had been planned long ago. I reminded them that I didn't hold hair back, clean chins, or scrub car seats. They were also responsible for entertaining me. I couldn't help wondering if I might've had a better time with Blue — then I forced myself not to think those thoughts.

"I'm serious. I want to have fun tonight," I said. "Today sucked."

97

Frankie was especially wound up when she was drunk; and, lucky for me, she was determined to be good company, telling jokes that involved a lightbulb, a platypus, and a dishwasher repairman.

Her pixie shoulders jerked up and down as she tried to contain her cackling. She quickly switched to a stiff, plain face when her humor began drawing an admiring crowd. Alcoholic inducements might make her gab in front of me, but she wasn't drunk enough to tell strange jokes in front of strangers — especially when all of the kids knew she was a lesbian. In Shitville, hardly the most cosmopolitan place, she was justified in her paranoia. But then the people around us proved her wrong. Kids said hi and smiled at her; she went wide-eyed and ghost-white with surprise. When it became clear that most people didn't care what she was, Frankie's sharp eyes relaxed. She stopped looking over her shoulder to see who might be whispering — no one was. She smiled devilishly, and I knew more jokes were on the way.

She and Kevin got caught in a moving crowd, probably on a mission for more refills, and I could've sworn that I was intoxicated, too. I was seeing things. Cherry the Cheerleader showed up as usual with a guy on her arm. But this time the guy was shorter than she was, and he walked funny. Matt Faulkner. *My* Barbie-loving, tree-climbing, salami-eating, flute-playing, plastic-glasses-wearing, girl-car-driving Matt Faulkner! Those were the things I loved about him — me alone. Was someone else finally starting to see how cool he really was? That was good and all for him but bad as hell for me. I was jealous. Before they even had a chance to stroll all the way in and greet the crowd, she had her arms draped all over him and her tongue down his throat.

Frankie came up behind me and spilled her Surprise on the back of my mother's white pants.

"Oh . . . to hell with . . . it." She stared at them and slapped my arm.

Kevin joined our gawking brigade and said, "Will you look at that?"

"How do you make a whore moan?" Frankie asked.

"How?" Kevin asked.

"Don't pay her."

Cheech and Chong fell into fits of laughter, along with others who had joined in on the staring. I couldn't see the humor in any of this. I wouldn't have cared if he'd stood there naked holding a rubber ducky; I didn't want anyone making fun of Matt. But I wasn't about to take up for him, either, not after what had happened between us. My emotions slowly drained out of my body. So Cherry was the girl Matt had a date with. It would've been obvious from the flirting at the locker if it hadn't been so outrageous. What was Cherry doing with Matt? Was he the reason she was nice to me? I wanted to cuss, and I needed a drink.

"Well, you know. That girl never shows up alone," Kevin whispered to me in a tone that told me it wasn't funny to him, either.

I was so mad that I almost got a cup full of Kool-Aid just so I could throw it in his face. He didn't want to be with me, but he would go out with *her*?

"Hey, Katie baby," Cherry said. When had she gotten so close to me? "I e-mailed you. Did you get it? I asked you to

99

come to the party with us tonight since I knew you and Matt were such good friends."

I damned myself for not checking my e-mail; I definitely could've used some warning. Matt was wearing a black-and-purple-striped polo shirt with dark, tight blue jeans. I'd never seen those clothes before, and he looked less geeky than ever. Even his shoes were different, more combat than orthopedic. He put his arm around Cherry the same way he'd held me last week. He stared at her, which was hard not to do because she was so friggin' pretty, and her red lips were so perfect. He looked triumphant, like when he won his tenth consecutive hundred-meter butterfly race. What did he care if she changed guys like day-of-the-week underwear? He'd been graced with the presence of a Very Popular Girl. His dreams had come true, and this was my nightmare.

He kept looking at her boobs. I nearly coughed up an intestine when it dawned on me that the two of them would be capable of having sex.

"Goodness, I didn't expect to see you here," he said to me.

"That makes two of us." I really was going to vomit, and I didn't want Frankie and Kevin to think I'd been sneaking drinks. I said, "Great to see you both. E-mail me again, Cherry. Um, I have to get Kevin and Frankie more Kool-Aid or something." They were standing right next to me with full cups but I walked off, anyway. I had no idea where I was going.

Frankie and Kevin followed. "Don't worry, Katie," Frankie said. "She's just looking for the thrill, for the unexpected. She's going geek chic this week."

I shot her a disapproving look, and she stopped with that line of reasoning. Putting down Matt — the Ivy League Barbie he'd given me still sat ceremoniously on my dresser — would never make me feel better.

"Oh, Katie, I'm sorry. I like Matt. He's just, um, Matt," she said.

"I know, I know."

"She'll just disappoint him," Kevin added. "He doesn't know what he's getting into."

I assured Kevin that Matt cared more about his rep than he did about Cherry.

Kevin added, "She'll demolish him, I swear it."

I was glad when some random girl batted her eyes at Kevin, because I wanted to drop the subject. My survival depended on hiding away somewhere and pretending they didn't exist. I was in luck. I moved Kevin and Frankie to the other side of the party where the wall of flesh crowded around the bong and glow sticks blocked my view of Matt and Cherry.

"Hey, cutie." I could hear the voice behind me only because the raging music had stopped for a few minutes. Voices of all kinds filled the air, still making it difficult to tell what was being said to whom.

"Hey, you. Cutie." I was sure the missive had to be directed to a boy climber. All of a sudden, I worried that my buttcrack was showing, and hoisted up the back of my jeans.

"What did you do that for?" the voice said. I spun around to see the hot deejay moving in on me.

We flirted all night, which eased the stinging sensations brought on by the odd couple. I spent the rest of my time hanging out by the truck with the stereo equipment, hoping that my eardrums wouldn't burst like water balloons. Every time I'd try to leave and talk to my wickedly drunk friends — all two of them — the deejay would say, "Why don't you stay here, baby? Why don't you keep me company?" I danced gently — very gently so he couldn't tell how uncoordinated I was — and watched him intently. He didn't say much; guys who look perfect like velvet don't have to. I guessed he was nineteen or so, and he probably lived a few towns away. None of that mattered one bit. He was hot, and he was flirting with *me*. The night wouldn't be a total bust if it helped me move forward with my plan.

I pondered taking off my top briefly (exposing the bikini beneath) because that's how badly I wanted to score a date for the next night. Luckily, I didn't have to resort to Vikki J.'s most crass tactics.

"You busy tomorrow night, because I want to chill wichoo." He handed me his business card, which was the kind you buy from a machine in the mall. It had seven different numbers on it. "You page me when I wake up tomorrow, around four p.m. I gotta bust this joint tonight and take care of some bizzness. But I want to see you tomorrow. Damn, girl. I got to see you soon."

His name was Ian, and he was smooth. I was smitten as a kitten (I really did think that, ugh), but inside I knew my interest in him was about the conquest and not real feelings. Whatever. Before he headed out, he spent even more time with me. We sat in plain view of the entire party in the bed of his black low-rider. The base bumped when he kissed me for what seemed like forever. I kissed back Cherry-style, hoping that a certain best friend might catch a glimpse. Kids were giving the truck little love slaps to tease us during our PDA.

"Watch it, that's my ride," Ian would say before putting his hands back in my deep-conditioned, straightened hair. He rubbed the back of my neck and head, stopping often to stare at me, eye-to-eye. Kissing him was more like slow, sensual dancing than making out.

"I got to go. I'll see you, baby girl." He was off, taking the music with him. Another boy quickly took over in his beat-up blue truck with a stereo system that sucked. So the party wasn't a total bust, I decided. I kissed a guy, and I scored a date for the next day; Frankie actually talked to people; and Kevin jittered around, flirting with cute drunk girls. I didn't see Matt or Cherry when we left. But the windows in Winifred were suspiciously, grotesquely fogged up.

"No [cussin'] way," Frankie said when we drove past. I ignored it; I mean tried to. What I didn't see or think about hurt me less.

The force of nature broke my old routine

At four the next afternoon, I tried to beep Ian. Bob had to explain how to do it. I thought only doctors, contractors, and other important people needed beepers. What was so important about a deejay?

"Hey, cutie." He called me back immediately, sounding like he'd just woken up. He left the party at one a.m., so what had he done afterward that kept him in bed till four?

"Hi."

"You're a hot kisser. What did you think of me, baby?"

Bob was within listening distance, making the conversation even more difficult.

"I had fun." Sure, he was good, but I didn't know what I enjoyed more: the kissing or the fact that Ian had helped me increase my lifetime tally to four — Paul, Matt, Kevin, and Ian. "But that's not why I beeped you." Honestly, though, I was nervous, considering what I had to do — and why.

"Whatup, cutie?"

"I can't hang out tonight. Please don't take this the wrong way, but let's get together next Friday." My whole plan had just changed, and I hoped I wouldn't be free next weekend, but I didn't know what else to say. I figured Ian would forget about me by then, anyway.

"You dissin' me, baby? Why you go doing me like that?"

"I have, um, a, um, family situation that came up tonight." Bob shot me a disappointed look, proving that he was listening. I was lying to Ian, and Bob knew exactly why.

"It's all good. Don't sweat it, cutie, I got your number, and I'll give you a shout next week."

After hanging up, I dialed the next number, a number I knew by heart.

"It's me," I said.

"Did you do it?"

"Yes, I canceled my date." What was I doing?

"Good, I'll be there soon."

Paul had shown up at my doorstep — again — at ten in the morning. And boy, was he ragged. He wore his worst baseball cap, which used to be purple when I first bought it for him. Now it was a faded shade of blue. He'd probably slept in the ripped, bleach-stained T-shirt he had on, but his puffy red eyes told me that he hadn't rested much. When he spoke, tears rolled down his freckled cheeks, and I let him rub my hand again.

Finally he was sad about what he'd done to us. Before, I couldn't understand why he hadn't missed me, and it made me feel better to see that he did. But I was frustrated, too. Just when I started feeling comfortable without him, as my new improved sassier self, he put me back in the emotional spin cycle.

He said, "I heard you kissed *another* guy last night. Katie, I cannot take it."

He cried more. It was horrifying. He was a confident, cool soccer player with a cute butt, and it broke my heart to see him shed tears even though he deserved every ounce of pain he was feeling on my behalf. The one thing I was learning from our breakup: The smell of other guys reels the old one back in. Another thing I hadn't learned: how to tell Paul to beat it.

"I don't want to fight with you anymore," he begged. "Don't be mad at me about all of the stupid stuff I said. Just go out with me tonight, Katie. Please go out with me tonight."

I cried, too. "I have a date, though."

"Cancel it. You have to do that for me."

And I did. I couldn't say no to Paul Green.

It was no surprise when I came back into the house and Vikki J. and Bob were less supportive than a cotton jockstrap. After he left, they talked eighty miles a minute. I needed to kick Paul to the curb forever. I should have been over him by then. I was way too good for his scrawny, cheating ass. They went on and on while sipping their morning milk shakes.

I tuned them out, deep in thought on how Bob was the one who should take his own advice. I loved Bob, but he crawled back to Vikki J. no matter what she did to him. The worst was when she jetted off to Panama City Beach during spring break by herself. It happened two years ago, and she asked him to watch me while she cleared her head and drank some good margaritas.

"But they have margaritas here in Shitville," he'd said, clearly terrified that she'd meet an even younger man. "I'll even make you the best you've ever had. I'll walk to Panama City and back for the recipe if you want me to."

"Stayin' in Shitville won't do no good for gettin' the gunk outta my cram-packed head. I have to go away for a few days. A girl's gotta do what a girl's gotta do."

Paul and I kept him company; Bob wanted to torture himself and watched sappy movies on the Women's Entertainment channel all weekend. During commercials, he'd sneak off to the bathroom and weep. We were torn up for him, and we made promises never to do anything so mean to each other. I was raving mad at my mother for demolishing a guy who weighed at least two-hundred-and-forty pounds, totally stripping him of his dignity. But I hadn't been able to get through to her ever, so there was nothing I could say to help him. I advised Bob to set her straight when she returned, and he assured me he would. Vikki J. got back into town on a Tuesday, and she whipped up some fried chicken, smiling at him all the while. She gave him a sack full of seashells, and he cried. He begged her not to ever leave him again — in the middle of dinner when Paul and I were chowing down on the legs. He never had any spine around my mother. Yet neither one of them understood why I lost mine around Paul.

Paul picked me up at seven, and we went to our favorite haunt, the Chinese restaurant. I was surprised to discover that I didn't feel happy, content, or satisfied when I spent time with him. Every night before I fell asleep, I had secretly fantasized about the moment when we might get back together. Yet now, there was no fairy-tale feeling about it. I was paranoid instead. Thoughts raced through my mind. Like, I wondered how many times Ho-Hawnnah had sat her boy climber bottom in the very same passenger's seat. I had the drowning, dreadful feeling that he'd brought her to our restaurant. What if they'd dined at the exact same table we were at then?

"Katie, what's wrong?" He grabbed my hand, and my fears subsided temporarily.

"Nothing."

We had lots to discuss. We'd spent four and a half years together, so nearly two weeks apart was two entire eternities. It was weird not knowing everything that had gone on in his life. He told me he'd missed me at his intramural soccer games, and he updated me on his friends. He'd spent the night with them Friday, which meant they weren't free to streak through the party I'd gone to. He'd also been accepted to the community college, the same one I'd probably attend, and he was glad that was all set. I talked, too. I explained that I hadn't understood just how isolated I'd been when I dated him, and I told him about my mission to make more friends. I didn't mention the date-twelve-guys-in-six-weeks, fall-in-love-before-prom plan. Instead, I talked about Kevin and Frankie, two people he admitted he liked. But I didn't dare utter Matt's name. Paul's jealous nature could handle me being friends with Kevin, who I just met. But he couldn't think about me with Matt. He didn't mention Ho-Hawnnah at all.

I loved him. I loved him. I loved him. But I hated him, too. The hurt he'd caused me overshadowed the intensity of my warmth for him. He'd taken away the trust between us — which sucked the joy out of spending time together. His presence infused me with anxiety and pain when I wanted to be content again. Despite all of that, though, I could still feel that

I cared incredibly deeply for him. Somehow he made me miserable in that lovesick, please-save-me kind of way. He didn't seem plagued by mixed feelings like I was. He rubbed my hand — crap! — and his eyes sparkled with lust whenever I spoke.

He hadn't paid so much attention to me since our four-year anniversary, the night we set up a tent in my backyard. His mother wouldn't let us really go camping; she was suspicious that we were making mad, passionate love every chance we got. My mother knew better and came up with the idea to camp out at our house. (She was impressed that I kept telling Paul no.)

We lit candles and roasted marshmallows over them that night. We looked up at the stars and kissed and hugged. We were happy together. I basked in good memories to make being with him more bearable. I hardly noticed that we had finished our sesame noodles, and Paul had paid the bill. That was unusual; we usually split it. I snapped back to reality when the waitress dropped the fortune cookies and the receipt.

"Your turn," he said. Like most couples, we had a ritual of reading our fortunes out loud.

"You first."

"No, you go."

"Um, okay," I said. "*A new friend helps you break out of an old routine.*"

"*The face of nature reflects all of life's ups and downs.*"

"Those fortunes are boring."

"Yeah, that's too bad," he said. "They totally suck."

Paul and I may not have had sex, but whatever you want to call our extracurricular activities, I hadn't done them with anyone else besides him. My mixed emotions were trumped by longing. I couldn't help it; I still wanted him. We gave each other a knowing look and headed out to his car. When he kissed me, my cheeks and chest flushed with color. Our love connection needed work, but our sexual one was still perfect.

He stopped and looked at me. "Your eyes get more violet when you're turned on. God, you are the most beautiful girl I've ever seen."

We continued to feel each other's bodies in the most pleasurable ways possible. When you've spent as much time together as we had, you become makeout professionals. He knew exactly where to touch me and when. He took my top off right when I wanted him to, while I squeezed him in his most private places. In those stolen, perfect moments we could forget everything that had happened. We savored them, making our steamy session last as long as it could.

I'd never worn skirts before. So Paul nearly popped out of his skin when he put his hand up my thigh and tugged at my panties. I hoped I'd done a good job shaving my legs — but really, that didn't matter so much.

"Being with you feels good," I said.

"There's nothing like it on the planet." He was really rubbing my thigh.

"This is what I want; the way we are now is perfect enough." That was the truth, too.

"I have to have sex with you, Katie. I have to. Please let me." He had lovelorn eyes, not just horny ones. I knew how he felt about me. But that was never the issue in moments like this one.

"This is enough. I don't want to do more than we're doing now." My sexual buzz was fading fast.

"You're kidding me." He sat up.

I couldn't believe we had to go through this old argument when we were just starting to connect again. He was clear on my feelings about sex, and of course he knew me well enough to figure out that my mind hadn't changed. I was disappointed. It always had to be more, more, more with him. I'd received what I needed, and so had he. Why did he have to be such a Neanderthal about it? It dawned on me that the race to have sex was propping up his ego. This was more about the conquest than his feelings.

"Here's the problem with us," he said.

"It's *your* problem with us. You need to get over it. If you really loved me, you wouldn't make me feel this way every time."

"If you really loved me, you'd do it."

"I'm sick to death of this argument. You'll have to find someone else if that's what you want."

"I already did." He stared at me, craving a strong reaction. When I looked back — it took me a few seconds to really hear what he'd said — he could only stare at his knees.

"You what?"

"Nothing."

"You did it with *her*?"

He could've told me my bedroom had burned down, taking my photo albums and childhood toys with it, and I would've been happier. I hadn't even imagined the possibility of them lying naked, body-on-body, sharing the most intimate act that exists between two humans. At least I didn't feel bad for referring to her as Ho-Hawnnah, since that's exactly what she was. I needed a name for Paul; he was a slut, too. He'd only been seeing her

111

since Monday before last, and they were already having sex. If I'd ever meant anything to him at all, he wouldn't even want someone who wasn't me. He could've kept waiting; it wouldn't have killed him. I would've been ready eventually, and I would've wanted him. I always thought Paul would be my first.

I imagined him sharing himself with someone else. I envisioned them in the act. I was so mad that I sat up, bumped my head on the roof of the car, fiddled around looking for the handle, and hopped out the door. I was standing outside his vehicle behind a large bush in the parking lot at our Chinese restaurant. My shirt was in my hands and not on my body, and my pink bra with flowers was in plain view and probably unhooked in the back. I didn't even care.

"I hate you. I swear to God, I hate you," I said.

His eyebrows furrowed again, this time in pain, as he realized how badly he'd screwed up — in more ways than one. He knew he never should've let that information slip. Even worse, he knew he never should have done it with another girl if he expected me to keep loving him. We locked eyes, and I told him everything without saying one word. I bawled so hard that the world went blurry as I stood there nearly naked behind a bush at the Chinese restaurant. He wept gently in the backseat of his car. Paul had hurt me enough, and I hadn't deserved it. I swore to myself that he wouldn't make me cry ever again.

"I never should have done it. Katie, I love you. I shouldn't have."

"You probably never stopped. You probably did it with her last night. You make me sick. I have never hated someone so much in my life."

He bit his bottom lip hard to keep it from quivering. He whined, showing desperateness and vulnerability. It was too late for any of that. "Don't say those things to me, Katie. Please don't. Whenever I'm with her, I think about you. I want to be with you. I know that now."

"It's too late. I'm going home."

"Get in the car. At least let me take you."

"I'll never set foot in that car again. Who knows what you've done in there." I turned toward the Chinese restaurant to use their phone. I wasn't going to give Paul the satisfaction of asking to use his cell. But I was so paralyzed by pain that when I tried to walk, I could barely move. I bent down to the ground and buried my head in my knees, which quickly became soaked. This would be the last time I cried over him, I swore again.

He didn't know whether to leave the car or leave me alone. "Katie. Don't. I'm sorry. I never meant to hurt you."

"You're selfish. I never would've done any of these things to you. I couldn't imagine hurting you this bad." My body relaxed, allowing me to stand up. I turned to walk away, pulling my shirt on as I went.

"You can't go anywhere like that!" He held my skirt and my shoes out the window. I put them on with my back to him. He slumped over in the backseat of his car as I went into the restaurant. I ordered some green tea and more fortune cookies, even though I knew I wouldn't be able to eat or drink them.

By the time Vikki J. and Bob picked me up, Paul was gone. My appearance — bird's nest of hair, eyes pink as raw mosquito bites — alarmed them. They fussed over me, and I assured them I was all right. I had stopped crying, and I had meant it when I made that pact to myself. He would not turn me to mush again. I was becoming Kung Pow Katie.

"What the hell did that silly-ass boy do?" Vikki J. asked. "Ah'll slash his tars if he ever comes in arr driveway again." Her accent was stronger when she was pissed.

Bob reached to the backseat to pat my head and gave me a look like he understood how messed up I was inside.

Vikki J. continued. "We're a-goin' to his house right this minute. I got to have me a word or two with that little turd. If he thinks he can just show up and mess 'round with a Jaymes, then he don't have the sense of a cash register."

"Let's just go home, Vikki," Bob said to her. "Katie's been through enough. She needs to go home."

"You gonna tell me what happened er what, punkin?"

"I will later, Vikki J. First, I need to go home and pray about it." I wanted to bury my head in her lap and cry. But I didn't have the right kind of mother for that.

"Have it yer way. You know that silly religious talk is the quickest way to shut me up." She turned up the radio and hummed to a whiny country song about love gone wrong.

I thought about beeping Ian to see if he still wanted to take me out tonight. I imagined us at a late movie holding hands and pretending to pay attention to the screen. I'd kiss him passionately and pretend that Paul was watching. Maybe I'd even have sex with Ian out of spite.

No.

Tempting as it was, I did not contact His Slickness. Attention from another guy wasn't going to ease the pain that shot out each of my pores. It would only numb me more. Ian — or any other random guy — might be able to make me forget about Paul for a while, but none of them could give me what I really longed for at that particular moment. I wanted Paul to have his virginity back. I wanted to be the special one to pluck it away from him. Now it would never be me, and I would never want it to be. I decided to stay home, tucked away in my bed in silence. I wouldn't stay there for days on end like I had the last time. But I needed to be right there for one night. I needed time to think and heal so Paul couldn't hurt me again.

I had to feel it.

I felt the pain completely until two in the morning. I concentrated on becoming stronger. Paul hadn't demolished me like he had two weeks ago. It hurt, but it didn't flood my veins the way it had before. Paul hadn't deserved any of my affections. I knew I had made a big mistake today. I would not make it again.

Ten Sausage Pizzas, Please

Sunday, April 13

I longed for Matt like some people crave chocolate to cure sadness. I couldn't count on cocoa for solace, of course, unless I wanted to be attacked by puffy scarlet hives. But I needed something sweet and comforting. The Muppet Babies were childish, Vikki J. was a fanatic, but Matt was always perfect. When we were little, every problem could be solved by climbing a tree. I wondered if we'd be too big now to take on the one in his backyard. Whatever I did, I needed to spend time with Matt; no one could lift my spirits like my best friend.

But pride wouldn't give me permission to pick up the phone. How silly was that? I was being psycho about his flamboyant choice in women. Embarrassingly, I was being jealous, too. We were never an item except for a few short hours on one drunken night, and I told myself to get the hell over it. After all, I was no better than Matt and Cherry after I superglued my lips to deejay Ian's in front of everyone. Surely Matt and I had a bond that was stronger than alcohol and longer lasting than sexual thrills. Somehow, we'd have to move past these petty romantic jealousies. I willed myself to call him, even though doing it would feel like swallowing a toad.

"Matt?"

"Oh, my goodness. Katie, I wasn't expecting to hear from you." He actually sounded surprised and uncharacteristically occupied.

"We used to talk almost every single day," I pointed out.

"Things have been crazy lately, haven't they?"

We talked about the party — deliberately avoiding the most obvious topics of Cherry and Ian — and our attempt to be normal felt surfacey and fake. At least it was civil, with undercurrents of warmth. We still loved each other. We just didn't know the appropriate ways to show it anymore.

"I went out with Paul yesterday, Matt," I confessed.

"For Satan's sake, why would you do a thing like that? Katie, it's hard to keep saving you. You keep making the same mistakes."

He was harsh, cold, even irritated. The Matt I could count on would have invited me over for macaroni and cheese, and he would've cooked it just the way I like it, with extra Velveeta. I might even have convinced him to climb that old tree. But this new, *not* improved Matt kissed Cherry and scolded me. I pictured him sitting downstairs in front of his TV cross-legged. His plastic cup of cranberry juice would be sitting on the end table next to the couch. His flute and sheet music would hog most of the carpet. He usually played for a while, then got caught up in a syndicated show.

"Where are you right now?" I asked.

"In the basement?"

"Did you practice the flute?"

"Yeah, for a while, till I started watching real-life forensic disasters."

"Have you had any cranberry juice?"

"Not yet, it's on the table over there. Why are you asking me all of these questions?"

"I still know you, Matt."

"Katie, goodness, you are being weird. Are you okay?"

Actually, I wasn't, and I told him so. I told him every detail of my evening, except the Ian stuff, including how I lay in bed last night making a real effort to process everything. He grunted the right uh-huhs and okays at the most appropriate moments. He listened. That's all I needed, and I was assured that there was one person in the world who still got me.

"I'm sorry I was harsh earlier. I didn't mean to be. I'd ask you over for macaroni and cheese, but I can't right now."

He always could before! What could possibly be more important than me? I wasn't angry, I was disappointed. That feeling was becoming alarmingly familiar lately. I decided to be silent. Not saying anything would be whiny enough.

"Oh, come on, Katie. Cherry's coming over here to study."

First, no female being — excluding me, his mom, his grandmother, and his cat — had ever set foot in the Faulkner house. Yet he mentioned Cherry's arrival as if it were as commonplace as Bob's marriage proposals. My fascination continued. Cherry wasn't exactly an astrophysicist. Neither of us were in accelerated classes like Matt was, but at least I didn't have to take geometry twice. I had passed out the graded papers for our teachers before. Cherry made crappy grades and was hardly the kind of person who would want to study, even if she could figure out how to do it. The only thing she knew was anatomy. I did not like this one bit. Maybe she wanted to teach him an X-rated cheerleading routine. I shivered with nausea.

"What, are you jealous?" Matt asked, reading my thoughts — damn him.

"No, no, are you kidding? I'm happy for you, Matt."

"I wasn't happy when you were all over Ian. I didn't like you dating Kevin, either, but he seems like a pretty good guy now."

"God, really? I had no idea. I thought you'd forgotten all about last Friday."

Matt sighed into the phone. "Don't be silly, Katie. It's just that we're so complicated."

"I know." I wasn't going to make a fool of myself and ask him why why why he didn't want to try. I'd already thrown myself at him once, and I didn't want to do it again. Besides, now that he was with Cherry, he was less appealing. She used guys, and she liked to be used. Fading jealousy aside, I hoped to God she didn't hurt Matt. If she did, I'd make her eat a pom-pom.

"This thing with Paul has me acting crazy," I went on.

"Exactly," he replied, not exactly saying the right thing, another out-of-character behavior.

His sentiments made no sense, and the ending to our phone conversation was hardly satisfying. But there was no one else I wanted to talk to. Kevin and Frankie didn't know me well enough. Calling Ian would have been a temporary fix. For the second time in two days, I wished for a wise, thoughtful mother who could help me sort out complicated traumas. I couldn't mention Paul to her, because she wanted revenge. She'd already threatened to order ten sausage-and-onion pizzas and have them delivered to his house. I couldn't talk to her about Matt, either — she thought our kissing was pure insanity.

Whether I liked it or not, I was alone. I had isolated myself for years, so it was no one's fault but my own.

"Katie Kay-Kay," Vikki called up the stairway. I pretended not to hear. When she used a pet name like that, she usually wanted to test a new hair product on me. Though I wasn't as opposed to those things as I used to be, I was in no mood.

"Katie goddamned James," she said again, alerting me that she meant business. "There's a phone call for you." I was sure my caller heard and once again I was annoyed at her lack of tact.

"Hello," I said hesitantly.

"Hey, baby cakes!" It sounded like a younger version of my mom was on the phone.

"Yes?"

"Do you know who this is, sweetie?"

"Um, I'm sorry, I don't."

"This is Cherry!"

Oh, Cherry! Cherry the Cheerleader! How'd she know she was precisely the person I was *dying* to talk to?!

"Hey."

"What is *up*? I hear you live just a coupla doors down the way?" I thought I'd break Matt's legs; I was getting that mean. But I took a deep breath, thought of chanting monks, and controlled my irritation.

"Um, yeah. You must be at Matt's."

"You're smart! How did you know?" I thought she was kidding, but I couldn't be sure. Then she added, "This sweet hot stud wanted me to call you. Ooooh. *Mwah, mwah, mmm-mmwah.*" I did not enjoy watching her kiss Matt on Friday, and listening to her do it was even worse.

"Well, I just wanted to know if you wanted to mosey on down here and study with us. I, like, brought these books and class notes, and I even have my geometry assignment." I could hear her flipping through her makeup bag in her purse.

"I already did my studying for the weekend." I had, actually. Either I could've spent the day wondering where the hell Paul's virginity went, or I could try to memorize the battles of the Second World War. The latter was a joyfest, if you asked me.

"That's too bad. Want to come over, anyway?"

"Oh, no, you two just hang out. I'm okay."

"Well, sweetie, Matt told me you were kind of sad. I just thought I'd be happy to try to cheer you up." Then she started whispering so I could hardly hear her, "Those broken hearts really suck. I know all about those."

"That's nice of you. I really appreciate you two calling me. I'm going to be okay."

"Well, let's talk soon. It seems like forever since we've had one of our chats," she said. "Matt says all of these great things about you. I hope we can get to know each other better, too, girlfriend."

"Okay, I'll see you tomorrow in typing class."

"Do you think I should study for that, too? Wait, I already did. E-mailing counts as typing, right?"

"Yeah, sure."

"Catch ya later, doll-face."

I kind of loathed her, but was starting to consider liking her at the same time. Had guys really hurt *her*? I didn't quite get how that could be possible, but it certainly made her more real. Maybe everything I thought about her was all wrong. Maybe she was just dying for attention. She was definitely a flaunt and a slut, but instead of her using guys, she insinuated that it was the other way around. Maybe underneath the high-volume laugh, brazen sexuality, and big mouth, there was a nice person in there. I decided to think about it tomorrow. At the very least, I allowed myself to keep hating her for the rest of the night.

i'm nobody's bitch

Monday, April 14

"She did what with who?" someone behind me asked.

I put my head down on my desk and giggled to myself. It would've been too proud of me, too obnoxious, to smile out in the open. The kids in homeroom couldn't believe it was me with Ian — him hitting on me publicly, then planting his lips on mine in the back of his truck. Girls asked me what it was like, as if he were a supernatural being. Guys watched after me with keener interest. That was always the case: Whenever a girl had a boy after her, she became more attractive than Miss Teen USA. I didn't take the renewed interest in me as a compliment; instead, it merely served the purpose of feeding their machismo. My theory: If I was being pursued by The Deejay, hopefully more guys would try to steal me from him, and then I would hopefully get a date I could stand for the prom.

I received an invitation to hang out on Friday from a rich sophomore who had the reputation of being a booger eater (I swear to God I'm not making that up). I declined somewhat gracefully, telling him I already had plans with The Deejay.

The sophomore slumped away disappointed and defeated. I, Katie James, had to turn down a date. My self-esteem jumped up about ten notches, if for the wrong reasons. But even more rewarding was the knowledge that Paul had to hear all about it. I was tempted to spread a rumor that I had slept with Ian just to make Paul jealous. But, well, that wasn't me.

Everything that had happened was enough to make Paul seem defeated, and because of that, I was finally able to pass him normally in the hallways. He may have acted like nothing was up, strutting past lockers and talking to his boys in the lunchroom, but the dark skin under his eyes and pursed lips told me otherwise. He was hurting . . . as he should have been . . . damnit.

Just when I thought everything was going my way, for once, I stepped innocently enough into the girls' restroom. Maybe it was payback for being a bit obnoxious that day — Blue was sitting right in front of me on the sink top as if we had arranged the meeting.

"Hey, I hear you had a good weekend," he said. And even though I didn't know him nearly as well as I knew Paul, I could tell that he was hurt, too. Human beings wear jealousy like emotional jewelry, myself probably included.

"I did," I said. Since no one had heard about the Paul fiasco, I could just pretend it never happened and bask in my present position of The Deejay's love goddess.

"I bet Pee-an, I mean Ian, was so *goooood*."

"Ewww. I am not that kind of girl."

He looked directly at me and his tone grew serious. "I know you're not. I'm teasing, Ms. Violet Eyes."

That surprised me. I had to remember why I hadn't gone

out with him in the first place. Once I did, I could go on the defensive again. "What are you doing here?" I huffed, newly self-confident. "I told you never to speak to me again. I think you're egotistical and disgusting." I also thought he was cuter than anyone I'd ever laid eyes on, but I didn't dare tell him — or anyone else.

"I came to explain. I don't know what Frankie said. I'm just sure it wasn't the truth."

"Are you saying my friend is a liar?"

"I'm saying there's more to the story." He smiled at me, locking eyes, moving closer to me like he'd done in that restroom before.

Stop it! Stop it! I repeated in my head. These charming males — Paul included — were not going to convince me to doubt myself anymore.

"On the other hand, I think I've heard all I want to hear," I said. "You can't spin your way out of this one."

"You wait one second, Purple."

"Is Purple some reference to being friends with Frankie? Because if it is, I don't think it's funny. Anyway, you need to get a haircut and a life. Go away."

"I merely aim to compliment you, O Charming One," he said, getting prickly.

"I have an idea, Mr. Alterna-weirdo," I shot back. "Why don't you take your compliments somewhere else? They are wasted on me. Go back to the CD store, and leave me alone."

He turned around as if he'd been stung one too many times with a flyswatter. I'd kicked the sparkle right out of his blue eyes.

"You misunderstand, Katie James. You misunderstand," he

said and walked away, shaking his head like an old sage and appearing less self-confident than he had before.

I almost felt bad for the awful things I'd said. But I just reminded myself of what Frankie had told me. I had never told someone off like that before. I was sorry, but I had to practice on someone, and it looked like it was going to be him. God, what a waste of great hair Blue was. What a waste of a sexy smile and interesting words.

What a waste.

i win — well, maybe

Wednesday, April 16, and Thursday, April 17

Let's make Paul jealous, teased the note I received in homeroom on Wednesday.

Visions of demolishing him in ways legal and not had filled me with delight all week. He was enduring the rumors about me and Ian, but that wasn't harsh enough. Paul deserved more pain, just so we'd be even. Paul took almost five years of my life — literally because he didn't let me have one of my own — and for what? So he could get his sexual quota filled, and then realize fleshy pleasures weren't all that, anyway? That was complete crap. I didn't admit to anyone that I still loved him a little — it would have been pathetic on my part. I couldn't help it, though. I'd had a good time with him, however fleetingly, on Saturday before I ended up crying in my underwear outside of his car. But the bottom line was, I *had* ended up crying in my underwear. That can never be good.

I could've lived without the humiliation of Breakup Part Two. I never needed to know what went on with Ho-Hawnnah.

Even worse, that information would have to keep us apart, maybe forever. I meant, definitely forever. I wasn't sure which sentiment was more painful: What he had done, or what it meant. I wondered if Ho-Hawnnah heard what happened over the weekend with me. I wondered if he'd finally dumped her. I half hoped that now she knew exactly what it felt like to be dumped. But, as much as I hated them both, I wasn't ready to wish that kind of pain on anyone — except for Paul.

I'll think about it, I answered to the query in the note.

You'd better hurry. My weekends fill up fast.

I folded the piece of paper we'd been writing on and tucked it into my back pocket. I'd have to sleep on that one.

My friends — I was finally used to the idea that I had some — were keeping my mind off of things. Kevin even asked me to go to the gym with him Wednesday night. He thought I might be good at aerobics if I just tried. Clearly, he hadn't seen me when I'd screwed up this year's cheer at tryouts.

"Come on," he insisted. "It couldn't be that bad." He said I just needed the proper training.

"If you want to train me, you'd better make sure I have a whiplash collar."

"If dogs can learn to serve blind people, *you* can make it through an aerobics class. Don't worry; I'll help you."

"I'm more tree sloth than dog. Ever trained a tree sloth, Kevin?"

Kevin had to cancel on me, and I thanked every deity known to man. He was called in to teach a class for his bubble-brained, bleached-blond boss who was "under the weather." Really, though, she was probably under some middle-aged man, because Vikki J. had done her up that afternoon in preparation for a big date. Her getting lucky was lucky for me. Instead of suffering in a foreign torture chamber called a gym, I decided to do something I was good at instead. I was going out to eat. Frankie, Matt, Cherry, and I — an oddball group I'd thrown together just for kicks or self-inflicted agony — were going to Big John's to see who could eat the most pepperoni. Matt and I called our competition The Great Meat Off. Our battle could be considered a physical activity, couldn't it?

I was trying to be open-minded about Matt and Cherry. I was slightly less jealous than before, because Ian had called me two times already, events that I bragged about often, especially in front of Matt. I chattered about it every chance I got because I was insecure, and I wasn't afraid to admit it to myself and no one else. I just didn't care, and I wanted to do anything besides talk about Paul. Anyway, Matt had Cherry; Paul had dumped me and boned someone else; and I was a loser with no date for the prom. I didn't owe anyone explanations. My new flirtation with Deejay Smooth — *my* new nickname for him — made me feel worthwhile. So did the facts that I had turned down Blue and Kevin Ebernackey and a rich sophomore geek for dates in the last few weeks. I never mention that about Kevin for obvious reasons; he had become my good friend. But it still inflated my ego to think about it. Was it okay to inflate my own ego? I vowed to stop doing it the next day.

"I got a C on our surprise typing quiz today, Katie," Cherry said. "How'd you do?"

"Um, I got an A. Didn't he tell us about the quiz yesterday?"

"Is that what he was doing? Heee. I couldn't concentrate. I was too busy thinking about Matt." She made more kissy noises and aimed them in his direction.

"Oh, for goodness sakes, Cherry, don't say things like that. You'll make me blush." And he did.

She got out a mirror — not the one I'd "given" her — and put on more red lipstick. She stared at it for an awfully long time. The love-pigeons cuddled together and stole kisses while Frankie and I rolled our eyes and glanced at each other uncomfortably. We willed the extra-large, extra-pepperoni pizza to arrive on our table in record speed. I hit Frankie's thigh and told her to remind me to tell her something later. I wanted to say that whenever I'd been to Big John's, Cherry had always chosen that booth and put her date on the inside of it next to the wall. That way she could squish over in the corner and make out with him easier. I didn't know if I could eat the pepperoni when I thought about what might have been going on under that table. Oh, well, I was getting over it. *Ian, Ian, Ian*, I thought to myself.

"So Ian said we were going to this great big party at a hip-hop club on Friday," I said kind of loudly when Cherry acted like she was going to swallow Matt whole. "He said I could hang out in the deejay booth and everything. He's going to let me choose the songs and teach me how to make noises with the records. I bet some really cool people will be there. I'm even kind of worried about what to wear."

"That's awesome, Katie," Cherry said. "I bet you'll have a lot more to play with than a bunch of records. That door probably has a nice, big, hard lock. You go, girlfriend." Clearly, she knew nothing of the recent Matt-and-Katie tryst. Matt glanced down at his knees and turned red — again. Frankie looked blank and bored as she buttoned and unbuttoned her flowered housedress.

"I hope so." I smiled as big as my mouth would allow. "I mean, he is the *hottest* guy I've ever seen before *in my life*!"

"Not quite, Katie girl," Cherry interrupted. "I think Matt takes the top prize. And you know what they say about swimmers."

"Anyway . . . he swears he's going to take me around to meet all of his 'peeps.' That's what he calls them, 'peeps.' Isn't that cool?" I was really hamming it up.

"Sounds like somebody's trying too hard," Matt said, squinting at me; he left his glasses on the table, and I had to admit he looked a lot cooler. "Um, we're going to the symphony on Friday," he added, smiling at Cherry and pulling her closer to him. If they squished together just a little bit closer, she would've been sitting on top of him. Despite myself, I worried that she might accidentally kick his legs.

"That sounds like fun," Frankie said. "The symphony is cool. You know what? I [cussin'] miss ballet."

They were right. Going to the symphony with someone you cared about sounded a lot more romantic than screaming at each other over the bass at a loud club. I expected it to be the kind of place where guys grabbed girls' butts as if that were perfectly acceptable. And the truth was, I really didn't want Smooth all over me in a locked box. The only point of going on a date with him was to make out in public where, hopefully, kids from school would see.

"You did ballet?" Cherry seemed genuinely interested. "That means you got to wear a tutu."

"I haven't worn a tutu since I was five."

"Did you wear shiny pink shoes with the hard tips? Did they hurt your feet? I bet they did because, girl, I can barely wear heels with pointy toes."

"They hurt like hell. Think of wearing those shoes when you're doing a pirouette piquee."

"Wow, you speak French, too. Frankie, you are too cool. I bet your feet really hurt, like when you wear four-inch heels," Cherry said. "Those are the *worst*."

"I wouldn't know — I only wear boots. The kinds with plastic soles."

"You don't know pain and torture, then."

"Oh, I think I do." Frankie kicked me under the table. The treads of her shoes made me grimace.

When the pizza came out, Matt and I explained the rules of The Great Meat Off, a game Vikki J. helped us invent in elementary school. At the count of three, everyone would start pulling pepperoni pieces off the pie, one by one, and eat them as fast as we could. Each person had to count out loud after we swallowed each one. When all of the pepperonis were gone, whoever ate the most won and got to eat more slices than the others if he or she wanted to. I usually won at this game, so it was my idea to play it.

"Cool," Frankie said.

"That's kind of gross," Cherry added.

"Gross? It's great!" Matt said.

"You're right, honey. This is *brilliant*!" Cherry wasn't even being sarcastic.

"I wish Ian were here to play with us."

"Go!" Matt yelled.

"One!"

"Three."

"Four."

"Five."

"Six."

"Two." Cherry wasn't doing so well at this game. "They're too hot!"

"Seven."

"[Cuss], I dropped one on my boots."

"Nine."

"Eleven." Matt was edging ahead of me.

"Fourteen."

"Four. Ewww, they're greasy."

"Fifteen."

"Nine." Frankie was plugging along. "You two just wait till next time. I'm gonna practice and kick your asses."

"Four and a half. Oh, God, my lipstick is coming off!"

"Eighteen."

"Twenty."

"Twenty-one."

"Twenty-three."

Matt and I exchanged death stares. I reached under the table and pinched his knee — I knew exactly how to do it just so I'd cause a distracting tickle. Luckily, Cherry's hand wasn't down there at the time.

"Twenty-friggin'-nine," I yelled, catching my breath after swallowing the last one. "Twenty-friggin'-nine, twenty-friggin'-nine, twenty-friggin'-nine." I had won, in case anyone hadn't noticed.

"Congratulations, Katie. You earned it. You deserved to win," Matt conceded. Cherry reached over and kissed his greasy pepperoni-splattered face. He didn't seem to care if he lost, which irked me.

"Woo-hoo. Just call me the Pepperoni Princess," I bragged, anyway.

"Don't get so cocky. I'll beat you next time," he said.

"But you won't beat me," Frankie added in a strangely void-of-emotion tone.

"I'll sit the next one out," Cherry said. She was a dim ray of light, and her comments were so unintentionally funny that Frankie and I were constantly nudging each other. While she lacked certain conversational skills, her ability to multitask was impressive. She got out Vikki J.'s compact this time, the one that used to belong to me, rubbed Matt up and down, and carried on a pseudo-conversation all at once. "Pepperoni is just not good for my complexion, doll-babies. In fact, all kinds of meat break me out. I'm kind of a vegan. I prefer pizza with just cheese."

Frankie snickered. Matt and I just looked at each other. Matt and Frankie began a discussion about science classes, and I could've killed them. They left me no choice but to converse with Cherry, and her favorite topic was — shocker — guys.

"So how was the sex with Paul? You never told me." What my body did — or didn't do — was no one's business. Matt knew I hadn't had sex, but he never wanted the details, and I never wanted to give them.

"It was fine."

Matt, who must've been listening, shot me a *you lie* look.

"I bet it was, honey. I bet it was. Me and Matt here —"

"I just may do it with Ian," I interrupted.

Matt frowned, and Frankie wrinkled her nose and peered at me.

"You should, girlfriend. He's hot. But not nearly as fine as Matt here. Right, snookums?" She wiped the grease off his forehead with a Big John's napkin.

"Yes, Ian is fine." I'd never called anyone "fine" in my life. Frankie reached into the pocket of her flowered dress — it was about two sizes too big for her — and put some money on the table.

"I have to go, you all. It was fun."

"What's wrong?" I asked. "Don't leave yet."

"I have to, man. I'm feeling all . . . I don't know."

"Just stay a little longer."

"No, thanks. You have a good time. I'm fine, really."

"You don't seem fine," I said.

"I'm just sitting here feeling, well, really lonely." She blushed from her cheeks down to her chest. She was so red that my scalp got hot from looking at her. "Every one of you has someone." She paused. "Oh, don't look so horrified. I'm just tired of being alone. I'll catch you tomorrow."

I wanted to leave, too, but I didn't think Frankie would want to take me. I wanted to tell her that I didn't really care about Ian. I didn't even know Ian. I felt exactly the same way Frankie did. Maybe she was giving me what I deserved by leaving me with the love crew. I sat there smiling and acting polite while Cherry asked titillating questions between kissing on Matt. By the time they dropped me off at home, I was more depressed than Frankie had been, but I still bragged about my date with The Deejay pretty much until I walked through the door. Being obnoxious didn't make me feel one bit better; it probably made everything worse.

Vikki J. was watching *Babes*. "I'm not surprised you're making so many friends, Katie. And you're getting more dates than a fruitcake," she said. "Honey child, you are so much prettier than Avalon."

"Thanks, I have to —"

"Baby, you go pray. You do that. I have to go downstairs and do something about this hair."

Thursday morning, I pulled the note out of the back pocket of the knee-length jean skirt with frayed edges. My mother was buying some cute stuff lately, and I was happier than ever to be borrowing it.

At the bottom of the letter, down where there was still some white space left, I wrote: *Yeah, I'm in. Let's make my ex jealous.*

The response? *Now, you're talking. When do you want to do it?*

Let's go out Saturday, I wrote back. I had plans with Ian Friday, of course, and the whole school knew it. But this time, I chose not to rub it in.

You're on. We'll do whatever you want. I'm your bitch. XO, Wren.

I just hoped Paul's best friend wouldn't streak when we went on our date.

No meat – Please

"Dude, you embarrassing me," Deejay Smooth said at the start of our date.

I couldn't help it if I nose-dived up the stairs to the deejay booth on the eighteen-and-under party barge out on the river. My nerves got the best of me along with Vikki J.'s kitten sandals, the same ones that recently attacked my poor toe at school. Who could blame me? This date with a local celebrity was high-pressure. Plus, I was twenty miles away from Shitville in a glam nightclub that seemed out of place in a state that boasted more ears of corn than people. I hated it; I was a cat pinned in a rabid dog kennel.

To make matters more miserable, I had taken one of my mother's old faded jean skirts and lopped the hem off. I turned it into a super-mini that made Bob wince, and I was terrified of providing a peep show every time I took a step. To add to the frenzy going on beneath my skin, Ian kept looking me up and down, making me feel like I was being evaluated for his personal approval test. I hadn't tried to land him, but now that he was with me, I had to step up. I wished I could impress him the way he impressed me. I mean, after Ian gave his name at the door of the club, he and I breezed past the kids waiting in line. The cover charge was comped.

He kept his hold on me as we made our way through a sea of bumping and grinding teenagers. The musty scent of perfume mixed with mousse mixed with body odor made me want to take a shower immediately. The sweaty girls kept touching my creamy smooth date, saying stuff like, "You da man!" or "Hey, Ian baby, come say hi to me later." None of them looked like they found me worthy of being in his presence. Green strobe lights flashed rhythmically in every hater's honor. I strutted through the scene in vain. As much as I tried to convince myself that I deserved to be there with a hottie, I knew the truth: I was just a glammed-up geek. Everyone else knew it, too.

The deejay booth was in an elevated box with windows in the front center of the room. The inside of it was empty, like a blank sheet of music paper waiting for its composer. Ian insisted I climb the stairway first, and then I really wished I hadn't cut off the hem because I knew he'd get a close-up of what was underneath my skirt. When I reached around to pull a tiny swath of jean material between the back of my thighs, my feet forgot where they were supposed to go and came crashing down. I barely saved myself from a bloody broken nose, thanks to my fast-thinking right hand and my brave shins that leaned against the steps to brace me up. My eyes were two inches from the wooden steps, and my heart beat so hard I thought it would crack my ribs. My burning shins brought tears to my eyes that were determined to drip down my cheeks. In the fall, my hand could no longer monitor my mini, so the small tube of denim rode up around my waist. I landed in a compromising position on the steps, my white thong gleaming.

"I'm so sorry, Ian. I didn't mean to cause a scene. Are you okay?"

"Damn, girl. The whole room is lookin' at your booty. Pull that skirt down. Sheeit."

I hobbled up the rest of the stairs into the deejay booth and sat down on the one chair in the corner. I rubbed my shins and hoped they wouldn't get too bruised. I realized that I'd forgotten to put on my deodorant. My armpits were sweat geysers, and my face was so red-hot it burned.

"I've had a rough day, kiddo," he said as he rubbed his temples. "My peeps got me up at noon today. They were talkin' some trash about how their car broke down, and I had to take them to White Castle."

"Wow." My own day flashed before my eyes. I'd been up since six a.m. because I needed to study more for my math exam. I crammed during other class periods and totally stressed myself out. I'd forgotten my lunch money, and by the time I got around to borrowing it from someone at our table, the only selection still available was hamster surprise, which was a mysterious meat substitute breaded and stuffed with mushy creamed vegetables that were green. Everyone made rodent jokes while I mumbled my math equations, and I was only able to swallow the peanut-butter ball. I was starved when I took the test, and I probably flunked. If I'd only had White Castles, I would've considered it a perfect day.

"I need a rubdown, baby. Bring me that chair so I can sit down. Then you can fix my muscles."

Ian was doing me a huge favor by a) going out with me and

b) parading me around a cool club. I just shut up and did what he asked. I thought if I gave him his massage, he'd forgive me for falling on my face, bruising my legs, and embarrassing him. I knew the situation was ridiculous even while I was living in it. But Ian owned this powerful, commanding charisma. When someone expects prince treatment the way he did, everyone around him — including me — gave it to him.

He rocked to the beat of his choice of songs and moaned when I kneaded the area just above his shoulder blades. By this time, my shins were on fire and so were my hands. Ian had the hardest, most rock-solid body I'd ever felt in my life. I wondered if he was made of human flesh or industrial steel. Most teenage guys were still skinny and soft, even if they were fit, and they had a lanky awkwardness about them that revealed their age. Deejay Ian was the opposite, an Adonis with the well-developed muscles of a twenty- or thirty-something. He also had the smallest waist I'd ever seen on a man — there was no way he ate *that* many White Castles. I peered over his head to study his luscious lips. They were like two perfectly inflated balloons, and I wondered what delightful things they might be able to do to a girl's body. But I didn't want the girl's body to be mine. I realized I'd take geek over god any day.

"How old did you say you were, Ian?" I asked.

"Dude, I'm eighteen. I come to this club all of the time when I'm not deejaying. Do you think they'd let me in if I was twenty-one, kiddo?"

"You're older than eighteen. I can tell by your body." And I know he'd said he was nineteen at the outdoor party.

"What's that supposed to mean?"

"You have these hard, well-developed muscles, you know."

"They sexy?"

"Of course they're sexy."

His smile was naughty when he said, "You just keep quiet on the age tip, and we'll get along just fine."

He showed me how to scratch records and asked me what I thought he should play. Ian called my song suggestions "rank" and played his favorites.

"Wanna see the hotties move? Check this." He played a banging techno song and the females gyrated as if possessed by poltergeists or dancing in tongues. His nose made a grease mark on the deejay-box window as he watched. For a second, I got all jealous of the pretty girls in no clothes. I didn't understand how Ian had that kind of effect on me. I didn't even like him.

"Hey, do you have to stare at the other girls?" I asked.

"What, you eaten up with envy?" He laughed. He checked his beeper for the seventeenth time — really, I'd been counting.

"I'm not jealous."

"Why don't you give me something else to do with my eyes, then?"

"You owe *me* a massage."

"Deejay Ian don't give rubdowns. Well, not on girls who don't dance for him, anyway."

"You want me to jiggle around in this little deejay booth?" That thought terrified me. My moves were about as smooth as a pig at a slop trough. I couldn't dance, and I didn't want to, regardless.

"Yeah, that'd be nice. Dance for me, cutie. If you don't, one of my girls will."

"Let them."

My ego was bruised beyond recognition, not to mention my shins. I couldn't believe I'd just given this undeserving slug a full back massage.

"Oh, come on, kiddo. See all those girls out there? They'd kill to be with me."

"I repeat myself — *let them*. I'm out of here."

What kind of silly, stupid chick fell for this kind of guy? I tugged my skirt down as far as it would go. I cussed myself for being tempted by this freak even for half a second. I had kissed him, too. Barf. It made me even more nauseous, though, thinking that I'd have to call Vikki J. — again — to come rescue me. Maybe Matt or, even better, Kevin, would be able to come out here to this party barge and throw me a life jacket. I was drowning in Ian's bullsheeit. I turned around to go, and he grabbed my arm and whipped me around. His inflatable lips were pressed against mine before I had the chance to pull away. This time, his lips were not soft or warm. They were more like jagged rocks, and his tongue was lizardlike, cold and slithery. I yanked myself away.

"Cutie, don't do me this way. I waited a week to see you."

I opened the door and went down the steps, being careful not to fall this time. I had no clue what was going to happen to me next, but I sure as heck wasn't spending another second with Ian.

"See ya, kiddo," he called out after me. "You don't know what you missing."

I pushed myself through the crowd, fighting off pimply teenage boys who humped my butt and called it dancing. I felt stupid. Actually, I was smart to leave that creep, I reminded myself. At least fifteen minutes later — that's how long it took me to fight my way through the sea of gyration — I found the door. I asked the bouncer if there was a diner or something around, and I refused to let him stamp my hand. If I was lucky, I would never have to step my shins in a place like that again.

"Walk three blocks that way and three more that way. There's a Dairy Queen next to Jail Bait Liquors."

It was easy to find, and I used a pay phone to reach Kevin on his mobile. I'd never been more thankful for the invention of portable communications devices. Kevin knew exactly which Dairy Queen I was at and promised to be there in twenty minutes. I sat down at a greasy booth that was only big enough for two. I wished I had a newspaper so no one would be tempted to talk to me. I thought about picking my nose and rocking back and forth for that reason. I was alone in an unsafe area. An old man tried to offer me half of his cheeseburger.

"Thank God you're here," I said to Kevin when he arrived.

"You look like you need cheering up," he said as he hugged me. "The first thing I want you to do is smile. Did you know that when you smile, you force your brain to think more positively? Studies show that acting like you have a certain emotion brings on that same emotion within ten minutes or less."

"Okay, I'm smiling." I gave him my cheesiest smile of the evening, thankful that, unlike the old man with the burger, I had all of my teeth.

"That's so fake, but it will do. Let's get some pizza. I'd take you to the party I was at, but it sucked. I didn't even get a phone number. Those boys Wren and Keith streaked through it already, and everyone else has already gone home or passed out. What happened to your shins? Holy crap. You need some ice."

We went to Big John's, and I was relieved. I'd take the beat-up gingham tablecloths, the crappy jukebox, and the familiar aroma of garlic powder any day. I never wanted to see that party barge ever again. The pizza joint was packed, but at least I could walk through it without getting groped. Two freshmen from school were hurling slices at each other to the dismay of the lone busboy. Others gathered in small groups to gossip about who knows what. Cheerleaders clearly had the munchies. And Blue sat in the corner — with another girl. Whoever she was, she seemed engrossed by whatever he was saying. Her eyes never left their private space, and every time he drank from his can of Coke, she took a sip, too. I guess I was staring at him. When he caught me, he jumped, clearly surprised, then winked.

"What's going on with you and that dude?" Kevin asked, not even looking up as he poured parmesan, garlic powder, dried peppers, and salt on his veggie slice of pizza. Good thing he didn't plan on kissing anyone that evening. "Isn't he the guy — one of the guys — who asked you out?"

"God, nothing is going on with him. He's just some dumb guy — he totally cheated on his ex-girlfriend. Frankie knows her."

"He did?" Kevin couldn't really talk with his mouth so full of pizza. I wondered why he was in such a hurry all of the time.

"That's what Frankie said. I feel sorry for that girl he's with."

"They're just friends," Kevin mumbled manically. "Sorry, I haven't eaten all day."

"How do you know they're not together?"

144

"Um, I've just seen her around with other people."

"Well, I hope not. For her sake. He's a real mean guy."

"He is? Oh, wow. Are you sure he did that to Frankie's friend? If so, I'm surprised. I don't know him or anything, but he gives discounts to all of the kids from the Y. You know, at the CD store where he works. What's his name again?"

"I don't even know," I lied, trying to erase him from my memory.

Finally Kevin looked up from his plate. "Katie, just smile, will ya?" He pulled up an extra chair and told me to prop up my legs so they wouldn't throb so badly. Kevin was always saving me from my own clumsiness.

Before Blue left with the girl, he plopped a cup full of ice on the table. "You look like you need this, Katie. For those bruises."

I ignored him. Blue was egotistical and assuming, and I couldn't take it. I'd had enough of narcissistic men for one evening. Kevin said I looked whipped and suggested we end the night, which inspired me to flash him my first genuine grin. He dropped me off, and we couldn't help noticing that Cherry's car was still at Matt's. I couldn't believe Mrs. Faulkner was letting her stay over there so late. Even Kevin seemed a little freaked out, for God knows what reason.

"Aren't you surprised about those two?" I asked. "I am."

"Actually, yes. At least she's interested in someone who'll be nice to her. Let's just hope she returns the favor."

"But Matt is such a —" I stopped myself from putting him down. Boy, I had been cocky lately. "Why would she want to be with him?"

"Katie, he's your best friend! You shouldn't say that."

"I know, but they're just too friggin' weird together. I can't stand the way she always has her tongue down his throat, either."

"It's nasty. Are you jealous?"

"No." I flashed him another fake smile showing every tooth I had. He shook his head and left me alone.

Brains are like mouths

Ian sucked. Blue disappointed. Paul strayed. I couldn't do anything about those guys; they had shattered my hopes, and they were history to me. But Matt, I couldn't give up on him. I'd had unshakable, sinking feelings ever since I'd seen Cherry's car outside of his house. I decided to do something about it — I called him up the next morning and said, "I've had it. I've just had it."

"For Christ's sake, Katie, with what?" Matt was mad.

"If you ever cared about me romantically or otherwise, you wouldn't be messing around all over town with Cherry the Cheerleader: The Ultimate Bag of Slut."

"For one, I have always loved you. We are friends, Katie. Do you know how hard it is to just be friends? I've been waiting my whole life for you to be single, and once you are, you're a total basket case. It's impossible to be with you right now — friends or anything else."

He stunned me. That wasn't the answer I was expecting. "Wait. What do you mean *just be friends* —?"

"Nothing. For two, you're only remotely interested in me now because I'm finally with someone else for the second time in my life ever. You don't own happiness, Katie. You've had more dates than I can even dream about — and more action, too. Now you're just trying to ruin everything because you're selfish."

That hurt because it was true. "I am not," I protested.

"For three, Cherry is not a slut, and if I do it with her, it's none of your goddamned business. Cherry likes you, anyway, Katie. Goodness, you should get off her case."

"She does *not* like me. She is more fake than your mom's Saturday teas with 'The Ladies.'"

"Now you've done it. Insult my girlfriend *and* my mom."

"That slut is your *girlfriend* now?"

"Stop calling her a slut! Like I told you already, she really likes you, though I have no idea why. Katie, you're so shallow lately."

"Shallow? Cherry comes from the kiddie end of the gene pool!"

"That is exactly what I mean. Makeup didn't do anything for you. You were prettier before. I've been thinking about this for a while, and I need a break from you. Maybe Kevin or Frankie can take you to school. I don't know how to say this but, well, you're kind of being too bitchy for me right now."

"Too bitchy? Too bitchy! Whatever." I hung up. Let him be with Cherry, I didn't care. Matt had changed, not me, I tried to convince myself. He went from Super Legs to Super Climber. He always wanted the latter, anyway, and he had the nerve to call *me* shallow. When he was a little kid, I used to worry that if the popular kids had taken him in, then he would've dumped

148

me. That wasn't a possibility then, of course, since no one wanted to play with either of us. But what about now?

Fighting with Matt made me nauseous.

Had he really said that it was hard to just be friends with me? His words were real, but I couldn't dwell on them, because he was lying. He'd chosen Cherry, after all.

To get Matt, our fight, and visions of him with Cherry out of my head, I carted Ivy League Barbie down to the basement and hid her behind the washing machine where the dust bunnies collected. I didn't need his gifts around shouting their constant reminders.

"What in the hell are you a-doin'?" Vikki J. asked. "And why are you cryin'? I didn't raise no goddamned emotional wreck, girl. You gotta get yerself together. There's been too many strange things goin' on around here lately. And now yer hidin' dolls in my laundry room."

I couldn't take it. Not then, so I spit fire at her: "Let me tell you about strange. You, Vikki J., are strange. In fact, I bestow you with the Weirdest Mother of the Year Award. Not only are you totally inappropriate as my mom, you are also a complete ice queen. It's no wonder that I can't handle my emotions. I certainly didn't learn how from you."

"Katie Jay, you will not speak to me like that. You say yer sorry right now."

"I'm not sorry. I'm sick of it. Just look. Thanks to you, I'm like Freak Show Barbie. Thanks to your infinite beauty wisdom, I can't go out of the house without getting into some kind of trouble like a crazy piece of white trash. And now it's too late to go back — I can't bear looking at my hair unless it's straightened; overalls make me feel dorky. There's no turning back, and you knew that before you did this to me." I held out my blood-red, perfectly manicured nails. "I'm losing my best friend, and I'm losing my mind. I don't know myself anymore. Nothing I do makes any goddamned sense."

"Goddamn! Don't say goddamned. Who do you think you are?"

"Maybe I need to change the spelling of my last name, too, you know, like you did." I was really being mean, and it didn't make me feel any better.

"I don't know what kind of crisis yer goin' through, girl. And here I was proud of you for stickin' to yer plan, but look atcha. Yer an ungrateful goddamned hotheaded brat who is insulting her mother."

"Don't call me a brat."

"I'm yer momma, and that means I have the right to say what I please. You are a brat. I've let you find yerself and do whatever you wanted to for yer whole entire life. I used to think you were a mature girl — that's why I let you babysit at ten and go to yer room with yer boyfriend when you were thirteen. Now yer about as grown up as a whiny baby without her binky. You get yer silly self all in a tizzy over boys like you've never seen one before in yer life. Whether I've agreed with you or not, I've stayed out of yer way, and this is the thanks yer a-givin' me. Before you speak to me again, you just remember that brains are like mouths. When they're empty, they blabber. When they're full, they digest." She stomped up the stairs, and I heard Bob ask what was wrong. She told him, loud enough for me to hear: "That girl is just a shiver lookin' for a spine to run up. I've about had my fill of her."

I cried loudly upstairs in my bedroom, which didn't ease my

mind, either. My tears were manipulative. I wanted my mother to feel sorry for me even though I had unleashed my darkest, most insulting thoughts, the ones I tried to hide away from the world, especially her. I imagined I'd be magically transformed — enlightened even — if I only had the courage to speak my hidden opinions. Instead, doing it felt like hell. So I cried more, not out of manipulation anymore, but out of useless rage. I was infuriated with everyone, myself at the top of the hit list.

After ten minutes, the tears slowed down. They only fueled my pity party, plus they made my complexion dull and veiny, which was unattractive. At that moment, I had one positive realization: I had not reached for the woe-is-me mirror. I no longer wanted to gape at my own misery; seeing myself in a heap offered no morsel of satisfaction. I ran to the kitchen and made a scene of breaking the mirror into a million pieces over the garbage can with one of Bob's hammers. My mother and Bob looked horrified, as if I'd just thrown a puppy in the compacter. They didn't comment and tried their hardest to ignore my antics.

"Katie, I think you should apologize to your mother."

"I don't need nothin' from her," she said. "Except my compact back. Where is that goddamned compact with the powder and the mirror?" To Bob she said, "Lord only knows what she'll do to *that*."

I went upstairs to pull myself together for my big date with Paul's best friend, Wren. I was in the perfect bleak mood to wreak havoc. I lined my eyes with thick black liner. I was finally skilled at applying whatever beauty product fit my mood. So I dared to get out the gray-black eye shadow and some deep purple, too. I applied the darker shade at the sharp edge of my eyelid. I flared out the color to create a catlike wave that made me look older, wiser. I swiped the purple over the lid and up to my eyebrows. I looked in the bathroom mirror and was pleased.

My eyes, crazy with emotional baggage, were impossible to miss. It didn't matter what else I wore that night. I didn't care where I went, either. I had but one motive: I wanted revenge, a sick kind of release from all of the rage pent up inside. Screw you, Paul. Go to hell, Matt. Wank off, Ian. Visit a shrink, Vikki J. I forgot about love and the prom and my plan. My rage and hurt were in search of freedom. Wren was in for a crazy night, or something.

"There's this great party at this freshman's house," he told me once I'd belted myself into his front seat.

"Forget it." I was not in the mood for meeting the general public, especially with a streaker by my side.

"Come on. It'll be fun. I don't know her name; I just want to trash her house."

"I will not go anywhere with you unless you promise to keep your boxer shorts on. And you are not capable of doing that at any party. So no."

Wren smirked in a way that struck me with sheer satisfaction. We were connected by intrigue and trouble. "I like a woman with balls. I'll try to keep mine to myself for the night. Unless you ask for a private viewing."

I had considered having a close encounter with Wren while I'd put on the third and final coat of mascara. I loved the idea of losing it to Paul's best friend — what glorious, rich revenge. I wasn't above following my ex's example and exhibiting my own set of bad judgments; another messed-up decision was mine to make, if I wanted.

"Maybe," I said, voice soft yet scratchy, to tease him.

"Really?"

"Maybe."

"Are you sure you're just doing this to get back at Paul?"

"Of course. And, by the way, don't ever mention his name to me again. I call him Weedkiller. So, I take it you and Weedkiller aren't hanging around too much anymore."

"Where've you been? I hit on Johanna this week when he dumped her, before he got back with her. He didn't like that too much. Now I'm moving on to you."

"So you just asked me out for the same reason I accepted — to piss him off? Nothing more?"

"You got it," he said. "And he tells me you're a great lay, too."

"What?" I was dumbfounded, which threw a kink in my icy, self-confident composure. I no longer appeared bewitching; I looked like a ding-a-ling. "What are you talking about? If he said that, I'll, I'll —"

"What are you going to do? What do you weigh, a buck?"

"Did you know he was prematurely losing his hair? Did you know that his thing looks like a jerky treat?"

"That's what I thought. Relax. He didn't really tell me anything. You're virgin territory." He shot another kidding-but-not-kidding-but-really-kidding grin.

We snuck into a theater through the exit door to watch a psychotic thriller about a woman who strangled all of her lovers. Then we slinked into the next room and watched half of another movie, too. When we got bored with it — no one was getting killed — we threw his Milk Duds and my Dots at the thin screen. We stopped by McDonald's and swindled a giggly cashier into giving us free value meals. Then we kissed in the car until it got really hot, and we had to roll down all the windows. I can't even remember what his lips felt like. I don't know if his skin was hairy or soft. Was he rough or gentle with me? I had no capacity to focus on him. My dark side turned me on.

"You're hot," he said, flashing that playful smirk again. This was the best of all worlds for him — he was getting some action *and* it was a big tease. But I didn't feel threatened or uncomfortable like I had with Ian. Not at all. This time I was not only in on the joke, I had helped orchestrate it. And, I must admit, it was crap-eating funny.

"Thanks," I said.

"Wanna see my balls?"

I laughed. "Not really, Wren. Another time."

"Damn, really? Seriously, you are hotter than *Hustler*. What are you doing tomorrow night?"

"It's Sunday, I have to study." That was so *not* dark of me. I really wanted to take off my makeup, too.

"What about Monday?"

"Maybe."

"Hang out with me at school. Be my chick. Spend time with me. Wear my *varsity jacket*."

"You don't have a varsity jacket. Can we go home now? I have to wash my hair."

Wren was hardly the answer to my problems with Matt or my mother or my life. Duh. But he had helped me forget it all for a few hours. After spending a few hours with Wren, I felt like toilet-papering a house or maybe playing mailbox baseball. Thankfully, I didn't take my visions of mischief and mayhem with me to bed. My goofball high hadn't lasted long, and I didn't need another hit.

I wanted more than shallow fun and mind games.

Get your boob out of my brain

"What a freak," Frankie said. It was Monday; we were in the hallway.

"Unbelievable — this is why guys get bad reps," Kevin added.

"This just shows that Paul deserved it, Katie. I'm glad you went out with Wren," Frankie said.

Frankie and Kevin watched the show with me: Paul and Ho-Hawnnah were leaning against my locker furiously making out. I wanted to disinfect the metal before I touched it again. It was gross. He had a fistful of her blond hair in his hand as he kissed her deeply. When I was close enough to hear, he called her "beautiful" and looked at me. Shivers shimmied up my spine and shot out of my ears. Who was horny at seven-forty-five on a Monday morning? They had planned it; Paul was practically broadcasting my payback for all of Shitville. It was beyond tacky, but it worked.

I stared for five full seconds in hurt disbelief. They'd probably been doing it all weekend. That thought, and not the way he was embarrassing himself in front of the whole school, hurt most. I'd hoped that he'd spent Saturday and Sunday sitting at home crying his eyes out in front of the video game player I had bought him. Wrong. Clearly, his level of post-breakup pain was measurable in millimeters. I was learning that mine was infinite.

"You are so not going to cry." Frankie grabbed me by the elbow and yanked me down the hall. She held a fistful of magazines to share with me later.

"I deserved it."

"Dude, you didn't."

We walked all the way to the other end of the school, near the wood shop, to use the girls' room. "Down here, no one knows what's going on," Frankie said. "No one cares. These guys are too busy building lamps for their mothers. We're safe from everyone here."

She was right. This end of the school was called the Fast Learners Wing. It was a demeaning title for the guys who did poorly in conventional classes. They learned to fix cars and plumbing and do complicated carpentry. I never understood how they were considered the dumb ones when the rest of us didn't even know the difference between a Phillips and a flathead. I bet the Fast Learners had cool parties and invited everyone in this wing. I envied them.

"The girls who work down here are cute. Look at that one," Frankie said, pointing to a short chick with a blue bandanna tight around her head. "Or what about that one?" The next one she picked out looked familiar; she was with Blue at Big John's. "I need to hang out here more often."

"Cool. That would be perfectly fine with me." We sat down on the carpet for a few minutes side by side, shoulders touching, her knee rhythmically tapping mine. No words necessary between us. Vikki J. used to rock me that way when I was little and had bad nightmares.

We were late to homeroom, but we didn't care. We went back during lunch to watch them work. Those kids were actually accomplishing something — fixing and making things. The guys would stop often to make jokes and sneak cigarettes while the mechanics teacher pretended not to notice. I got involved in their world, and I forgot about my own. These boys winked at me; it was as if they were letting me in on a secret. None of them would waste away behind a keyboard — they'd do things like Bob and my mother had done.

By the end of the school day, Wren broke the tranquility of my new hiding spot, tarnishing it with his presence. I had no clue how he found me. He was such a stalker.

"What do you want?" I asked, embarrassed at his too-chic, all-black outfit.

"I have a plan. Tomorrow morning, I'll pick you up, and we'll do exactly what Paul — I mean Weedkiller — was doing with Johanna. Only we'll make it hotter. Then later, I'll put my hands up your skirt next to the vending machines, and you can lift your leg a little and moan like you really enjoy it. I mean, you *will* really enjoy it."

"What did you say?" I asked.

"I want to make out with you all over this school. Then I want to take you out. We'll go to the CD store and try out this new gadget I bought online that switches off stolen merchandise detectors. Oh, man, it will be so fun. We won't have to pay for a thing."

"Look, Wren, I'm not interested."

"Yes, you are. You were all over me. You wanted me."

"I think you might be confusing me with yourself, Wren."

"Whatever. You loved it."

"Seriously, it was fun then, but I'm done now. Really."

"God, it's like you *used* me. I mean, that's cool, but are you sure you don't want to go out with *me*?"

"I'm completely, one-hundred-percent positive." I hoped the Fast Learners weren't watching. The scene was embarrassing.

"Not even to make *them* really jealous?" he begged.

Tempting, but . . . I'd decided to pack that game up and place it back on the shelf. "Not even."

When I made myself go back to my area of the high school, I saw that Matt and Cherry were following Paul and Ho-Hawnnah's lead, though they were slightly less pornlike. Why were the two guys I knew upside down and backward acting out on the exact same day?

Oh, probably because I pissed them both off. Kevin seemed distressed by everything, too, especially when he saw Matt and Cherry kissing before sixth period. Kevin hurried inside the classroom to safety; I walked straight up to them.

"Matt, what is going on? Do you hate me this much?"

He wiped the spit off his lips. "What are you talking about? Not everything is about you all of the time. We're just having fun. Buzz off, goodness."

"Stop it, Matt," Cherry said, then directed her attention to me. "I wish you two would make up. Matt is miserable without you, even if he won't admit it." He huffed off.

"Really," Cherry continued, "just make up. Then you and I can hang out again soon."

"Um, yeah." It was my turn to head to safety.

In the few minutes before the teacher was ready to start, Kevin asked me, "By any chance, did you have a bad horoscope today?"

"Yes, it said, 'Past lovers take revenge, and your worst enemies will rub salt into your eyes.'"

"Wow, those things are right on," Kevin said. "I have to do some research on this astrology stuff."

"Actually, I made that up. But it sounds about right."

"I'm checking mine when I get home tonight. If tomorrow's supposed to be as bad as today, I'm staying home."

"You're having a bad day?"

"Feel my forehead. I'm sick, right?"

"Definitely." Kevin was healthy. "But you have to come to school tomorrow. I need you to."

I hadn't seen Kevin upset; bad moods skipped him and landed on people like me. I was worried. His enthusiasm usually didn't waver, even when he had to do things like rescue me from the Dairy Queen. He was the one who told jokes to underclassmen instead of hazing them, and he made teachers feel good by paying more attention when class was boring. Yet, during sixth period, something was wrong. He was scribbling as fast as he could in his notebook, biting his lip so hard his eyes glazed over. I passed him a Jolly Rancher, and he still didn't smile at me. He just kept writing.

"Is something wrong?" I asked after class.

"Nothing, I, um, just didn't understand something we went over today."

"Want to borrow my notes?"

"No, thanks. I'm fine. Totally fine." I didn't believe him.

After school, I stuck around the common area waiting for Frankie to complete her latest punishment. For someone so quiet, she got into mischief quite often. This time, she had rearranged a bunch of figurines in the back of the honors English classroom. Frankie placed Jane Austen on top of Hemingway, and John Steinbeck laid underneath James Joyce. When she put Sylvia Plath underneath Emily Dickinson, she got caught and had to stay after for thirty minutes.

My head pounded. I went down to the Fast Learners Wing and it was empty, so I walked back to the commons, sat on the gross orange floor, and leaned against the cheerleading mural on the wall. I closed my eyes, but visions of Paul putting his hands up Ho-Hawnnah's shirt were all I could see.

"Talk about a shit day," a voice said.

"Totally." I turned around. "Oh, it's you."

Blue was standing in front of me, looking tall and alternative and cute. He was putting his earring stud into his eyebrow. Maybe they're called browrings. I stopped myself from asking him since I wasn't supposed to talk to him as per Frankie's orders.

"I heard what happened — everyone did. You didn't deserve it. Any of it."

"Thanks. Wait a minute. Why do you keep talking to me? I don't like you."

"You will because I want you to."

"Not now, okay?" I had no witty response, no comeback. But

161

he was clearly not the kind to back down. Totally surprisingly, though, that's exactly what he did.

"You got it," he said. "You get yourself some quiet, and good luck on the peace. You make like a monk, and I'm the flying nun."

He walked away, and I watched him until he diasppeared down the hall.

one big bizarro jigsaw puzzle

Thursday, April 24

"Dude, that guy is so lame," Beefhead #1 said. "He's Cherry's charity case. What's his name?"

"Matt something," Beefhead #2 said. "You know, Super Legs."

"Oh, yeah, the guy who played the flute during the morning announcements once."

"He's a good swimmer."

"He's a total dork."

"Dude, you're right."

"Cherry will come to her senses soon. Right now, she's hawking her body on Geek Street."

"Geeks are not chic."

"Dude, no one is ever going out with her again. She's ruined."

"No way, man. I'd go out with her. She's got a killer body. What a waste."

The two guys, big fleshy ones with no necks, stood near my locker watching Matt and Cherry chicken-peck each other good-bye. Why they were still parading near me was a mystery. The other torturous couple had stopped — and hopefully gone to hell or something.

"Hey there," one of the sausages said to me.

"Uh, hi."

"You're that girl who wasn't hot but is now, aren't you?"

"You must be thinking about somebody else."

"Didn't you used to date Paul Green?"

"His name is Weedkiller," I said, causing a baffled look. "Why don't you ask him?"

"Dude, I knew it was you. What do you say . . . you and me?"

"We what? Stand over there and grope each other and make fools of ourselves?"

"That's not my style. I like to wine and dine my women, and I'm free this Friday."

I did not want to go out with snotty sausage-head number one. He wasn't my type. He played football, which I couldn't even pretend to understand or like, he obviously gossiped too much, and he had called Cherry hot. Before I said no, though, I remembered that I had three more weekends to fall in love before prom. I still needed a date for Friday night, and no one else had asked me.

"Um . . . I have to see if I can cancel my other plans first," I totally lied. "I'll call you after school."

While scribbling his phone number on my notebook, he said, "Whatever. You make the right decision, dude. You won't be sorry."

I used my teeth to trim my nonexistent cuticles. My week of weirdness and confusion continued. Caring if I was late to second period was not on my agenda, so I walked down to the Fast Learners Wing by myself to see if a cute guy might wink at me. I hoped for someone like Blue, but not actually Blue. I considered doing something out of character. Maybe I'd have better luck if I picked someone and did the asking. But which one? I liked the skinny red-haired boy with the confident walk. He winked at me, and I blushed. Another guy, reasonably cute, stood on his head in the corner even though the floor was covered in grease. I decided against him. One more caught my eye from behind. He was wearing a torn-to-pieces flannel and had a dark mop of hair on his head. Upon further inspection, I knew it was Blue. He was taking a Fast Learners class! I had him pegged for one of those kids who spent all of his time in art.

My surprise didn't stop there. A girl was luring him out into the hallway — Fast Learners didn't sit at desks and had a lot more freedom. The girl was Frankie! The way she shyly shook her head and shoulders, I guessed she was thanking him for something. I was completely confused. I bolted before they saw me, and I couldn't concentrate for one whole second during the rest of the day.

Maybe I should've checked my horoscope and stayed home like Kevin did. After lunch, someone broke into my locker. The lock was missing, the door was open, and I figured everything would be gone — my makeup, a sweater, my new backpack. If someone really hated me, they'd take my homework, too, just to be mean. But to my surprise, everything was scattered around in its proper place. It didn't make sense. Then, I saw something on top of my pile of books. It was a CD. The title was hand-written on it: "You Make Me Feel Religious." That was a love song from the chanting monks. I didn't know if it was creepy or cute because someone clearly knew me way too well. Maybe it was presumptuous of me, but I thought of Blue, the one with lots of CD access. Or maybe Wren, who was crazy enough to do something like that. What about Paul? No way; we were too busy hating each other. Anyway, chanting electronic monks were pretty popular, so it could've just been a coincidence. I went to the office and got a new lock. The whole day was one big bizarro jigsaw puzzle.

I was glad to get in Frankie's car and go home. At least she could give me some answers and solve a mystery or two.

"So, I skipped the first ten minutes of second period today and spent some time downstairs," I told her.

Her eyes widened for a split second. She pretended to be completely preoccupied with finding a good song on her car stereo. She gnawed her chewing gum like she was trying to kill it.

"Frankie, did you hear me? I went to the Fast Learners Wing today."

"Yeah, so. What were you doing, hunting for dates?"

"Actually, yeah. But you wouldn't guess what I saw."

"What?"

"I saw you, silly! I saw you talking to Blue!"

She deadpanned for a second, expressionless and therefore incomprehensible. "Katie, why are you spying on me? This is creepy, I swear," she finally snapped.

"I wasn't. I was —"

"You know, I need my privacy. I don't tell everything to everyone all the time."

"But I thought you hated him."

"Now you're really pissing me off. I said I didn't want to talk about it. If you really need to know, I still [cussin'] hate him. Can we drop this now?"

"Um, okay. Why do you have to get all mad at me, though?"

"Because you were spying on me."

"I WASN'T SPYING!"

"You don't have to yell, Katie."

Me? She started it! "You don't have to be all bitchy." But then I decided I'd better do some damage control. "Sorry," I relented. I didn't want to keep fighting about what amounted to very little, really. Friendships — girl friendships — were confusing like calculus, but I still wanted to keep the only one I had.

"Okay," she started. "Okay. . . ." She was really holding on to that steering wheel again. I was nervous — Frankie was either going to fly off the handle, or what I didn't know. After several weighted seconds, her freckles got bigger, accommodating her big smile that I liked so much. "I will tell you one thing," she said. I exhaled deeply, wanting to laugh with relief. If she became testy easily, at least she forgot quickly. Yes, I could wrap my mind around this friendship; I was fond of it.

"Just one thing, for the record," I interrupted. "I was not stalking you, it was a coincidence. The whole thing confuses me, but if you want me to stay out of it, I respect that. Also, I want to tell you that I don't need to know everything. Just tell me about stuff that's important to you whenever you're ready. You know, like in a friendship."

"Okay, okay, now let me just [cussin'] tell you my good news." She hadn't heard my speech. In fact, she wasn't even concentrating on the road and clocked an orange construction cone. She was so excited about whatever it was that she pulled off to the side of the road to tell me about it. Thankfully, she spit her gum out first.

"I have a date tomorrow!"

"Oh, my God!"

"I know. It's surprising."

"That's great. I had no idea. . . . With who?"

"Well, just because I told you I had one doesn't mean I'm ready to spill everything else. Just let me see how it goes first. I'll tell you more after. I swear."

"Seriously, I really would love to know. That's awesome!" I just said awesome, surprised at my own perkiness. My mood was improving.

"So you want to hang out after school tomorrow before I go out with this football guy?" I asked her.

"You have *another* date?"

"Of course. I mean, yeah," I answered. "With Travis the Beefhead. I have to go out even if I don't want to. It's the plan."

"Right. This has nothing to do with your ego."

"What did you just say?"

"Nothing. Listen, Katie. I've stayed out of this whole thing, but I . . . oh, never mind, I'm the last person who should be giving relationship advice. Really, I am."

"What were you going to say? Now you have to tell me."

Frankie didn't take much convincing. She laid it all out. "Okay then. I just don't think you should go out with that all-beef patty, that's all. What a loser. He's not your type, he's definitely just as much of a player as Ian was, and you know it's not going to work."

She was right. I examined my hand on my lap, and I vowed to put a Band-Aid on my gnarliest fingernail.

"Katie, think of it this way: You'd rather spend the rest of your life in after-school suspension than go to prom with him," Frankie continued. "So why bother? Okay, I'm done. That's all I have to say."

"But I have to! Go out with him, I mean."

"Who the [cuss] says? Didn't you learn your lesson with Ian?"

Then it all clicked. Of course, I didn't want to go. I didn't like the guy. At all. Frankie was dead-on in her assessment. Still, I found myself — knee-jerk reaction, I guessed — whining, "But I need a date!"

"Go on one by yourself, then."

"Huh?"

"I'm serious. I saw a woman do it on some life makeover TV show. She took herself to dinner, then out dancing, and she spent the time thinking and contemplating and feeling whatever it was she needed to feel. You need it. I'm serious." She was still pulled over on the road, looking me tunnel-vision in the eye, fully immersed in what she had to say to me.

"What's that supposed to mean?"

"Why don't you go out with someone cool for a change, that's all? Think about it, Katie. You're always judging yourself by whether or not you're with a guy. Now for obvious reasons I'm totally against that. That's beside the point, though. What I'm trying to say is: Why don't you get to know yourself without a boy in the picture? You might like who you really are."

I thought of my mother; her speeches were sometimes similar — feisty and empowering. Vikki J. would've used more cuss words, though, and definitely some goddamns. I was flattered and floored by Frankie at that moment. I was also terrified about what she was challenging me to do. My neurotic side won, and I answered, "But I don't have a car to pick myself up." That excuse should've bailed me out.

"Take mine," she offered, as generous with her wheels as she had been with her homemade desserts and music magazines. "I have a date, remember. I'll ask her to drive."

"Oh, crap," I said, giving into the brilliant idea. "What kind of excuse can I come up with after that?"

"Nothing I can think of," she answered. I don't know why — my brain just wasn't on, but my emotions were — I reached over to the driver's side and hugged her. She reciprocated, and we held tight to something really important.

Lonely expletives

Thursday, April 24 — night

I was greeted at home by another complicated female, one I hadn't figured out yet. Only this one was completely silent. Ever since our big blowup, my mother only uttered words when absolutely necessary, like when she let me know that dinner was ready. I would sit at the kitchen table by myself while she ate on the couch using a TV tray. She grunted at all other times, like when she handed me a sack from the drugstore full of deodorant and tampons. I thought I'd enjoy the peace and quiet. I had always prayed, hoped, and dreamed for a Vikki J. break. As it turned out, though, I didn't like it one bit. The house was freezer burnt.

"Bob, will you please talk to her for me?" I pleaded when she was down in the salon. I wanted to try; I just didn't know how.

"You two have to work through your own problems. I can't get in the middle of it, Katie." He took a swig from his lukewarm bottle of wine while sitting on our La-Z-Boy. He seemed mad at me, too.

I sighed.

"Katie, I know it's not fun," he said, seeing that his tone had hurt my feelings. "You've been doing two years' worth of growin' up in the past three weeks. You're allowed to make a few mistakes. But sometimes you have to apologize for them."

"But I'm scared of her."

"And I'm not?" He rubbed his bald head and went back to his snack.

I stayed in my room studying and being bored. I needed a hobby desperately, and I also needed a set of wheels. Vikki J. never bought me one because she liked my dependence on her. She loved making me sit through *Babes* before taking me to the mall or CD store or wherever else. Now, though, I bet she would've bought me an airplane to get rid of me. I didn't like it, but what did I do about it? Nothing. I couldn't make myself talk to her; I hadn't figured out what to say.

On that note, I decided I deserved a little torture, so I called Beefhead.

"I can't go, sorry," I began. "I have this family thing I have to go to tomorrow night, and I can't get out of it," I lied.

"What about Saturday night, then?" he asked, making juicy mouth sounds, obviously chewing tobacco.

"No, I'm sorry, um" — I couldn't even remember his name — "but I just don't think it's a good idea."

"I'm the best idea *you* ever got, that's for sure," he said, charming and chewing as ever.

"You're right," I went along, just for my own amusement.

"I can't believe this bull. You know how bad I wanted a piece of you?"

Did he really say that? And was it supposed to be a compliment? He didn't care what my reaction was — so I didn't bother to give him one. He just kept right on going.

"Your friend Wren said you really wanted to do it bad," Beefhead added, "and I was damn excited."

"What? Wren's an idiot." I didn't know if Wren had really said that, or if Beefhead was making it up. I couldn't care less either way. Meanwhile, the monster truck of a boy had no interest in what I had to say. He just continued to gripe, swishing his tongue through a mouthful of spit.

"Your friend Matt bangs Cherry, a cheerleader, and I can't even get a piece of *you*. Freaky geek." Then he unleashed a stream of X-rated expletives, words that would've shocked even my mother. Well, maybe not.

"Wait, Matt and Cherry what?" I asked, ignoring his insults that didn't insult me, anyway.

"Where've you been? Oh, I forgot. You're a loser," the loser said. "You don't know anything."

Hanging up on him seemed a wise move. I was demolished, but not by Beefhead. Matt and Cherry were doing it? Matt and Cherry were doing *IT*?!!! It didn't take much brainpower to figure that one out, but I had still held tight to my hope that they hadn't had sex yet. And their activities were common knowledge? Crap, crap, crap, and other expletives.

Matt was doing someone. That meant Matt was taking her to the prom, too. Weedkiller was doing someone. Ditto regarding Weedkiller and prom. Why weren't they pining for me? I was secretly and guiltily pining for them. I was longing for a lot of things, though. I wanted to make up with Vikki J. I fantasized about meeting the perfect guy. I longed to be in love the way I had been before. I wished I had something to do with myself so I wouldn't sit at home all of the time indulging myself in my own pining. I wanted to feel wanted. *But wait,* I thought, *I didn't even want myself.*

I had to stop my cycle of feeling bad then feeling worse. I needed to make a major change. So, insane or not, I looked in my dresser mirror: "Katie," I said, "would you like to go out on a date with me?"

I batted my eyes and replied, "Why, yes, I'd love that." The matter was settled, and I was more nervous than if it had been a boy-girl date.

"Who'd you go sneakin' up in yer room, girl?" I heard Vikki J. yell from downstairs. "You'd better be up there alone, or I just may have to kick yer ass."

She was worried about me! She was paying attention to me! Things with guys weren't looking up. But at least they might be getting better with my mother. I guessed I would just have to see to it myself.

Problems – solved

Frankie and I rode home after school, but we stopped for ice cream first. I gave her pep talks about her date — she was so nervous that she dropped her sundae. It was a good thing I'd have her car that night. In her basket-case state, she would not be a safe driver.

"You'll be great," I said. "You're amazing."

She'd turned so red I thought she'd burst. She shook her head in disbelief and tugged at the long laces on her shiny black combat boots. Then she told me she didn't want to talk about it anymore.

"Are you going on your date?" she changed the subject.

"I guess."

"You guess? You're going."

I dropped her off at her house and drove on to mine. I laid down on my bed for a nap. Disturbing fictional sights and sounds refused to give me any peace. I stared at the knobby paint flecks on the ceiling. A sad, anxious rumbling vibrated in my belly up through my throat. I brought a glass of milk to my bedroom from the kitchen, but it could hardly soothe me. I left it on my nightstand and lay back down. Through the spider-webs and tangled vines in my mind, only one thought broke in clearly: Something had to change. I slept for thirty minutes.

I woke up, and the house was as still as a burial ground. Usually, voices and commercial jingles wafted from the living room where Bob watched TV. I would have been comforted by the sound of blow-dryers muffling high-pitched voices in my mother's salon downstairs. Sounds of chaos didn't bother me. The silence did.

A note scribbled on the table said, *Out all day. Love, Bob.* I had no other messages. Matt had still not called, to my dismay. Even more depressing, the last person I wanted to spend Friday night with was myself. The girl who cried into her pillowcase, watching colors change for entertainment, would've been bet-ter company, but she didn't exist. I had beaten her up and stripped her down because she was not strong; she was not any-thing. She was not good enough, but for what? I liked myself softer, less superficial, and not as driven. The new me was an alien.

I poured a bowl of cereal for dinner. I was reduced to con-versing with soggy Rice Krispies on a Friday night. Then my mother's voice vibrated through my head. *Get off yer god-damned ass*, it said. *Go out, do something. Stop bein' a crybaby.*

I thought of Frankie, who was going out on her first date since God knows when. I rooted through my mother's closet and found a cute outfit in the back. I pulled my hair into a ponytail, and I slathered on some makeup. It was a little too thick, but I was in a hurry. Plus, I was too nervous to do a good job on it, anyway. I grabbed the forty dollars hidden in my sock drawer, hopped in Frankie's car, and sped away. I was going on a date — with myself.

"Are you waiting for anyone?" asked the waiter at a new Italian restaurant.

"I'm not," I said, tightening my ponytail and trying not to shake. "I'd like a table by the window." I had decided to be unashamed. I wouldn't sit in the back of the restaurant in hiding. So what if anyone saw me alone? I didn't care. I wanted to feel good about myself again. I ordered a glass of red wine, something Bob would've done.

"Can I see some ID?" the waiter asked, trying to look serious and not chuckle.

"No. Coke, please."

I ordered a salad and eggplant parmesan. I crunched through the greens and savored the tangy vinegar dressing. My appetite was whetted. I devoured the eggplant with the perfectly thick crust. I looked at my empty plate quite satisfied. I had never eaten at a restaurant by myself. I was proud of myself because I did it, and didn't think I could. Yesterday, I wouldn't have guessed that I'd actually go through with this date.

"Can I get another Coke?" I asked, hoping the refills were free. I decided not to get dessert, though, because I didn't want to spend too much money.

After dinner, I went to the movies. A girls-kick-ass chick flick seemed appropriate. I enjoyed holding my own hand. It wasn't so bad. *I* wasn't so bad. I watched the fictional team of three too beautiful actresses save the world from self-destruction. After two hours of estrogen-infused entertainment, I was pumped. Just like two of the characters in the movie, I didn't need a man. (Only one of the three had a Prince Charming in the end.) Just like them, I could take care of myself. At least, I would try very, very hard.

When I got home, Vikki J. and Bob looked at me strangely. She still wasn't speaking to me, so I gave Bob the signal that I was okay. I marched to my bedroom, and I knew what had to change. It would be the dating. A little over halfway through the plan, my so-called brilliant and empowering mission, I would stop completely. My quest to find love would not keep me up one more night. If I stayed alone, I could not cause myself any more problems. And maybe I'd be a nicer person again.

There would be no more dates, no prom, no love. But at least there would be sleep.

The kissing parade stopped

Saturday, April 26

I was cleaning my room when the phone rang. I raced to get it.
I was, I hated to admit, getting lonely.

"Katie!" It was Kevin.

"Hey," I said, happy to hear from him. "Where were you
Friday?"

"Just sick and tired, I guess. You know, the last time I missed
school was when I had mono sophomore year. I needed a day
off. Did I miss anything?"

"It was relatively uneventful. The infamous couples seemed
to have better control of their lips — the kissing parade
stopped," I said.

"That's good news. I couldn't take it anymore."

"Me, neither. You okay?" I didn't know Kevin well enough
to be too demanding, but something had been off since
Monday.

"I'm great. I'm much better now. I worked out all day yesterday and did a few one-on-one classes with kids at the gym. I'm

out of my funk now. They say the best way to stop feeling sorry for yourself is to do something for others. It totally works."

"What was wrong?" Kevin was too saintly sometimes. I'd totally misjudged popular people — Kevin was proof.

"Nothing, really. I'm good now. You don't sound too cheery. What's going on over there?"

I wasn't even embarrassed to tell him I'd been on a date with myself. I was surprised to find myself giving him a scene-by-scene rundown of all the things I'd done and found. When that subject wore out, I mentioned that my mother wished me dead and admitted that the house was way too cold lately.

"Put on a pair of shorts and some tennis shoes. I'm coming to get you."

"Oh, no, not aerobics."

"Something better. I swear."

He arrived within twenty minutes. We dropped Frankie's car off, and then he took me to the YMCA. We made it just in time for the couples' salsa class.

Yippee. I tried to tell him no way, but he made me.

"We'll try it. As your friend, I do not believe that you dance like a frog in a blender," he said. "If you're that bad, you'll just have to prove it to me."

That, I could do. Some people were graceful, others clumsy. But no one was as pitiable as me, and I'm not even exaggerating. For starters, the counts for the Latin dance were funny: one, two, three, five, six, seven. Don't they count to four in Spanish? Kevin had lost his mind taking me there — at least his toes believed me.

"You weren't that bad," he said, leaving class halfway

through because I pleaded. "Let's try something else." He had another idea: Kevin was taking classes to become a trainer, and he needed a guinea pig. That was fine with me; a well-monitored workout sounded a lot safer than salsa. To impress my friend, I ran hamsterlike on the treadmill, lifted weights eagerly (even though they were no heavier than a Chihuahua), and stretched catlike afterward. He pushed me, and I actually accomplished small athletic feats. With his help, I had done it. I was a mini-jockette — at least for a few minutes.

"You're pretty flexible. I'm really surprised."

"I can almost do the splits, which is why my mom always thought I should have made it for cheerleading. That was fine, I guess, except for the actual cheering part."

"Ah, who cares? We won't assess your weaknesses; let's find your strengths. You're pretty flexible. I want to try you on the balance beam."

"But I can't even walk straight down the hallway!" I made a goofy face, eyes crossed, to show him just how much of a goober I was.

"Just humor me."

"Remember when I stubbed my toe the first time we talked?"

"You were wearing *heels*," he said, as if that were a crazy thing to do. Yes, I liked Kevin. "Take off your shoes. I'm going to teach you balance, which is the first step in gaining coordination."

We walked across the thin little beam, and I fell off a few times at first. Fifteen minutes later, though, Kevin had me standing up straight and looking at the walls ahead instead of the ground. I didn't even wobble. A few more tries, and I looked like I belonged on the catwalk of a New York fashion show. Well, not quite — but that's what it felt like.

"Now get off and do a cartwheel."

That was easy. I had learned something from all of those try-outs. As long as he didn't ask for flips, aerials, or back hand-springs, I was game.

"Do it on the beam."

"No way."

"Katie, humor me."

I fell a few times, but bruising my body parts didn't scare me. We clumsy people have high risk-of-injury tolerance. Within ten minutes, I did a perfect cartwheel on the low balance beam. I wouldn't have believed it if I hadn't done it with my own body. Then Kevin took me to the high beam, a full four feet off the floor. I followed his lead, walked up and down, did dips and struts. In two more hours, I was also doing cartwheels and small, slightly graceful jumps when I landed on the floor. I hadn't, um, beamed with athletic confidence since I was twelve. That's when I set the record for highest branch climbed in Matt's maple tree.

"See, I told you. You are athletic."

"Did you say pathetic?" I crossed my eyes again.

"Katie, stop it. You know you did a great job." He scratched his head, eyes flashing around the room. I couldn't believe twitchy Kevin had been able to focus his attention on me for a serious amount of time, but I was glad.

"Thanks, Kevin."

"Pleasure was all mine." He bowed, an odd gesture that made me laugh. He ran upstairs to check his messages and fiddle with papers before taking me home. I hugged him when he came down, for raising my spirits. He had made me feel better without complication. We didn't talk about anything important, yet we had bonded and laughed and accomplished things together. It sounded stupid, but I had this apocalyptic revelation that I didn't have to think about things constantly. I didn't have to make everything — especially friendship — a drama. Because of the afternoon, and last night, I looked forward to spending the rest of the day and evening alone. No date? No problem. I really meant that.

My main concern changed from self-serving destitution to making restitution. I was determined to set things straight, starting with Vikki J., who was back at home. No other cars were at our house. I smiled — taking Kevin's advice for psyching myself into a good mood — and walked in the door.

Sprawled out on the shaggy living room floor, flat on her back, arms and legs spread in opposite-end Vs, was my mother. Her eyes were open and blinking, but she had no makeup on, which made her look older and more mom-like. She didn't turn my way when the door opened; she didn't even flinch when a cold shiver of spring wind followed me in.

"Oh, my God! Are you okay?" I was concerned; Vikki J. was never so disheveled.

She pah-shawed at me. "Please, like you give a rat's ass."

"Mom, really, are you all right? Do I need to call the doctor?"

"Goddamnit no. Just go away." I don't know what was more disturbing: her messy hair, pasty naked face, the turned-off television, or her odd position that took up most of the carpet.

"I want to talk to you. Tell me what's wrong."

183

"Goddamnit, I said go away."

She didn't have a can of cheap beer or a soda sitting next to her as usual. Instead, there was a plastic tumbler filled with orange mystery fluid about two feet to the left of her head. I knelt down beside her and lifted the oversized, dingy cup. I took a whiff and winced before deciding, unwisely, to take a drink. The alcohol fumes burned the back of my throat and took a layer of skin off my nasal passages. My verdict: She'd mixed some Tang with stiff vodka. Thankfully for her sake, she hadn't sampled much of the concoction.

"Just let me be!" she said to me.

"You don't have to tell me what happened. But let me say this: I'm sorry for everything I said. I shouldn't have been so awful to you. I really didn't mean all that stuff."

"You meant every word. Those eyes a yers always give you away. Everything you said was true accordin' to you."

"I'm so sorry." I reached up to touch her hand, located arm's length above her head. "I owe you a huge apology."

"I'm only talkin' to you because I ain't got it in me not to, not today, anyway."

"Um, not that it's odd or anything — really, it's not — but why are you lying on the floor like that?"

"Bob dumped me like a load of garbage. And he meant it this time . . . serious as a goddamned heart condition."

I went into the kitchen to get a long straw. I came back, put it in the drink, and tilted the cup to her face. She took an extended sip and swallowed without wincing. She said, "Oh, to heck with it," and sat up to take another big gulp. I sat close to her on the floor with the plastic-covered ottoman in my face — it would've been too disruptive to shove it out of our way. I noticed how deep her laugh lines were once her face had the opposite expression. Her sadness gave her worn skin, the kind that had lived and played hard. Oddly, I couldn't remember the last time she'd looked so pretty. A few more sips, and she told me the story.

Bob had brought her breakfast in bed, a move that wasn't unusual. He couldn't make a peanut butter sandwich, but he would sneak away to the Waffle House and bring her takeout. Then he told her to get out of bed because he wanted to go swimming. She told him it was still too cold, and he said he didn't care; he'd already rented a little boat to take her out on the river. So she canceled all of her appointments and slipped into her bikini and a sweatshirt. They launched a little john-boat, the kind old men fished in, by the pier near Jimmy's Bar. He started the engine, pulling the cord like a lawn mower, and took her to a scrub of land called Six Mile Island where they swung from a rope-swing someone had strung up on the shore-line.

I told her I'd been there before when Paul and I hijacked his uncle's rowboat.

She smiled at me for the first time in ages. "It's romantic, ain't it?"

Bob exerted enormous effort into his record-setting swing. When he crested in the air, he hollered, "Vikki J., you're going to marry me today," before splashing into the river water. When he came out, he took a diamond ring off his pinky and held it up to her.

"I can't wait for you anymore. You love me, so let's do it. I talked the justice of the peace into waiting for us down at the courthouse. I even had to pay him to be there on a Saturday afternoon. And he's got a marriage license just waiting to be signed."

At the time, she laughed and laughed. This was the most elaborate plan he'd come up with yet. She was not making fun of him, though; she was happy whenever he professed his love even though she always turned him down. For past proposals, he'd spelled out *Will you marry me?* in French fries at McDonald's; he'd also printed an ad in the local newspaper. She never took him seriously, and this time was no different. But he'd never had a ring before — "a real sparkler," she called it. When he tried to put it on her finger, she hedged. She would only hold it in her hand.

"Well, girl, you put your jeans on and get in that boat. We got ourselves a wedding to go to."

She hopped in and rubbed his back, kissing up to him as usual to lessen the blow of a no. About ten minutes later, she put the ring back on his pinky. "I love you," she said, "but I cain't. You know I just cain't."

He cried so many tears that Vikki J. thought he'd flood the boat. He wouldn't accept her kisses. Instead, they sputtered to shore without speaking; they docked, and he helped her out. He told her to walk into Jimmy's Bar and ask for Rob.

"He's sitting there waiting to take you home because I already figured what the answer would be," Bob said, and then he pushed the little boat back away from the dock. Before he started the engine, their eyes met.

"Ah, come on back," she said.

He replied, "I love you more than there are stars in the sky. More than there are fish in this river. I love Katie, too. But you've done me over for the last time, Vikki, and I'm finished.

186

I'm moving to my sister's in Texas because I'm tired of you breaking my heart. Isn't that sad? I can't even be in the same town as you." He threw the ring in the water before disappearing into the wide Ohio River.

She finished telling me the story and did something I'd never believe unless I'd seen it myself. She reached over, hugged me tight, and she cried.

Up in Smoke

Vikki J. got herself together with the help of that plastic tumbler. Once it was empty, she washed her face and put on a full pound of makeup. Then she said, "So, who's yer date tonight?"

"I don't have one," I told her.

"Well, why the hell not?"

"Because I quit, that's why. My plan was dumb," I said.

She shook her head. "Oh, no you don't, girl."

"Don't what?"

"I didn't raise no goddamn quitter. You are going out tonight, and I'm a gonna tell ya with who."

"Who?" I asked, a little afraid.

"Me. Sittin' home alone won't do me no good a-tall. So you have a date now; you have one with your mother."

We dressed in matching skimpy outfits with bright colors, lace, and tight jeans, and we headed to a bar in the next town. It was called Fast Eddies, no apostrophe, and was situated between Nightcap Hot Dogs and the Moose Lodge. She

188

assured me that no one would give me any trouble there, especially since she knew the bartender. But she put fake eyelashes and heavy makeup on me just in case. I still didn't look twenty-one. I just looked like an underage stripper. We walked through the door arm in arm, and every man stared at her.

"It's been a long time," said one, probably a post–high-school Fast Learner.

"Great to see ya again, Vikki J."

"Now there's my gal. Where've you been hidin'?"

They asked how Bob was, and she didn't flinch when she said fine. She had met him there, and she didn't want anyone to know that they were done for good. She ordered a Michelob for herself and an Amaretto and Coke for me.

"Let's sit at that table right over there," she said. "It's got the best view."

"Of the pool table?"

"No, of cute butts."

We didn't say much. Her game face didn't work with me; her mind was occupied. I willed myself to keep my mouth shut. If I had begged her to marry him, she may have done the opposite — like when we were getting ready, I told her to wear red, so she promptly put on purple. She was a spitfire, all right, sometimes with inflated pride and bloated self-assurance. I was on edge, too. She didn't have much time to come to her senses.

"Vikki J.," I finally said, finishing off my last drop of Amaretto.

"Don't you start on me."

"I am not going to say a word about Bob —"

"Don't you say his name. You call him Ringkiller."

"Okay, okay. I just wanted to tell you again about how sorry I am. You know, for —"

"Oh, stop, I know that. You don't have to keep sayin' it." She ordered me another Amaretto even though she hadn't touched her Michelob. When I polished that one off, I hugged her.

"Honey, you're sloshed," she answered, patting me on the back. I had driven us to Fast Eddies, but it didn't look like I'd be getting us home. "Just remember one thing, somethin' I'm always remindin' myself. Be careful whose toes you step on today 'cuz they might be connected to the ass you gotta kiss tomorra."

She walked to the pool table to talk to old friends, and I sat there alone, fully entertained by the scenery. The smoke drifted out of the drinkers' mouths in thick, artistic waves. I studied the translucent puffs, each exhale its own little galaxy, and wondered if I'd ever produce something so lovely. I was transfixed, content, mesmerized. When one cigarette was tapped out, I'd search the room for another to stare at.

The skinny red-haired boy from the current Fast Learners Wing was there with an older buddy. Like nearly all the guys in the bar, he was smoking, too. I jumped when his eyes met mine. He winked, and I turned my attention to my drink, sucking through the straw, only noticing the loud hollow noises when Vikki J. abused my shoulder with her two-inch fingernail.

"Katie, go over there and talk to that boy. He's cute. His friend's pretty nice — he works for Ringkiller." She paused before giving me a playful slap. "Jumpin' Jehoshaphat, is he ever checkin' you out! Now go on over there; it ain't hard to say hi."

I stood up and walked with relative poise to the bar where he was standing. My balance-beam lessons were helping me out; he could hardly tell I was tipsy.

"Hey," I said, dropping my drink to the floor and smashing the glass to bits.

"Hey." He laughed and kicked the broken glass closer to the bar, away from the stool. "Can you get that?" he asked the bartender. He had the smile of the century, crooked and controlled like a mischievous genius.

"You come here often?" Was I a comedienne? He laughed again!

"Just sometimes with my cousin here. So, I've seen you around quite a bit lately. What's your name?"

"Katie James. That's my mom over there."

"Ahhh, Vikki J. She's real cool. Put in a good word for me. If I ever need a job around here, I'd like to work for her boyfriend."

"I will. What's your name?"

"Jesse."

While my mother stayed busy at the pool table — cracking up her admirers, men ten or fifteen years her junior — I got to know Jesse. He was a year younger than I was, but would be graduating with us. I tried to listen to his story, but I kept staring at his blond eyelashes. He had one of those small, compact bodies that effervesced testosterone. I did catch most of what he was saying; he'd been taking summer school classes for the past two years, trying to graduate early. In July, he was moving to Germany to help his older brother open a car repair shop. I was impressed; after school ended, my grandest goal was to finish reading the romance novel I'd started.

"So why've you been down in my 'hood lately?" Jesse asked. "You know, at school?"

"Well, I was just tired of the people upstairs, especially my ex, who kept dry-humping his new girlfriend on my locker."

"He dumped you? And they say the kids are smart up there. From what I hear, there's a better guy out there who's interested. I wouldn't sweat your ex."

"I'm not." My armpits were wet because of Jesse, not Paul. A better guy? Was he flirting with me?

He talked and I mostly listened for another forty-five minutes. I loved when he lit his cigarettes, because he used only one hand to strike a match in his matchbook. He was a cocktail of gentle manners and pure sex. I loved the way he moved, from his deep inhales to the money he threw on the table, all bills facing the same way.

"So, do you change your own oil, or do you go to Jiffy Lube?" he asked.

"I don't know. My mom's boyfriend does all of that. Anyway, I don't even have a car."

From Jesse's expression, you would have thought I'd just told him that I didn't have any knees or elbows. "That's crazy!" he said. "You should. My old Bug is for sale — you want to take a look? It's real cheap, and it actually starts about ninety-nine percent of the time. I've been toying with it since I was ten. I learned on it."

A car! "That'd be great," I told him, "but I don't have any money."

"You could pay me slowly; I trust you. I know your mom and her boyfriend. It'd be like a loan."

"I don't have a job."

"You what? Are you rich?"

"Hardly."

"That's crazy. I've been working since I was eleven. I guess it's better if you don't have to."

"I should, I'm always broke. But I just never thought about it." Thankfully, even through my Amaretto fog, I thought I'd better not admit to him how I make forty dollars every year.

It was quarter till eleven, and I knew Vikki J. might want to leave soon — *Babes* replayed at night, and she hadn't watched it all day. When she made her way to me, she didn't strut or flirt with the guys on the stools on her way. She was uncharacteristically tired, probably exasperated from acting playful when she was heartbroken. She managed a smile when she said hi to Jesse.

"How ya doin', little gal?" she asked me as she twirled a piece of my hair into a tighter ringlet. I hadn't bothered to straighten that day.

"Great." I wanted to seem enthusiastic and sober so she wouldn't make me go.

"You know I cain't leave you alone in a bar. You ain't even eighteen till this summer. Sorry, honey, but you've got to come home with me."

"Um, Vikki J.," Jesse cut in. "Do you mind if I drive her home? We'll go next door and grab a hot dog. I'll bring her home by midnight. She'll be safe with me, I swear to you."

"You're in a bar, boy. You can't drive my Katie in that state."

"I don't drink; haven't had a drop."

"Hey, you." She poked his cousin. "What's this boy been drinkin'?"

"Nothin', ma'am. He's boring, he don't drink. That's why I always bring him . . . so he can drive me home." The bartender assured my mother that it was true, and Jesse's cousin went on, "If he wants to see that beautiful young lady home — your sister, I take it — I can get a ride with one of my buddies." I tapped my feet like an itchy rabbit hoping I'd get to spend a little more time with Jesse.

"You on weed?" Vikki J. asked him.

"No, ma'am. The hardest thing I ever have is Coke. And I mean the kind you get at the grocery store."

"Well, okay. But you bring her right home, I mean it."

"Are you sure you don't mind?" I asked her. My first concern was that she'd be okay, and that I wouldn't find her sprawled out on the floor anymore.

"Girl, I'm gonna be just fine," she said as she kissed my head. I was drunk, of course, but I thought I felt a tear drop on my scalp.

"I won't be gone long," I promised.

"No more drinkin', you're done. I mean it. Have fun."

We walked her out and watched her drive away. At the diner, we had to sit in the smoking section, which made my hot dog with gravy taste like sawdust and stale water. His only fault was the constant smoking. We finished the food in time for him to swing by his house — what Vikki J. didn't know wouldn't hurt her. He was anxious to show me his '70 SuperBeetle. He had painted it a shiny, sparkly shade of violet. The Bug was so dark it almost looked black. I hopped into the driver's seat, which was the perfect size for me. I rolled down the window.

"Katie, you have to buy it. It matches your eyes."

It was cheap — just a few thousand bucks — but it might as well have been a million. I had about twenty dollars at home, my life savings.

"I wish I could," I told him.

"Well, you think about it. Let me know if you want a job. I know one of the managers at McDonald's."

That was an idea I'd never taken seriously. I never had

wheels or any motivation to save money. Maybe I needed that little Beetle.

"I'll think about it."

He stamped out his cigarette in the gravel driveway and wiped his permanently oil-stained hands on his jeans. When he coughed, his whole body quaked. A tear in his battered jeans exposed his skin, and I wanted to see more. He caught my stare and made good use of it. He leaned into the driver's side and kissed me. His skin was rough, but his lips were soft. He might have been a good kisser, but I couldn't tell because his mouth tasted like toast burnt beyond recognition. I wished he didn't smoke.

"Well, I better get you home. I wouldn't want to make your momma mad."

In my driveway, he just chicken-pecked my cheek, not asking for my phone number or anything. He gave me a charming mischievous expression and told me to think about the car. I didn't get it; most guys I'd met lately were in hot pursuit. This one acted like he had all the time in the world to get with me, and he was leaving the country in July. But I doubted if anything made him feel nervous. At least I had an excuse to find him at school — I could ask him about his Bug.

I walked toward the door wondering what he thought of me. Admiration? Attraction? Nothing? He made me anxious, and I wondered if he'd call or act like he knew me. Dating was awful — either I didn't like them at all and suffered, or I liked them a lot and suffered more.

I noticed how empty the driveway looked without Bob's Econoline in it. The house looked vacant as well. Fewer lights were on; silence greeted me in place of questions and laughter.

I was worried about Vikki J., and I wished I were clever so I could say the right thing to make her feel better.

As usual, she was in the living room — but the TV was off, and she was already asleep. There she was on the couch, wrapped in my soft, old Muppet Babies sheets. She was fully dressed and smelled like the smoky, liquory bar even though she hated cigarettes and hadn't touched her beer. Her perfume, Tommy Girl, was struggling to hang on. I brought a pillow from her bedroom and tucked it under her head.

"What? What's wrong? You're okay, right?" she asked, half asleep.

"I'm fine, get some sleep." I just watched her for a while as she burrowed into the pillow, facing the back of the couch.

And then I said, "I love you, Mom."

i have vertigo

I've never been more content to see a weekend end. My mother had been lying on the couch all Sunday looking at the TV without even noticing that the remote was in the other room. She didn't change her clothes, speak, or have an appetite. She rose from her favorite spot only to go to the bathroom. I brought her Cheez Balls for breakfast and macaroni and cheese for dinner, but she barely touched either. I kept a glass of cherry cola by her head and a box of Kleenexes on the floor by the couch. She didn't want them, either. She might have felt better if she'd just let it all out. I asked her if she was okay, and she nodded her head yes. The only time she smiled was when she asked me about Jesse.

"I toldja your plan wasn't a failure. It's gonna work out just fine. I'm proud of you, Katie."

On Mondays, her salon was closed, and I hated to leave her at home alone. But honestly, I'd been counting the seconds till I got back to school. I wanted to run into Jesse, find out about Frankie's date, hear what Kevin had done on Saturday night, and hope that Matt would at least acknowledge that he hadn't called me back. As for my grand plan — keep dating every weekend — I wasn't sure if I was really quitting or not. I did know one thing: Something still had to give. The change wasn't tangible; it was something I couldn't explain inside of me. I didn't want to hurt other people; I didn't want to hurt myself, i.e., no more Ians and no more activities that are totally not me.

Regardless of my high hopes, my first indication that Monday would be a bust came early. Frankie refused to tell me anything about Friday on our way to school.

"What happened? Did it go well? Did you two kiss?" I asked before my butt was even situated in the front seat. I immediately regretted it because she told me to buzz off. I don't know what got into me; I understood wanting to keep to herself. Usually, that's exactly what *I* did. But I'd never had a girl as a friend — I never cared enough to be nosy.

"Katie, we talked about this. Will you just be patient? It's kind of embarrassing." Luckily, I could tell it went pretty well despite her unwillingness to share. She drove slower and didn't get irritated when she got the red lights. She sang the words to cheesy pop songs. She didn't go off about one single thing — not even when I wanted her to.

I missed Frankie by third period when Paul invaded my space at my locker. I couldn't read him, so I didn't know what I was in for. I just didn't want to see him at all.

"Hi," he said, looking a bit doe-eyed and trying to be sexy about it. I was basically more turned off than a broken table lamp. I didn't want anything to do with the locker-side makeout king.

"Did you have to go out with Wren?" he asked.

"This isn't the time or place." I was really rattled by Paul; he still had that power despite everything awful that had happened. He probably always would.

"That was disgusting," he had the nerve to say.

"Don't talk to me about disgusting." I really didn't want him to get me riled up and make me embarrass myself and then scream things that would make my teachers think badly of me.

"[Cuss] you, soccer-ball brain," Frankie said. She had my back, surprisingly, and heard the whole thing. She was awesome.

Paul and I had a staring match, and he looked away first. He was no dummy; he knew he couldn't take on two of us.

"See ya around, Katie. See ya, Frankie," Paul said, walking away. He had lost the battle, that was clear. But there was still a war between us.

"It'll be okay. It'll be okay," Frankie assured me. I was teary-eyed despite myself. I don't know how that boy still got to me. I really hated him; I really, really did.

"Looks like perfect timing for me to come rescue you," Frankie added, taking my hand. "Weedkillers suck."

We took refuge down in the Fast Learners Wing for about ten minutes after the attack. She winked at the girl who'd been with Blue, which gave me a few hints about her mystery date. I was confused, though, because I thought Blue had gone out with her. I forced myself to hush; Frankie would tell me when she was ready. Blue hopped down from a stool where he was busy hanging a new light fixture. He winked at me, and my body tingled even though I didn't want it to. I smiled back at him before I thought not to. My eyes darted around; I hoped

Frankie hadn't seen. I hoped Jesse hadn't, either. She hadn't, and Jesse was nowhere in sight.

"Here, for you," Blue said, making his way closer to me and Frankie. He handed me a lightbulb, whatever that meant. That time, I took it from him without smiling or giving any expression. He was dangerously close to inciting the wrath of Frankie. He'd have been wise to steer clear of her; she was good at being protective of me. But she didn't even notice him standing there. She was making eyes with Bandanna Girl.

"Um." I just couldn't think of anything to say.

Blue went back to his ladder and the light fixture.

"Ahhh, Katie," Frankie said. Before I could get the story out of her, she was flirting her blond hair off again.

The rest of the day was pure entertainment for everyone except for me. Boys snickered as they passed notes about me in all of my classes. They made a calendar and picked different days to go out with me because rumor was I'd go out with anyone at any time. They passed my name, secretive and sinister, the same way they'd share an X-rated magazine. Stories sprouted legs and took off running, and by the end of the day, I was a slut, too. The guys were all planning sex dates with me. I was not amused; I was hurt at what was being said in my dishonor.

It didn't seem appropriate to tell everyone that I'd gone on a date all by myself last weekend (what would they make up about that?), and that I'd recently turned down three guys — the Booger Eater, Beefhead, and Wren. I didn't know how to defend myself, so I didn't even try. Frankie wasn't much help because she ran down to Fast Learners between every class. Thankfully, Kevin met me as usual before last period. I knew he'd be on my side. He hugged me and told me not to worry. "They'll find a new rumor soon."

"I know." I hoped.

"It only takes a couple of days, another weekend at most," Kevin said. "I promise. Someone else will get the heat."

Strangely enough, Cherry and Matt were there again, and neither of them had a class near ours. They weren't making out, but talking intently. They came over to us.

"Katie, oh, my goodness, is it really true? I mean, I know you're going through some changes and all," he said, looking down at his cool new shoes, shoving his glasses back up his greasy nose. His voice quivered, and he rubbed his temples.

"Matt, please. You still know me." I was just glad he came up and spoke to me. I missed him, I missed him, I missed him.

"No, but Wren is certainly spreading a lot of stuff, and everyone saw you and Ian."

"Wren? Again?" I asked. Being un-invisible was exhausting. "Anyway, if you'd just call me back, I'd tell you what's going on. I've been wanting to apologize for everything I said, you know. I was wrong."

"I'm sorry. You're right. I know that's what you wanted. I've been meaning to, you know, call you back," he said, still looking down at God knows what on the floor. "Cherry and I have just been so busy lately."

I was in no mood to imagine with what. Why wasn't *she* the butt of nasty rumors? Probably because they were true, and nonfiction was never much fun.

"He's such an amazing guy, girlfriends," she said, looking directly at Kevin. "I should start a few rumors about *him*. Really, I'm lucky the rest of the school hasn't caught on to Matt yet.

Anyway, Katie-Kay, don't worry about it. Those guys are idiots, and everyone knows it. Even I know it."

"Gee, thanks."

"Katie, I'll talk to you soon," Matt said while Cherry kissed his cheek. Again, she was staring at me and Kevin. "I'll give you a call," he added, and I hoped he would — Matt had always done what he promised.

"I'll call you, too, girlfriend," Cherry said to me. "I want to make sure that you're okay."

"Let's go," Kevin said, ushering me into class. "See ya, Matt."

I did not enjoy infamy. I was furious at Wren, but I couldn't beat him up. And I couldn't stoop as low as him no matter what I did. To get my mind off everything, Kevin offered to take me to the gym after school. But he had to help one of our teachers grade papers first. So I was stuck waiting for him in the commons, hiding in the corner praying that no one would notice me. I just wanted Kevin to hurry the hell up.

"Hey . . . Katie," Blue said. I had awful luck. "Your eyes sparkle more today than they did yesterday, I say."

"I'm in no mood . . ."

"I come in peace," he said, towering over me. I looked up at his face from where I sat cross-legged on the floor. He was tall and pierced, reminding me of a beautifully warped poem that made dying sound romantic. How could a guy with such soft, emotional eyes also be such an ass to his girlfriends? Just when I was about to overlook what a jerk he was, he reminded me.

"I will try again," he said quietly to himself. He stood up straight, positioned his shoulders, and made a show of self-confidence. "You'll go out with me now," he said.

"What?"

Blue had classes upstairs — he was only in Fast Learners for one period — so surely he'd heard the Katie rumors. He had honors English with Matt and was on the newspaper staff, where he wrote music reviews. In the past few weeks, I'd taken time to learn about the teens who lived and died at Shitville High.

"You and me," he said. "*Vertigo*. This Friday."

"How dare you! First of all, I still think you're disgusting for everything you've done. Second, you win the Biggest Dick Ever Award for asking me out today of all days after . . . you know . . . everything."

"I never thought it would be bad to get the Biggest Dick Award. . . ." His usual smirk left his face again. As he walked away, he added, "What other people say means nothing to me." He seemed awfully wounded by me, which made no sense since we barely knew each other. I wondered again if he could've been the guy who left the CD in my locker a few days ago. Maybe that's what he was talking about, and not the slut stuff. *Think of Frankie,* I reminded myself. *Loyalty.*

"What was that all about?" Kevin asked. "That guy is always around you, watching. It's kind of odd, don't you think?"

"He is?"

"Well, yeah. Is there something you're not telling me about?"

"No, I told you already, he ruined Frankie's friend's life. He keeps asking me out, today even — the jerk — and I keep saying no."

"You're a challenge. He's probably in love."

"He probably wants sex."

"Who doesn't?" Kevin said with a shrug.

"Kevin!"

"I'm kidding, I'm kidding. I'm telling you not to worry. Try not to act upset, even if you are. Studies show that it's only fun to pick on a person when she reacts to it. So don't react."

"Yeah, right. From now on, I don't care if anyone calls me Katie James the Makeout Queen."

"Come on." He held out his hand to help me get up off the floor. "Just stop. You know you're awesome; I know you're awesome; Frankie thinks you're awesome. Want me to continue?"

Kevin ruled. He told me all kinds of stories that had nothing to do with me. We goofed off, we did sit-ups, and we jumped on the trampoline. Eventually, he went off to do his own thing. As I made my way up to the high beam at the gym, I fantasized that my life was in perfect balance. I wouldn't be a phantom whore; Bob would be at my house when I got home; Matt would be my best friend; and I would still have a chance at finding love. I turned off my thoughts the best I could. Kevin would not approve of my obsessing.

I concentrated on walking straight ahead without wobbling, and I didn't lose my balance once or make any other mistakes. I had done fine on the beam by myself. I could even jump off flawlessly, all without a lot of practice.

"See, Katie, you're Queen of the Beam."

I smiled. Then a pun occurred to me, and I threw my scrunchie at him.

"Oh, come on. I didn't mean it that way."

Kevin took me home and had to run back to substitute-teach a class. Vikki J. was still wrapped up in sheets on the couch. At least she had changed into pajamas.

"You okay?" I asked.

"What don't kill me makes me stronger."

"Do you think you should try to talk to him?"

"I think he's already gone."

"Well, did you call him? I'm calling him right now. Where's the phone?"

Vikki J. didn't move but shot a deadly look. "Goddamnit, Katie, don't you dare. What good does it do to call if I'm not gonna say yes?"

"Please, just say yes."

"No. After your daddy died, I never wanted to get married again. I promised myself I wouldn't ever. For him."

"What if he'd want you to?"

"I just ain't me without my independence," she said, fists full of wadded tissues. "Now go away, I have to pray."

"You have to what?" Her mouth would set fire for saying that.

"I have to pray — ain't that what you say to me when you wanna be alone? I know you don't know shit about religion, Katie. I know when you're just tryin' to get rid of me," she said. Barely moving, she was still fiercesome. "And don't I leave you alone?"

"Yes."

"Shoo, child. Goddamnit, shoo."

The phone interrupted our conversation. Once again, I hoped it would be Matt — or even better, Bob. It was neither.

"Katie." It was Paul.

"What now?" God, he was the last person on earth I wanted to talk to.

"Really, tell me it isn't true." His voice quivered just as much as Matt's had earlier.

"What do you care?" I couldn't believe it — I had a breakthrough, an ah-ha moment. Clear as plastic wrap, I knew I didn't have any feelings — not one — when I heard his raspy voice. I didn't smell Zest and grass just thinking about him. The memory of him holding my hand didn't make me cry or cringe. The day wasn't a total bust after all, because I knew I was over Paul.

"Wren?" he asked. "Just tell me you didn't, and I'll be okay." He sniffled and crackled. I could hear the rustling as he shifted around in his chair. He was calling me from his cell phone in his bedroom. I wondered what he'd done with the love collage I'd made him last Valentine's Day. I hoped he'd gotten rid of it. He needed to move on once and for all.

"You owe me an apology," I said. "What you did by my locker was cold. It was kind of embarrassing, too — to me and to yourself."

"What about you and Wren? By the way, he and I aren't best friends anymore. Like, duh."

"You know, Paul, we could get into an endless loop over who owes who what." That was the first time I'd spoken his name out loud since we'd broken up, and I was fine with it. "But I don't want to do this with you. I probably shouldn't have taken revenge like that. You probably shouldn't have gone around sleeping with a freshman. Let's just call it a truce. We spent too many years together — we know each other too well — to hate each other this way. I don't want to fight with you. I don't want to hate you."

"Katie, just tell me if you did him."

"God, Paul. No, I didn't. Ewww."

"I didn't think so." He sniffed again, and I heard the hollow hushed sound of a tissue bursting out of its box. Then Paul blew his nose.

"I want to see you again," he said.

I would've loved those words a few days ago, coming from him. But now — no.

"We're never getting back together," I told him, and as I said it, I was sure it was true. "Ever. Let's try to be civil, and maybe we'll even be friends one day. For now, stop this so you don't hurt your girlfriend the way you hurt me."

"Katie, go to the prom with me." That was a line I wasn't expecting. I have to admit it threw me off guard. If I was over Paul, and I swore I was, I wasn't over the fact that I was dateless and loveless for prom. "It would be so awesome. We'd really go this year. Just me and you," he added. "I know if you gave me a chance, I could make you feel the way you used to about me. I know I could."

"No, no. This is exactly what I don't want us to do. Friends don't beg friends to get back together. But if you promise not to bring up anything romantic, there is one thing you *can* do for me."

"What. Anything. Tell me." He was breathless. His sniffling stopped. "Maybe I'll help you, but you have to at least consider going to the prom with me. We could go just as friends."

"No."

"Okay. How about this: I'll only help you if you agree to one thing. My offer to go to the prom with you will always stand. If you change your mind, and I don't care if it's the very last minute, I'll take you. You got it?"

"That's screwed up. What about your new girlfriend?"

"That's my problem. Just say you got it, and I'll do whatever you want. Anything."

"Got it." I wasn't sure what I was agreeing to, but I knew what I needed.

In this case, Paul was the only one who could help me.

Things to hold on to

Turned out my ex was good for something besides becoming one with my metal locker. After school on Thursday, I asked him to stake out Fast Eddies. I didn't have a car, so I couldn't do it. Plus, my mother, more disillusioned than usual and grief-stricken as hell, had already forbidden me to contact Bob. But if Paul, the one guy Bob knew, "accidentally" ran into him? Well, I could *not* be held accountable for that. I hoped.

Paul didn't expect to find Bob at the bar at that time of day. He *did* find the bored bartender, though. Paul discovered that Bob had been around a lot, drinking heavily and saying good-bye to friends before heading to his sister's in Texas. Paul pretended to be one of Bob's hired hands, and the bartender didn't believe him. Paul decided, for once, to be completely honest.

"Tell me where he's working today," he said. "I've got a plan to get him and Vikki J. back together."

The guy called Bob's cell and asked him to stop by Fast Eddies that night around eight. The bartender made up some story about people from the neighborhood who wanted to say

209

good-bye. When Bob arrived, Paul made sure he was there waiting.

"So, I hear you're leaving," Paul said once Bob sat down. It was a mystery how one bar stool contained him. Bob ordered a red wine even though he was at a beer-only kind of place — a guy of Bob's size could order whatever he wanted without it threatening his manhood.

"Boy, you've got a lot of nerve meeting me here like this. I oughtta teach you a lesson after everything you've pulled on my Katie. But you're too scrawny." Bob turned his attention to the wine. "Nahhhh, no, you're not." Paul was no dummy. He trembled, and his tennis shoe slipped off his bar stool footrest and kicked Bob's shin. The clean-cut kid glanced around the room wondering if any of the patrons would protect him. Nope, probably not.

But he was lucky, because I was watching the whole thing. Vikki J. and I, bar maidens extraordinaire, saved him at precisely eight-fifteen p.m. I knew we'd be late because I knew my mother. I told him to be there at eight because, well, he .deserved to break a sweat. He wiped his brow when he saw us.

"Katie, thank God."

"Thanks, Paul." I kissed his cheek, and Bob's forehead wrinkled.

"It's okay," I told Bob, hugging him hard as I could and kissing his cheek, too.

Vikki J. stood back, fiddling with her fingernails and looking at the floor. I'd never seen her — the almighty woman who roared and cussed — hold herself like an innocent little girl.

Bob jumped off his seat, and he put his hand on her shoulder. She was trying not to look up, not to see his gentle eyes, but she couldn't stop herself.

I stepped back and stood beside her. I thought I might have to hold her up.

"I'm gonna kill you, girl," she said to me.

"No, you're not," I replied. In order to get her there, I'd told her she had to get dressed and drive me back to Fast Eddies. I had lied and said Jesse wanted to see me there, and of course I couldn't go there alone. ("Damn right, you cain't," she yelled, fixing herself up for the first time in days.) The truth was, I hadn't seen Jesse all week; I'd heard he was visiting his brother in Germany till Sunday.

"I knew you was up to something," she said to me, with Bob standing right there, too, his red wine flopping out of the glass he held it in. He was literally too shaken to speak. "Or, at least, I hoped you was."

"Why didn't you do it yourself?" I asked her.

"I guess I ain't as independent as I thought I was."

I took Bob's red wine and gulped it down while they kissed. The entire bar — only six or seven people, mind you — yee-hawed. I don't think I have ever been that happy. Paul hadn't moved from his bar stool. Wisely, he'd chosen to stay back out of the way. But he beamed; he knew they belonged together, too.

"Thanks," I whispered to him.

"Anytime."

We sat next to each other in silence while Vikki J. and Bob did God knows what. It was nice being close to Paul again. When we were like this — not fighting, not worrying about who was sleeping with who, not being jealous or hateful or desperate for each other — he was comfortable, like a favorite slipper or old friend. He knew me and my family so much better than anyone else ever could. That wouldn't go away if we wanted it to — and that was the one thing I wanted to hold on to most. We smiled at each other when Bob yelled:

"Ya'll are invited to Main Street next Saturday afternoon at one o'clock sharp. There's gonna be a marriage!"

He pulled a diamond ring out of his pocket and slipped it on her finger.

"Well, goddamnit, I thought you threw that thing in the river," Vikki J. said.

"I'm not that dumb. When you weren't looking, I put it in my pocket. The only thing I threw in the river was my old empty key ring."

We all yeehawed again.

Hamsters get cancer?

Friday, May 2

I managed to contain myself, I have no idea how, till lunch. I hunted down everyone and made sure to give them a note begging them to please sit together in the lunchroom just for today. I wanted Kevin, Frankie, Paul, Matt, and even Cherry if it made Matt happy, to be together. I had something to say.

"My mother is getting married!"

They sat on the edge of their seats as Paul and I told them the entire story. Matt got mustard all over his face; Cherry didn't look in her mirror once; Kevin actually sat still and stopped eating; and Frankie listened intently as usual. They cheered just like the guys in the bar had done.

"Oh, my goodness gracious!"

"Well, get out, girlfriend."

"Awesome."

"Holy [cuss] —"

I invited them all to my house at eleven a week from Saturday, so they could help me decorate for the small wedding in our backyard. We'd put up streamers and piñatas or whatever the heck else struck our fancy. Vikki J. and Bob didn't mind what we did; they just wanted it to be small, nonreligious, and fun. The justice of the peace would arrive at one.

"Katie, I would not miss it. Can I bring my mom?" Matt asked.

"Doll-face, did you know I bake?" Cherry asked. "I've got the cookies and cake covered. It won't be fancy, but it'll taste great." So Cherry was good for something. I felt obligated to invite her because I wanted Matt's friendship. She wasn't that bad, I told myself, especially if she was going to provide food. After all, I didn't know a chocolate chip from an M&M. (I just knew I couldn't eat either one of them.)

"I'll bring some cool music — even some stuff that you don't have, Katie," Kevin offered. "Let me deejay. I can set up the chairs and help you clean up, too."

"I'll pick everyone up," Frankie said.

"Wait, what about prom?" Paul asked, everyone a little surprised to hear him speak. They had been cold to him on my behalf; I hadn't had the chance to tell them they weren't required to hate him anymore. They were probably shocked to see us making the announcement together. Well, not together together, but sitting next to each other as friends.

"I was thinking about that," I said. "Why don't you all bring your stuff, and we'll get ready at my house after the wedding? If you want to, we can all go together." I was shocked at my own event planning. First of all, I didn't even know I was going to the prom until I said that. Second, I'd never asked friends over to my house for anything, because I'd never had a group to invite. I began to understand why those second-grade girls got so giddy the week before their birthday parties. I had missed out; celebrating felt good. Like buttercream frosting on a golden vanilla cupcake, some things just went well together.

"That's great, I'll drive," Frankie said. "But can I talk to you, Katie? Not now. I'll do it on the way home."

"That idea rocks," Kevin said. "I'll meet the rest of my friends at the prom."

"That's the peachiest idea ever. You are brilliant, Katie girl," Cherry exclaimed, Matt nudging her as she spoke. I bet he wanted the two of them to have their privacy before the prom. Devilishly, I was glad to be ruining it. Them alone? Yuck.

"Well, Katie. I can't," Paul said. "I'll be at the wedding. But unfortunately, I have a date for the prom. And even more unfortunate, she isn't you."

Paul made everyone uncomfortable, including me, so we all ignored him politely with plastered-on smiles. We just changed the subject quickly, which was easy. I couldn't remember ever having a better time in the Shitville lunchroom. We must've whooped it up too much, because the lunch monitor kept telling us to tone it down.

I was naturally high, so the rumors didn't have their same acidic effect on me. People I didn't care about, not anymore, anyway, could call me Queen of the Backseat all they wanted — and believe me, they did. Even that couldn't bring me down. Not when my mother was getting married to the best man alive, and all of my friends would be there to celebrate it with me. To make things even better, I didn't have to stress about a date for the prom: I had four of them, my friends. The dress was another matter, but I'd think about that later.

"Okay, so here's what I have to ask you," Frankie said, speeding faster than usual down the street. "Maybe can I bring this girl, Renee, to the wedding? Or would Vikki J. and Bob think we're too weird?"

"Oh, so that's her name. Is she the girl in Fast Learners I've seen you talking to?"

"Well, yes, I was ready to tell you that, too." She was nervous; she white-knuckled the steering wheel again.

"Frankie, that is awesome. I'd love it if she came along. *They'd* love it, too. They love lesbians!"

"Are you sure?"

"Yes, I'm sure. Vikki J. and Bob are very accepting, very cool. You don't have to worry at all."

"Awesome, man. One more thing . . ."

"Anything." I meant it. The world was my shrimp cocktail that day — er, I meant oyster.

"You don't have a date tonight, do you?"

"No, but I'm not all that concerned with my stupid plan. I won't be in love by prom, but I would love it if you'd go to Fast Learners with me next week. I have to flirt with that guy Jesse." I didn't mention Blue, but I did think about him just then.

"Um, sure. But tonight, well, Renee's cousin is in town. I haven't met him, but we were going to see if you wanted to go to Big John's. The four of us."

"Do I know him? Does he think I'm as easy as everybody's saying? If so, no way."

"He lives in Michigan. He won't have a clue."

"Okay then, you've got a deal."

"And somehow, almost magically, you're staying on top of the plan. How many dates has this been?"

"Well, this is the fifth weekend, so I guess I've had" — I

stopped to count on my fingers — "eight dates including the one with myself."

"You rule. I'll pick you up at seven."

Once home, everything was back to normal. It was Friday afternoon, and the blow-dryers downstairs were whirring. By six o'clock, Vikki J. was cooking up a storm, fried chicken and potatoes for Bob. I couldn't wait till his Econoline became a permanent fixture — you know, legally required to park — in our driveway.

I called Matt, who I missed as much in happiness as I had in misery.

"Hi there," I started casually.

"Hi, Katie." He was still not thrilled with me. I could hear him fiddling with his flute case, and I was sure a glass of cranberry juice was nearby. "Pretty good news today, huh?"

"The best, really." I was nervous to talk to him, and I didn't like it one bit. "Listen, we're okay, aren't we?"

"You didn't really do those guys, did you?"

"God, no, I told you that! What is your problem?" His fixation — and everyone else's — on that subject irritated me to no end. I had to stay focused on the task, which was to make amends with Matt, and not say anything about it. It took willpower not to scream.

"I would be so disappointed if you had."

"Matt, I called because I miss you," I said, losing my patience. "I want to make up with you. I've heard things about you, too. But I'm not telling *you* that I'm disappointed." I was, though. "And the rumors about me aren't even true!"

"I know, I know. You're right. Katie, you're always right."

We were silent for thirty whole seconds. At least long pauses between us were never uncomfortable.

"Do you want to hang out sometime? Maybe go prom dress shopping with me? I mean, I know you have a date, but I don't," I said, not sure if that was a wise thing to do together. "I could use moral support when I go to the store."

"I know you hate those places." He paused and made terrible squeak, squeak noises as he shined his wind instrument. "Cherry would be jealous."

"So go with me and don't tell her. Again, I am truly sorry I said anything nasty to you a while ago, Matt. You are still my best friend."

"You're right. I just won't tell her. You're my best friend, too."

"Barbies forever."

"Gracious, did you have to bring that up?"

"Sorry." He made plans to pick me up in Winifred and take me to the mall on Sunday. I was half relieved, half nervous to hang out with him again. After all, our Amaretto love had still gone mostly undiscussed. I did a Kevin, and stopped obsessing long enough to look on the bright side: Things with my true friends were busily working themselves out.

Take Frankie. She was ready for me to meet her new girlfriend. She picked me up, her woman in tow. Renee was the girl I'd seen at Big John's with Blue, all right, but there was plenty of time to find out about that. Renee wore a red bandanna on her head, and ripped jeans, and I swore her outfit matched Frankie's red-and-blue flowered dress. Renee was soft-spoken, but managed to cuss a lot. I could have been entertained just watching them all night. Relationships are so positively airy when they start, and theirs was blossoming.

218

The guy they brought for me was another matter. His name was Eugene.

"Um, what do you do, like, um, for a job?" he asked me.

"I don't have one, but I might try to get one soon."

"Really?" Frankie interrupted.

"Yeah, I want to buy that guy Jesse's purple Beetle." There, I had stated it out loud — I had only *thought* about the job and car before.

"Oh, cool. I totally love that Bug," Renee added, tightening her bandanna, which was about to fall off. "I love Jesse, too. He's a [cussin'] good guy."

I liked him, too, but he wouldn't get back until Sunday.

Eugene chimed in with, "Well, um, I'm glad you have the freedom to save for something fun like a car. I don't. I have to save money, like really fast." He had curly hair, and he'd be fine with a makeover. But the poor guy had boogers hanging out of his nose. I just couldn't get past that, among other things.

"What's wrong?" I asked, trying to remain polite for Frankie and her date's sake.

"My hamster's about to die. I'm saving up for radiation treatments. It's gonna cost me more than a thousand dollars."

Frankie cracked up; Renee nudged her. I had to act horrified, or else he would have thought that I was a big fat bitch.

"Oh, my God," I gasped. "Really?"

"Yes, she has ovarian cancer. The vet thinks he can save her."

"[Cuss]," Frankie and Renee said at the same time. I just covered my mouth; it was too difficult not to laugh. Hopefully, he didn't see it. I really wanted to hand him a tissue. Not because he was about to cry, which he was, but because his nose luggage was really disgusting.

"It's not funny, Renee," Eugene whined. "I know you're laughing up there. Jeezus."

I pulled on Frankie's seat belt from the backseat where I was sitting. She totally deserved to be squished for getting me mixed up with the likes of Eugene.

The Great Meat Off wasn't even any fun. Eugene was a vegetarian who ordered a separate pizza with extra vegetables and no cheese.

"The entire American meat industry is incredibly cruel to animals," he tssked. "I can't believe you all eat that stuff."

"So, Renee, how did you and Frankie meet?" I asked. If Frankie wasn't going to tell me anything, maybe she would.

"Oh, I thought you knew."

"Um, no." I kicked Frankie under the table for not telling me *and* for setting me up with Booger Man.

"My friend Blue got us together. You know, that guy has a huge crush on you."

"What?! He did what? Frankie!"

"Crap." She pushed her parmesan crumbs off the table and onto the floor and her combat boots. She fidgeted. "Can I talk to you in private?"

"Why? Can't you tell her in front of me?" Renee asked.

"You girls are being so rude," Eugene said, wiping sleep from his eyes with his sleeve.

Frankie pulled me into the girls' bathroom.

"Look, we're really good friends now, Katie. We weren't as close when I did this."

I didn't like the sound of *that*. "Goddamnit, what?" I demanded.

"Well, um . . . [cuss]. I made up the story about Blue. It's a total lie. The real reason why I won't go back to ballet is because a girl there broke my heart," Frankie said shyly and with a lot of guilt. "I loved her, and we dated for a year. She finally dumped me eight months ago because she liked Blue."

I was still willing to give Frankie the benefit of the doubt. "Well, did he steal her from you?" I asked.

"No, he didn't even go out with her," Frankie said.

"What?" I was steaming mad. I pinched my leg to control my anger.

"But I was totally immature about it, and I hated him," she pleaded. "Katie, I quit ballet over it."

"Why did you go and do that?"

"I was crazy with a broken heart." She touched the upper part of my arm, and I pulled it away. "I was completely crazy," she said again.

"I can't believe this!" I yelled. My pinching trick wasn't working.

"Don't get mad. Please don't. You know how I had this big, um, crush on you a while ago . . . remember?"

"Yes. I thought we were over that." Oooh, I was irritated.

"Well, maybe you were, but I wasn't. Then of all the people in the entire world to ask you out, it was him. I was out-of-my-mind jealous. I couldn't stand to watch you hook up with Blue. So, well, you know what I did about it."

"What a mess." On one hand, I could understand what she did. On the other, I was totally disappointed — in a lot of things.

"Well, Blue knew that I hated him," she explained. "And he had seen you and me hanging around a lot, you know, after that

221

embarrassing scene at the CD store when we first met. Anyway, he found me after school one day and begged me to get out of the way, so you'd give him a chance. He has such a bad thing for you, Katie. What did you do to him?"

"I don't even know his real name." I was numb inside. He excited me beyond what I thought was possible, and I had only hated him on her behalf. "Frankie, why did you have to make this such a mess?" I wanted to be really, really mad at her. But I kept thinking of all the ways she had helped me. I was torn. I pinched my thigh harder.

"I'm good at it." She touched me again on the arm, and I let her. "So let me explain. Last week, Blue made me an offer. He's friends with Renee, and he thought she and I would really hit it off. He offered to set us up, and if I liked her . . . which I do *sooo* much . . . he told me that I had to convince you to at least give him a chance."

"Oh, my God!" I went from mad to excited at that moment. "When were you going to tell me all of this?"

"Um, right now," she said, her eyes pleading with mine for forgiveness.

"While I'm on a date with the hamster-saving, vegan booger man?" At the very least, she could have spared me that.

"Clearly a mistake," she said. "I didn't have time to set you up with Blue yet. But that's not important. Katie, listen, I didn't expect us to really become friends. I never would've lied if I thought I'd start depending on you — you know, as a real friend."

"You do? Depend on me, I mean?" I was happy; that was an amazing thing for her to have said.

"Yes, of course I do," Frankie added. "I care about this relationship, and not in *that* kind of way."

"Me, too." Our barriers were coming down; our emotions were clearer to each other. I felt closer to her than ever. But Eugene? But keeping me from Blue? Oh, that was still annoying. If I had gone out with Blue a long time ago, I wouldn't be the Makeout Queen. "But I'm still mad at you," I said.

"You should be," she said, clearly worried that she'd screwed things up between us. "I'm so sorry."

"Okay, I tell you what . . . I'll forgive you."

"Just like that?" She smiled tentatively.

"Yes, but only if you'll fix it. I don't know how. Just fix it," I said. "One more thing: You have to get me out of this date with Eugene in the next thirty minutes." I figured I might as well use Frankie's indebtedness to my benefit as soon as possible.

"We'll go to the CD store and look for Blue tomorrow. I'll make it all up to you, Katie. I swear." And without any more fuss — neither of us were experienced with friendship and its frailty — we left the restroom.

Back at the table, Eugene had cleared his nose. He and Renee were laughing, and he didn't scare me so badly. He looked less like a psychopath and more like an everyday weirdo.

"What happened to him? Did he take his medication?" Frankie asked Renee.

"I made him eat a piece of pepperoni — and poof!"

He laughed again, his spit hitting my arm. He talked too much for the twenty-five minutes, spraying saliva the whole time. That's when Frankie said, "Renee, Katie's not feeling too well. We have to take her home."

I coughed and sputtered, "Oh, only if it's not a problem. I wouldn't want to be rude," I said.

"It's okay," Eugene added, shielding his face from my so-

223

called germs with his hand. "I really don't want to get sick myself."

And with that, the evening mercifully ended. I took a shower the second I arrived home, after telling my soon-to-be parents (yippee!) good night. I loved the way the hot water prickled; it took the endless tingling away. I couldn't calm myself down over this Blue news. Tomorrow, if everything went according to plan, everything would be perfect with him.

Never Party on an empty Stomach

Saturday, May 3

Frankie was kissing my butt, all right. She showed up an hour early for our trip to the CD store. We sat at the kitchen table, drinking the Hawaiian Punch and eating the Pop-Tarts she'd brought, while the hefty scent of peroxide wafted up the stairway. She told secrets to win my good favor. For example, Renee was a good kisser. Eugene had been homeschooled, and he was one person who could've used the social skills. Blue had been such a terrible dancer that his own mother wouldn't let him take classes. She kept talking, much more than usual. I pretended to listen, trying desperately not to show how anxious I was to see Blue.

I imagined what I'd say: "Hey, let's go out tonight" or "I'm ready; *Vertigo*" or "Baby, I'm finally ready." Some things never changed: I was still a total geek.

We arrived at Ear Bangers just as it opened, and there he

was, flipping through CDs in the world music section. He wore his piercings with his thrift-store shirt and a pair of brand-new faded jeans. He danced around to the music overhead as he wrote titles down in a small, back-pocket notebook.

"Blue, I brought her."

I stood behind Frankie until she grabbed my wrist and yanked me in front of him. He flashed the same mischievous look I'd seen when he stood on the toilet in the girls' room.

"Well, look who's here," he said, scratching his mop. "So, Frankie finally told you. It's about time, *Frankie*."

"[Cuss]. Gimme a break." She was still annoyed with him; her short fuse around him gave it away. At least she was trying; she even gave us some privacy.

"So you have something to say to me, I take it." He was beaming. "I'm not a toilet licker. I am an angel. A serious dream boyfriend." His cheesy lines were satire, not earnest. He had a knack for taking any awkwardness out of our situation. Plus, with a little humor, he was letting me off the hook.

Next, it was my turn. "I hereby take back every negative thing I ever said about you." I was so excited, our banter was pure fun. "I shouldn't have been mean to your face or behind your back."

"Alas, I am honored to be in your good graces." He kissed my hand, and placed a CD in it. It was called Hip-Hop Zen.

"I only said those things because I was standing up for Frankie," I added, not wanting to be remembered for being a total bitch without good reasons.

"I know. You're a good friend," he said. "That only made me like you more."

"So let's not stand here and look at each other — let's go

226

out," I offered. "You and me, *Vertigo*." There, I had said it. It felt good to be around him.

"As much as it causes me pain, I must refrain."

Lottery addicts had better luck than me! Oh, what pain he was causing me! There was no way he'd understand how crushed I was. I tried desperately to hang on to my composure. What were the odds?

"Is it because of the Makeout Queen thing?"

He was offended. "No way, man. Those clowns don't exist in my world. Katie, I must be honest. It's because of another girl."

There I was, being sucked heart-first into the ground, as usual. I don't know why I was so surprised; none of this dating stuff had ever gone the way I had it planned. It was like trying to get an A on a test by studying your butt off and then it just doesn't happen. And you get stuck with a B. Well, today I was getting an F.

"So this whole thing, me coming here to grovel and ask *you* out for a change, it was for nothing."

"Not nothing," he said. "I had it bad for you, for a long time — three whole weeks. You broke my heart." He snapped a CD case in two for dramatic effect. "So last week, I asked another girl out. I am trying to replace you. She wants to see *Breakfast at Tiffany's* tonight. And the thing about me, you see, is I am a one-woman guy, Katie." He was obviously satisfied when he said that. "But if it doesn't work out with her, believe me, you'll be the first one to know."

"No, thank you. I'm not your second helping."

I ran out of the store in a mortified panic. He would not see me cry, but unfortunately, Frankie would. She cussed him, putting one-hundred-percent effort into making me feel better. "He still has it for you," she insisted. "He'll come running. I swear it." She was whiter than milk, her freckles shrunken due to her furrowed frown. She knew this was all her fault. "I'm going to a party tonight with Kevin and Renee," she continued. "Come with us."

"This will be my first night without a date this whole time." I'd always managed to scare one up somehow — with myself, my mother and Jesse, even Eugene.

"Ahhh, [cuss] it. You didn't care about that plan, anyway."

"I know, but something always came through, even if it wasn't the best thing. Something always happened to make it count, you know."

"Well, there's always Eugene," she said as if that were really an option.

"Oh, my God. Are you trying to make me hate you?" Oooh, this was not the time to push my buttons.

"Sorry, kidding. Seriously, I'm kidding," Frankie said more softly. "You're going tonight, though," she added. "I'm not letting you sit home alone."

She dropped me off, and I called my cheerleader. Kevin was born with the superhuman ability to know exactly what to do and say in every situation. This afternoon was no different. He took me to the gym, hoisted me back up on the beam, and ran off to multitask or something. I had twenty minutes all to myself before the gymnastics girls would take over the space. I did a cartwheel on the high beam. Only there could I be on top of the world. I relished the experience; it didn't happen to me often.

"We have to go, Katie," he hollered from the upstairs office.

His voice echoed all through the gym. "Come up here for a minute."

I wondered what I'd done wrong or had broken. I was careful climbing the steps, no reason to out my inner klutziness, and entered the ransacked office with papers and fitness books exploding everywhere. It was gross; I had an urge to organize it.

"This is my boss, Heidi," Kevin said. She was the tanned bleached-blond, my mother's loyal patron, and she reached her hand to me. I guessed I was supposed to shake it.

"So, I hear you're getting fit for the first time ever."

"Uh, yeah, I guess. Kevin is great." I was not comfortable around adults unless they were overgrown children like Vikki J. and Bob.

"I need an assistant to help me return phone calls and manage this mess of papers. Interested in a part-time job? I need you fifteen hours a week, and you can work whenever. Kevin said he'd pick you up, and you could do your hours when he was working. Your mother is talented, reliable as a whip. I'd love to hire her daughter."

"Really, me?" I couldn't imagine I was qualified.

"Yes, you."

"That's really nice of you and all. Thanks. Could I ask my mom about it first?" She wouldn't care; I just needed to buy time to think. Why get a job? I wondered. I did covet that Beetle.

"You can also use the gym whenever you want. You're getting pretty good on that beam," Heidi said.

"And I can give you personal training, too," Kevin added as he flipped through a nutrition book.

She told me to let her know in the next week, and I assured

her I would. Kevin and I strolled out to his car, and I was kind of excited about it. The offer gave me something to think about besides my disappointment with Blue.

"Why are you always doing such nice things for me?" I asked him.

"You deserve them. There's another reason, too. You know how I said the best way to feel better when you're down is to do something good for someone else?"

"Yeah."

"Today, that's what I'm doing for you."

We made plans to meet up at the party, and he assured me the evening would be fun. Feeling cruddy yet inspired, I decided to do something Kevin would be proud of. I called Frankie and told her my plan first. Then she called Renee, who was instructed to see if her cousin was game. Renee rang me immediately.

"He loves the idea," she said. "You're brilliant. He's taking my car and will be there by six."

"Perfect." My wonder date, Eugene, and I would meet them at the party at eight.

I ran downstairs, and Vikki J. was just finishing a friend of hers, an older woman with nails longer than her own.

"Two words for you," I said to my mother.

"Girl, you know I'd do anythang for you." It was like she'd been taking Prozac for a year; she was that elated and sweet. Bob was good for her.

"Another makeover."

"Yeehaw!"

Before Eugene showed up, she took me up to her closet. I tried to explain that the makeover wasn't for me, it was for a guy — not even a cross-dresser — so her clothes wouldn't work. We'd just have to work with what he showed up in.

"You silly gal." She opened her closet, and it looked like a rainbow. "Choose one, baby-dawl. Any one you want. Ain't nothing in the world I want more than for you to have fun with your friends."

"These are gorgeous," I said, dumbfounded at the prom dresses that peered out at me. "How did you pick them? How did you know what I'd like?" They were straight out of the pages of a teen magazine, not her usual Frederick's of Hollywood style at all.

"Little one, I know you're more uptown than me. Why do you think all of them clothes in the back of my closet look like they was built for you? You didn't seem like yourself in my outfits, so I boughtcha some new ones. I stuffed 'em in the back just for you."

"You did that for me?"

"Well, of course I did, Katie-Kay." She kept all emotions at least fingernail's length away, including the ones she had for me. Vikki J. had her ways, though, and those were okay with me.

"Thank you." I hugged her hard.

"Awww, stop that. Just pick one and go on. I got some settin' up to do downstairs. I ain't used to havin' men down there."

Sure, my luck sucked sometimes, but really, I knew I still had it pretty good. Way too many people had gone out of their way to be nice to me. It was time for me to return the favors. Eugene showed up, ten minutes early, and he had more crust dangling from his nostrils. He was dressed in pleated khakis and a flannel. I wasn't sure what I would do, but I would make him work. Eugene needed to fit in with society just a little bit better.

Not to boost my ego — I had none left — but for his own good. I mean, Eugene would never get a job — I don't care if it was at a fast-food place or a science lab — looking and acting like that.

"Katie," he whispered in the empty living room. "Katie." I had to come closer, and at least he smelled normal, like Ivory soap and Speed Stick. "I have a zit on my butt. I have a zit on my butt!!!"

"Okay, Eugene. Rule Number One: You do not talk about your body parts with other people. You do not talk about hamster body parts with other people. You do not talk about veganism with people who are eating pepperoni pizza with extra cheese."

I tried to explain social graces, the little that I knew about them. "When in doubt, Eugene, stay silent." I told him others don't want to feel put down or pressured. "Basically, to be friends with anyone, all you have to do is let them do ninety-nine percent of the talking and drench them with compliments. The key to success in life is feeding everyone's ego."

His eyes and nostrils went wide. "Katie, you're really good at this."

"See, you're already learning. Thanks."

"I think you're real cute, too," he breathed. "Maybe we should kiss later."

I had to set him straight. I told him, as gently as I could, that I was not interested, but I wanted to take him on a platonic date. I hoped we'd become friends, and I promised to help him hit on other girls. He thought that was a good idea, clearly excited about being around any female, whether or not she was me. We didn't have much time, so we went right to work. I taught him how to walk moving both arms in opposite directions. He stopped swinging them in unison, and I swear, that made him stand up straighter and sucked the schlepping off his stride. I coached him on what to say to girls — simple things like "Hey, what's up?" and "How are you?" He practiced on me, and in an hour, he was far less nervous and awkward.

Vikki J. took over next. She plucked his busy brow first thing, and he had nice eyes once you could see them. She cut his shaggy, curly hair into a cool MTV 'do. She gave him special soap to wash his face so his skin wouldn't look so greasy. Next, she attempted to dress him. She had him wear a plain white T-shirt, a man's V-neck that she liked to wear to bed. It looked dapper compared to the flannel, and the pleated pants were fine. We both insisted that he go out and buy some jeans. She complimented and flirted with the vegan, and he glowed. She was successfully boosting his self-confidence. He was so smitten by her, he even ate her hot dog.

"You don't never go to a party on an empty stomach, *Yoogene*," she said. "If you drank any beer without somethin' in your belly, you'll git sick."

"I can't just eat tofu and rice before?"

"You can, but this here hot dog will soak the liquor up better. You won't get such a bad hangover the next day."

"I don't drink. It hardens your liver."

"That's good, I think that's better," I told him. "But when someone asks you what you'd like, just say no thanks. Don't mention internal organs — that kinda goes along with the no-body-parts rule."

We asked him what he was interested in, and really, the guy was okay. At the public library he tutored people who didn't know how to read; he went to Sunday school; and he hoped to be a vet one day. I advised him to talk about those things with girls, and just try to keep his nose clean and relax.

We arrived at the party, and I made a big fuss over him in the hopes that other girls would take notice. He was still a little weird with his James Dean white T, but he really was cute. Most important, he didn't stand out. Eugene at least looked totally normal. Frankie and Renee couldn't believe their eyes. Kevin poured him a drink, which he politely poured out without mentioning cirrhosis. When I left, he was chatting with boy climbers, the perfect naïve females for him. I was proud of my smiling transformed spaz. It was fulfilling to make someone feel better. With my efforts looking like a success, I kissed Eugene on the cheek — right in front of all the girls. I said my good-byes, called Vikki J. and Bob, and went home.

"Your momma told me what you've been up to," Bob said. "That's mighty fine of you. All the things you've been doing lately are mighty fine."

"Do you think I should take a job at the Y?" I asked.

"Doing what?"

"Just organizing the office and making phone calls. That woman you know, Heidi, offered me a job. And I think I'd like to save up for a car."

"Wow, them things will keep you busy," Vikki J. said. "Think you can still watch *Babes* with me?" Bob gave her a pinch and a *no* head shake.

"You should do it, Katie," he said. "I'll take you until you've saved enough for your car. Anytime."

"Me, too," my mother said.

We pulled up in the drive, and Cherry's car wasn't at Matt's. That was a first for a Saturday night. I did not dwell on the two of them. I did not let myself suffer imagining that I could've been with Blue at *Breakfast at Tiffany's*. I did not obsess on what could've been different from what was my reality. If I wasn't in love, at least I wasn't alone. I stayed up late with my family, falling asleep in front of the TV.

The planets and
my new good mood

Sunday, May 4, through Thursday, May 8

"Katie, I can't take you shopping today," Matt said on Sunday. "Cherry is coming over and, boy, is she ever mad at me."

I had picked out the blue dress Vikki J. bought for me, so I was hoping he'd help me take the others back. It was just an excuse to see him, of course. "No way. What did you do?"

"Nothing, as far as I know. You women are such a handful."

"But we haven't talked in forever. We haven't had a chance to hang out since we kind of made up. We did make up, right?"

"Goodness, of course. Things haven't been the same without you, to be honest. I just can't see you today. Sorry, Katie, but I have to go."

I had always known what was going on with Matt, but this time I was stumped. The guy who was somewhat cool, who had sex with a pretty cheerleader, was mysterious to me. My feelings were more mixed up than ever. Sometimes, I wished we could hop back in Winifred on the night we kissed. If I could have a do-over, I wouldn't have gone out with Kevin the next night. That's what doomed us; I mean, Matt watched me say yes to that date while we were still out. I would've been pissed at me, too. Did things happen for a reason? If I hadn't gone out with Kevin on a less-than-satisfying date, Kevin and I wouldn't have become friends, and he is someone I wouldn't want to be without. I hadn't screwed it *all* up; dating spun its own tangled web. I wondered if Matt would want to be with me if he were free from Cherry. Could I get over my disgust for his social climbing, for his sexual interludes with a girl who's known for her sexual interludes?

School was a nuisance; I wanted to fast-forward to Saturday. The prom would be fine, whatever, I didn't care. The wedding, now that would be amazing. Vikki J. wasn't sweating it; she didn't like big to-dos. Even so, she didn't fool me. She shopped for a new red dress — like she'd wear white — and cleaned the house. I was the only one who'd touched a mop or rag as long as I could remember. She hated it, but this week, she scrubbed till things shined, singing the whole time. On the phone, we ordered fifteen folding chairs from a party rental store. We got out the tablecloths and bought white paper plates for the cookies and cakes. Bob and Vikki J. bought wine and beer by the case even though seven of the attendees would be underage. Monday after school, Frankie and I bought decorations to hang all over our house. I told Frankie to tell Renee to bring Eugene to the wedding, even the prom if he wanted, if he was still in town.

"Let's keep helping him," I said. "He's doing so well."

"You feel okay?" Frankie teased. "Renee will be thrilled that we're being nice to her cousin. That's really cool of you."

I tried to come up with other things I could do, too.

"Let's get flowers and silver tinsel and party favors!" I suggested to Vikki J., itching for more to keep me busy.

"I don't want none of that fancy stuff. Them piñatas you bought suit Bob and me just fine. We're gonna have a good time, don't you worry. Now, tell me about the prom."

"I am only going so I get to wear that gorgeous dress," I said. I'd made a pact with myself to go, and I was going. I tried hard not to be disappointed about the rest. "Really, it'll be okay, even if I am just going with my friends."

"Don't forget, your friends are folks who know ya and love ya anyways."

I scrunched up my face and stuck my tongue out.

"Awww, hell, Katie. You'll have a boyfriend again. Maybe you'll even meet someone at the prom." She kissed my kinky hair — I had given up on straightening it — and whistled Disney songs.

Kevin took me to the gym after school to keep me busy, and I told Heidi I'd take the job. I would start the week of May 11, right after the festivities had ceased. Next up, on Wednesday, I looked for Jesse. I'd been avoiding the Fast Learners Wing despite Frankie always sneaking down there to see Renee. I was doing just fine, and really, I didn't want to see Blue. But I did want to find Jesse, who was surely back from Germany. I had an excuse — I wanted to buy his Beetle, and, well, maybe he'd flirt with me. Bonus if he'd do it in front of you-know-who.

I stood away from the door, peeking into their cavernous workroom like I had done so many times before.

"You have to make *psst psst* noises, Katie, or they won't even look out here," Frankie, my wingwoman, said. "Look, I'll do it for you."

Immediately, Renee came out and gave Frankie a kiss. They were so cute together I wanted to puke. But I couldn't be jealous; I was too happy for them.

"You want me to get Blue?" Renee asked.

"No way, he's got some girlfriend. Jesse instead, please."

She went inside and tapped the skinny Casanova's shoulder. Fresh from Germany, his hair was cut in a spikier, Eurotrash style. It made him look more modern and — damn him — cuter. He wasn't Blue. Instead, Jesse was raw, rock-solid. Somehow, he seemed giant even though his body was small.

"Hey," he said, coming over. "I was hoping I'd see you at Fast Eddies this week."

"How was your trip?" I asked.

"Awesome, I can't wait to move. I'm going now in June."

Whatever hope I had left for love — and believe me, there wasn't much left in me — it was flying away on an international airplane.

"Ah, that's too bad," I said, giving him flirty eyes just for the heck of it. What did I have to lose? "I got a job."

"At McDonald's? Shoot, I could've helped you get the better shifts."

"Nah, I'll be organizing the office at the YMCA. My friend Kevin helped me get in."

"That's cool. Sounds better than flipping burgers."

"Except I won't get free Happy Meals."

He smiled. "Right. So, do you want to buy my Beetle? Because now I'm in a hurry to sell it."

"Yeah, I would, actually. That's why I came to talk to you."

"You sure you didn't have any other reasons?" He was tough — making me blush from my face to my feet. I tugged self-consciously at the jean skirt I had on. He had the power to make me incredibly nervous. I hated feeling nervous.

"Well. I was wondering if maybe . . . maybe you could show me the car Friday. We could talk about how I'd pay — I don't have any money yet. I'll buy you pizza, and we can figure it out."

"You askin' me out on a date?"

"Yes," I said. "I guess."

"How about this — I'll swing by and get you in the car around eight."

I was elated. If things went well on Friday, I could invite him for Saturday. Maybe he'd stay for the wedding and that little event afterward. Suddenly, the planets were in better alignment with my mood. I had hope as Jesse strutted back into the classroom to work on an engine. He turned around and winked at me. Blue was suspiciously close to the door, purposely avoiding eye contact. I hoped he'd heard the whole thing.

I didn't have time to sweat it. I had to run upstairs — I was already five minutes late for class. Frankie and Renee were all cuddly, a pair of horny Kewpie dolls, pixies in love. I grabbed Frankie's sleeve and literally had to drag her away.

"Geez, Katie," she said when I accidentally stepped on her combat boots. "Where did you get all of these balls lately?"

Me find Jesus

Jesse strode inside our spotless house looking like he owned the place. He wanted to meet Bob. But getting Bob's attention wouldn't be easy — he was busy concentrating on my mother, who was busy making fried chicken. They were having their own private rehearsal dinner after I left. I was starving, so I snuck into the kitchen and nearly burnt my fingers off when I stuck them in the squished potatoes.

"Well, girl, that's whatcha git," Vikki J. said, lifting her foam can-huggie.

"Bob, Jesse has the Beetle," I said, hoping to move their meeting along so we could hurry up and go.

Jesse explained that he'd fixed it up himself, then he went on about a million Fast Learners type of things.

"That's great," Bob said, half listening, eyes still on Vikki J. "Tell you what," he added. "I'll check it out next week. If I think it's in good shape, I'll pay Jesse the money since he's going to Germany soon. Katie, you can pay me back. We'll set up a loan."

"But it's your wedding," I said while I tried not to act too thrilled. "Shouldn't *I* be buying *you* presents?"

"You already gave me the best gift I could ever get. She's standing over there in the kitchen — see her sneaking those Doritos before dinner?"

"They're appetizers!" she yelled.

Jesse's mind was still on the car. "If Katie'll drop me off at home, you can just keep it for a few days," he offered. "I've got a bunch of cars; I can do without that one."

"You're a fine boy," Bob said. "Now, you take good care of my Katie."

How did Jesse make bowlegged look so sexy? His shoulders shook up and down when he walked in a boisterous blue-collar strut. It was like everything he did — walking, studying cars at school, shooting the shit with Bob — turned out perfectly. Thanks to him, it looked like I'd be getting my own car, after seventeen years of crawling, walking, and biking. I couldn't believe it. I was so impressed by him. He was just sixteen, but he was more mature than any boy I'd ever met, while still managing to be the very definition of cool. Jesse was worlds away from Paul — one was full-bodied German beer, the other a cheap bottle of Chardonnay.

I was going out with a guy I truly admired, and I vowed to keep my standards this high. He may not have been headed to college, but he still had a grand plan. He didn't just talk about his dreams, either; he was going off to live them in just a month. I just wondered why he had to smoke so much.

"You drive, Katie," he said.

It was embarrassing to admit that I couldn't even do that. I still hadn't learned to take control of a stick shift. Immediately,

Jesse put me in the driver's seat, anyway. He didn't flirt with me like some guys would have. Instead, he gave me clear instructions. He kept cool when I killed the engine in front of Matt's house.

"Come on, girl. You can do it. Now, press the clutch, turn the key, and hit the gas while letting off the clutch slowly." His last words kind of jerked out of his mouth due to my version of driving. "That's okay, you're doing it. Now, when you hit twenty miles per hour, listen to the way the engine roars. That's when you hit the clutch again, and shift the stick to second. Let off the gas when you switch gears — just for a second — there you go. Now keep goin'."

The Beetle was a tough old insect. I gave the transmission a pounding, but I did it with a mission. I was determined not to be so one-dimensional. I'd drive my own stick shift on my way to and from work! I'd visit my friends — *my friends!* — and maybe I'd even start looking into college. After all, I couldn't sit around and watch *Babes* all next fall.

"You're a really cool guy, Jesse. I can't believe how cool this is," I said, trying to pull in to Nightcap Hot Dogs. "Totally friggin' cool." I got about halfway into the parking space before yanking my foot off the clutch too soon. The car didn't ride into the curb, it hopped.

"You got any Tylenol?" Jesse asked, faking wooziness. "Just kiddin'."

I was gearing up to make my move, dive in, and be brave like Jesse was. I was going to ask him to the wedding and to the prom. It wasn't a big deal. I'd just tell him that there would be a big group of us.

"Me need go home. Me need find Jesus," a middle-aged,

five-foot bald man yelled in a high baby voice, interrupting my moment as Jesse and I were finishing up our meal. He didn't look like he was on drugs. He just seemed distressed and maybe disabled. If anything, he hadn't taken his medication. After bursting through the glass door of the hot dog joint, he ran right up to our table. Maybe we looked friendly. While his dementia was alarming, he was about as dangerous as a ladybug.

"Me brother, he find Jesus. You take me to brother? Please?"

Jesse stood up and took his right elbow. I followed his cue and grabbed the left. We walked the man up to the counter to call for help.

"No one care about me. Jesus care me. He do. Take me brother to find Jesus. Please. Please care me. Take home please."

The owners took the man, named Mike, behind the counter to an office.

"Thanks, kids. He comes in all the time," said a guy with a name tag that read DogMan.

"Whew. And I complain about my life," Jesse said, sitting down, pushing his hot dog away from him.

"I know what you mean." I glanced at the purple Beetle outside and thought of the wedding tomorrow.

"So, anyway, Katie, you looked like you were going to say something."

"Um, well, I better wait till later." What I had to say didn't seem important just then.

We drove around in the car, me behind the wheel, and Jesse smoked while I shifted gears. We went to the cemetery, and he smoked some more. We went to the car repair shop where he works, and he showed me the before pictures of the purple

SuperBeetle. It used to be yellow except for the driver's-side door, which was light blue when Jesse first got it.

"So, anyway," I said, "I'm having a nice time."

"Me, too." He blew galaxies of smoke that didn't intrigue me at all anymore.

"I was thinking, if you weren't busy tomorrow, um, you might want to come to my house around one. Bob and Vikki J. are getting married — it's really small and informal — then me and my friends are going to the prom afterward. If you're interested, it would be fun."

"Ah, man, I can't. I'd love to see your man Bob get hitched, that'd be fun. But I have to work, and I was off all last week. I can't take off again. I'm sorry, man."

"Well, you could meet us when you're done with work?"

"Wait a second," he said, kicking the dirt around on the floor. "It's not that I don't think you're great. It's just that me and prom don't mix. My friends and I don't do high school stuff like that. Maybe I'll wish I did one day," he said, touching my waist. "Besides, Katie. I couldn't do that to my buddy Blue. He's had a thing for you forever. I shouldn't even be hanging out with you now. I just wanted to teach you to drive and all."

I was humiliated. I was an idiot. I was pathetic. I was very, very disappointed. I'd made it this far — on eleven dates (I counted date equivalents). But I would be alone for prom. I reminded myself that I had great friends. I loved them, and it didn't matter if no guys loved me.

"I wish you'd change your mind," I said. "Blue has a new girlfriend, anyway."

"I think he likes you, though. He'd kick my ass, and man, I don't do people like that, you know."

"I'm a loser." I couldn't help crying. He hugged me tight, which would've been more soothing if he hadn't smelled like an ash factory. I told him the whole story, about Paul, my plan, getting new friends, losing new friends, and busting tail to win them back again. I told him what had happened between my mother, Bob, and me, how we all drifted apart and got back together. "I missed out for almost five years and tried to make up for them in a month and a half," I concluded. "A loser, a total loser."

"Have you been sniffin' gasoline?!" Jesse yelled, lifting my chin back up with his right hand. "First of all, do you know that I haven't been on eleven dates in my life? Teenagers only 'date' in movies." His little waist rocked back and forth and his arms flailed in the air. "I'm serious. What made you think the rest of us haven't pissed away the last five years, too? There are a million things I wish I hadn't done — and I have never even had a real girlfriend, let alone been in love. You've had a serious relationship, and you followed it up with eleven dates in a row. Now that's impressive. You're the queen of something, all right."

"That's what I've been told," I said under my breath, digging my kitten-heel sandals into the greasy gravel.

"Look at me. I wish I could be you. You've got it all, especially amazing luck, and things are only going to get better." He kissed me on the forehead and hugged me again. Our bodies were the perfect match. I was petite, and he didn't tower over me. "Let's get you home. You have a wedding tomorrow."

Weddings and other revelations

Vikki J. and a small gaggle of women friends hid away downstairs. The scent of perfume, nail polish, and Aqua Net wafted into the kitchen where Frankie and I busily hung the streamers.

The words *Congratulations on your wedding* hung from the window, in big tinselly bubble letters, over the table, and extended to the opposite wall. I would've pinned everything up with masking tape but, luckily, Frankie was more artistic and crafty. She brought double-sided everything so ugly things like tape couldn't be seen. We had red and black streamers to match Vikki J.'s dress and put them everywhere we could think of, over every window and bare wall space. We filled the coolers with ice and loaded them up with beer cans and wine bottles. We put a red paper tablecloth out and placed plastic and styrofoam cups along the edge. Paper plates, forks, and red napkins sat in front. We dumped two cans of cashews into a glass bowl and two bags of Doritos into another. Those were the centerpieces, along with red tea candles in tiny metal holders. We left large spaces for the cookies and cakes that Cherry was bringing. The traditional piñata — it looked like a cross between a muscular horse and gentle donkey — was in the kitchen with the snacks and drinks. Another one, the color of a burst of sun in the summer, was a tiger. We removed the swings from my old rusty set and hung the feline in the middle of the bar. We added a few streamers (though red didn't exactly match) and designated that as The Spot. Vikki J. would want to exchange vows right there. As for Bob . . . he would marry her anywhere.

Maybe a girl from a more sophisticated — aka wealthy — family would've been horrified, but my friends and I were right at home with the kitsch. We dared not think of the place as tacky. Whatever you wanted to call the place — cheese or chintz — Vikki J. was going to love it when she emerged perfectly coiffed from her salon in the basement. I could think of nothing that mattered more.

Kevin and Matt arrived to set up the chairs. Renee was prompt, and her main job was to flirt with Frankie whenever she could get away from Eugene. Her booger-free cousin wore jeans and a T-shirt. His attire was perfect for the occasion. Kevin and Matt took him in and kept him busy, thankfully, because Eugene had an alarming affinity for the piñatas. His eyes were glued to the tiger, and I was half afraid he'd come unglued and bust it.

"That boy's not quite right," Cherry said, making her grand entrance. She was dressed up far more than the rest of us. And she was done up from her hair down to her blood-red toes. Her arms were dramatic, helping her to take up as much space as possible in the small, 80s-style kitchen. I noticed her hands were empty.

"Holy crap, you don't think she forgot?" Frankie whispered. She didn't talk to Cherry much.

"Oh, my God," I said, panicked.

"Hey there, lovebirds." Cherry chicken-pecked Frankie, Renee, then me. How did her lipstick stay so red? It was on duty twenty-four hours a day, like the fire department. I smiled at her, reminding myself that I cared more about Matt's feelings than my own. I wouldn't hate her — or anyone else — at least not today. Unless she forgot to make the cookies and cakes; then at least I would get away with extreme dislike. I scratched my head through my mop of curly, frizzy hair.

"Oh, Katie baby, I didn't forget. What kind of friend do you think I am?"

Matt came running from the car with foil-covered plastic plates, his glasses barely staying put on his ears. He tore off the top from one plate and yelled, "Voilà!" Renee and Eugene were behind him with more plates and two simple layer cakes, all looking like they needed to be eaten.

"I can't wait," Renee said, diving into the first plate of cookies. I guessed it was okay. There were five or six plates full of sugar, chocolate chip, and peanut butter cookies, and one large sheet cake, and only fifteen people tops to eat it all. Everyone grabbed a handful — hadn't these people eaten? — and gobbled like mad. Then they went back to what they were doing. I had to admit, I was a tad hungry, too. I gobbled two sugar cookies.

"These are sooo good," Frankie said, adjusting her dress.

"I just want to make sure you used all natural ingredients,"

Eugene added. "I don't believe in food coloring or dyes. They cause cancer of the intestinal lining."

"They do not. Shut up," Renee said, giving him a little kick.

"Stop it, I bruise easily," Eugene said, then he started laughing. "Guys, that was a joke."

I glanced at him till I got his attention, then I shook my head *no*. I think he got my drift.

"Sorry," he said and went back outside to jiggle the chairs and stare at the candy-stuffed tiger. He took apart the stereo in my bedroom and put it back together outside. Boy, we were glad to keep that one busy.

Guests arrived, Bob's employees and Vikki J.'s friends and the justice of the peace.

"Sure am glad it's really happenin' this time," the justice said. "Right, Bob?"

"You're damn right," said a voice from the crowd. The crackle of cans opening filled the air and cork tops popped off. My friends and I poured drinks and made the adults laugh. We snuck a few sips of our own, but not too much. We had a prom to go to afterward.

My mother emerged in all her soap-opera-inspired glory, three big-haired women in tow. Her makeup was expertly executed, even if it was slathered on as thick as peanut butter. She radiated. She was proud of her self, her life, her house, her husband-to-be. "Look at all you've done around here!" She play-danced with the streamers and kissed the piñatas. Then she saw Bob, and she stopped dead still, the smile melting off her face. He and I exchanged glances of terror. Would she bail out again?

"Psych!" she said, dancing around, grabbing her can-huggie and keeping it company with a beer.

Paul showed up at ten till one when we were all outside.

"Hey, beautiful," he said.

I smiled. "Glad you could make it. Drinks and snacks are inside." I saw that longing puppy dog look in his eyes. I smelled Zest when he came up close, way too obviously admiring the way my legs stretched out of my jean skirt.

"I wouldn't miss this, Katie. You know, we got together right before they did."

"That was a long time ago."

"I wish it were yesterday."

Eugene put on some soft country music, and the justice of the peace said his thing. I wasn't listening. The wind whipped the tiger around in the air, causing it to whack into Vikki J.'s and Bob's backs. Matt saw Eugene head straight for it, and he held him down.

"Do you take this man, Bob, to be your lawfully wedded husband?" the official asked Vikki J.

"Hell, yeah. I do!"

"Do you take this woman, Vikki J., to be your lawfully wedded wife?"

"I do," he said, wiping his tears off his cheeks with the sleeves of his button-down shirt. "I surely do."

He pulled out the ring, the one that never made it into the Ohio River, and put it on her hand. I kicked my sandals off because they were seriously making my ankles itch.

"I now pronounce you Mister and Missus Bob Jaymes."

"His last name is Bryant."

"Oh, I mean, I now pronounce you Mister and Missus Bob Bryant."

I ran up to them with my bare feet and hugged them tight.

Then I got out of their way in case they wanted to kiss. They jumped up and down first, which made locking lips tricky. Finally, Bob just heaved her up into his arms to hold her as if he were carrying her over the threshold. "You've made me the happiest man alive today," he said. They kissed for five whole minutes while the volume on the country music went up. The justice of the peace came out of the house with wine in one hand and beer in another, both for himself. The adults said things like, "Remember when . . . ," and my friends and I headed back inside.

"Katie, I miss you," Paul said, kissing my cheek. Everyone, especially Matt, was giving him go-to-hell looks. "I'll see you all tonight. I have to go." I watched his cute butt walk to his car, and I was happy that I didn't long for it anymore. I followed him out to wave good-bye. He rolled down his window and yelled, "You have two more hours or so, you know. You just call me if you change your mind."

"Bye, Paul. Have a good time."

Back in the house, Frankie and Renee were missing, probably hiding out in my room doing God knows what. "I think they got into the romantic spirit," Kevin said. "Have you noticed that Matt and Cherry haven't really even spoken?"

"No," I answered abruptly.

Matt's ears must've been hot. "What did you two say?"

"Um, nothing." I didn't want to get into anything with him — I was having an amazing day, and I was just thankful to have my friendship with him on the mend.

"Katie, can I talk to you? Kevin, you stay, too." He sounded way too serious, ruining our party mood. "Sorry, but right now while Cherry's still talking to one of Vikki J.'s friends."

"What is it?"

"Katie, I have something embarrassing to admit," he said, watching me intently for my reaction. "You know that love CD you found in your locker a few weeks ago?"

"Yeah."

"I put it there."

"You what?" I was shocked, then confused. "I thought you loved Cherry."

"I loved doing certain things with Cherry. The whole time, all I thought about was you." He watched intently for my reaction. I didn't have one. I had dreamt of true love, but I knew romance would sacrifice some part of our friendship. That made me sad.

Kevin's contact popped out of his eye. He licked it and fiddled around to put it back. He clearly didn't want to go to the bathroom to fix it — he would have missed out on something good.

"Oh, my God." I started to sweat. "Kevin, will you please scratch my back?"

"Gimme a minute."

"I don't know why," Matt said. "I just wanted to. You were having such a hard time, and, well, I wanted you to know someone was thinking about you."

"Why didn't you just tell me, for God's sake? I couldn't get you to say boo to me that week."

"I don't know what my problem was; I was just nervous," he said hopefully. "You weren't ready. You had this plan, this mission, and I could tell you were committed to it. I didn't want us to get together until you'd been out with other guys — even though it sucked watching you with them."

He paused, for dramatic effect, I guessed. I stared at him, not believing the words.

Matt went on, "I knew you needed more time to get over Paul before you could ever possibly be with me." He was slightly nervous telling me all of this but also comfortable and natural with it. Basically, Matt was just being his sweet old self.

"Holy shit," Kevin said, thankfully scratching my sweat-soaked back.

"Why now, Matt? Why?" His timing was more than confusing. I had just accepted the fact that he was happy with someone else. I had just decided to forget about him — in the "us" sense at least.

"Because I told Cherry about it today, and she didn't even care. I thought she'd be mad at me, or at least upset. But she wasn't. She just said, 'So, I'm still invited, right?'"

"That's just like her, you know," Kevin interrupted, adding fuel to the white-hot scene.

"What?" Matt and I said in unison.

"She did the same thing to me," Kevin said.

"*You* went out with Cherry?" I was shocked; they just didn't seem like each other's types. But Matt and Cherry were not the perfect match, either.

"You know all of those condoms in my glove box?" Kevin asked. "She bought them for me — said I'd need them. But then, well, then . . ."

Matt blushed, looking guilty, and I wondered what might be hidden in Winifred. Matt and Kevin were spilling their guts, and it was too much information. The wedding had provided all the drama I could handle that day, but clearly, there was more to come.

"Oh, my goodness," Matt said, rubbing the top of his head.

"We started off seeing each other secretly because she was still seeing some other guy." Kevin was twitching all over, very clearly distraught. "I told her we'd stop sneaking around once she was ready to commit. She never could commit to me, even though she knew how I felt. This went on for three months."

He paused.

"Finally, I just couldn't take it anymore. I told her it was over." Kevin paced around in a small half-circle. "Then she begged me to take her back, and a week later, she cheated again! I made myself stop seeing her that time — ending things with Cherry was torture."

"You're still not over it!" I said, hugging him.

"I am too," Kevin replied, watery-eyed.

It all made sense — those two had unfinished business. So that's why Cherry and Matt made love scenes near my locker. The displays had nothing to do with me, I realized; Cherry just wanted Kevin to see. Why were those two continuing to be such jerks to each other? Why continue the cycle of revenge over romance gone wrong? Paul and I had tried it; and we agreed to a truce. It was then that I finally started to get over him. Kevin needed to call a cease-fire. If he didn't, he'd continue to harbor a broken heart.

"I hope she didn't cheat on me," Matt whispered. That made me mad. Was he professing love for me, or was he really into Cherry? Oooh, that Cherry — I didn't care how good those cookies were. I was mad at her.

"I sure as hell didn't cheat on you, baby," Cherry interrupted. She had seen the whole thing. "And I'm sorry I cheated on Kevin."

"You lie," Kevin growled. He looked freaked out, ready to bolt out the door. Renee and Frankie ran into the room, too. They must've heard our emotionally charged voices. Oh, my, we had made a mess on my mother's wedding day!

"I don't lie — not too much!" she said.

"Why weren't you more upset about me and Katie, then?" Matt asked her, looking a little too hurt for my comfort.

"I, well, ahhh, doll-face. . . ." She went to hug him, and he pulled away. I did not like their display one bit. "The whole time you were with me, it was to make Katie jealous. I knew that. It hurt at first, but I tried to be patient and give you time . . . I learned how to do that from Kevin. You were never over her, so I just played along. I guess I . . . I guess I really liked you and your friends. I wanted to belong."

"To us?" Frankie asked. "Why the hell for?"

"I started it to make Kevin jealous, I guess. But then, I don't know, you all were nicer and smarter than all of the beefheads I'd hung out with before," Cherry said. "I really loved being a part of the group. You all were this great group of friends."

"You only did all of this for revenge," Kevin interrupted. "You tell the truth for once."

"She is telling the truth," Matt interrupted. "She loves all of you."

"She couldn't tell the truth if she tried," he said.

"For [cuss] sakes," Frankie yelled. "You two — Kevin and Cherry — go into Katie's room and settle this once and for all. Either get back together, because clearly you still have feelings for each other, or be adults about it and work it out. I can't take all of this [cussin'] fighting!"

She and Renee pulled them into my room, really tugging. Then they didn't return. Frankie was a smart one. She knew getting rid of them meant Matt and I would be alone together. I was so wound up, though, it was hard to concentrate on anything he said.

He walked over to me, hugged me, and sat down on the couch. He patted the seat for me to join him. "I'm sorry I was with her," he said.

"If you really wanted to be with me, why would you screw around with her?" I demanded, hurt by it all. "Why, Matt? This doesn't make any sense."

"She was there, Katie," he said. "You weren't. She treated me like a sex god . . ."

Ewww, I thought. I grimaced.

". . . she gave me all the attention in the world."

"You were just climbing social ladders, Matt, and you know it."

"That was part of it, too." He really looked ashamed, slumped over and pushing his glasses back up. "It was a mistake. But Katie, what about you? You weren't sitting around waiting or anything."

"I called you, Matt. Several times."

"I know, I know," Matt said. "I really screwed up." He had tears squirting out of his eyes. There was no way I could stay mad; I knew him too well for that. He'd fallen for Cherry, at least a little bit. He wasn't using her completely. I was sure of it. He had feelings for both of us, probably. I decided to be more understanding because he was right. I *had* been kissing half of Shitville.

I hugged him hard, and he hugged me back. Before I knew

what was happening, we were kissing. I mean really kissing. He had weird, sugary salami breath. His lips were soft, but my insides weren't excited. Why oh why was this happening? Did I see my feelings for him through Amaretto-tinted glasses? I stopped. "Matt, wait."

He pulled away. "What?" He was really sad.

"I can't."

"I know," Matt said, tears still streaming down his cheeks.

As always, we had our unspoken language. I didn't have to explain that romance between us just wouldn't be right. I didn't have to tell him that he meant the world to me as a friend. I didn't need to explain that I could try until I died, but I just couldn't feel that kind of love for him. Everything became completely clear in those moments during our second, sexually uncharged kiss. We didn't have to say it; we both just knew. I was crying, too.

And we hugged again, for a long time. Our embrace meant everything.

"Katie," he said, pulling away from me.

"What?"

"Turn around." He lifted up the back of my shirt in a totally mom-like, unsuggestive way. "What's on your back? Oh, my goodness gracious!" He yelled. Frankie and Renee and Kevin and Cherry quickly filed back into the room on that cue.

"What? Will you scratch it for me?" I said, suddenly realizing that this was very, very bad. "Oh, my God! Matt, did you tell Cherry I was allergic to chocolate?"

"Oops. I forgot."

"You're allergic to what, Katie-Kay?" she said, running over to me. She gasped in way-too-much horror when she looked at my back. "I have to get you some of that pink stuff that takes the itch away. Where's Vikki J.?"

"Do not get her," I demanded. This was her day; I didn't want her to freak. "But I only ate the sugar cookies," I said.

"I accidentally put chocolate chips in those, too, girlfriend," she admitted, looking genuinely frantic about it. "I fished them out, but those daggone crumbs were probably still in there. Didn't you notice they were a little brown?"

"I thought they were just overbaked," I yelled. My skin was certainly cooked; my arms and legs were hot and turning bright red.

"I just can't believe this!" She threw her hands in the air, a total drama queen. "I am so darn sorry, Katie-Kay. And worried, too!"

I sat there itching my ass off, literally. How was I going to wear a blue dress in welts? And why wasn't I freaking over Matt, my best friend? And what the heck was going on over there — Cherry chicken-pecked Kevin's cheek, and he had a serious lovey-dovey look in his eyes! I just wanted to jump into an oatmeal bath . . . I needed time to think.

Kevin ran out of the room, probably to get my mother, despite what I'd said. Cherry trembled. Renee and Frankie held hands tightly, and Matt scratched me some more. Eugene showed up in the corner of the room, and I caught him picking his nose.

"Goddamnit, what the hell happened here?" Vikki J. was taking off her high heels, pointing the stilettos right in Cherry's direction.

"She didn't mean to do it," I said.

"Oh, well, then." Vikki J. threw her shoes on the floor. She fussed over me, wondering if my tongue was swelling up, if my throat was closing in.

I assured her that it wasn't. It was just like having a thousand mosquito bites. "I'm totally fine." She dashed up the stairs to run the bathwater for me. I worried that the humidity in the room would ruin her makeup and hair. I didn't care about those things, of course, but she did. And I had wanted her day to be perfect. I was ruining everything! The hives were wreaking havoc on us all!

Cherry started to cry, and Kevin, the softie, rubbed her back and whispered something in her ear.

"It's okay, Cherry," Frankie said, surprising everyone. "It was an accident."

"Can I at least get Katie-Kay some pink lotion or somethun?" she whined. "I'm just so full of sorries!" Cherry hopped in her car, presumably headed to the drugstore for any and all anti-itch gear. Kevin went with her — they had obviously come to a romantic conclusion, and I hoped that their third try would turn out better.

"What are you gonna do now?" Frankie asked.

"I'm gonna make sure Bob and Vikki J. go off to their fancy dinner on time, watch you guys get ready, and then I'm gonna lay in the bathtub all night long. There is no way I'm making it to prom." So the decision was made for me. I was partly disappointed, partly relieved. Some things just turn out the way they are supposed to be.

Eventually, everyone calmed down. Cherry put pink lotion on me, though it didn't help. We let Eugene break both the piñatas before Bob and Vikki J.'s company cleared out. Then Kevin cleaned everything up in fifteen minutes flat.

"This is all my fault," Vikki J. told me when only Bob was in the room. "I should never a-rigged that Easter egg hunt years ago."

"Oh, stop it. I'm fine." I didn't tell her I could still feel my welts growing. She hugged me and whispered she loved me. The first time I'd heard her say it since I was five.

"I love you, too," I said. "Promise me you'll go out and celebrate tonight."

"I cain't."

"I'm seventeen! I'll be fine," I insisted, trying hard not to scratch myself in front of her.

"Better listen to the girl," Bob said. He promised to call me every couple of hours, and she still wouldn't go. Then he said he'd call every hour, and she finally relented. He pulled Vikki J. away, and she nervously fixed herself up again to go out to dinner.

I pulled Matt aside. "We have to talk."

"We do."

"Let's try something totally unheard of," I said. "Let's really be friends again."

"I want to try," he said bittersweetly. "Goodness, I just can't take all the weirdness we went through last time we kissed."

"It was torture," I answered, sensing that things were truly okay between us for the first time in six weeks. "I don't want to be without you. It was awful not telling you things." I definitely planned to dig Ivy League Barbie out of the basement and put her back where she belonged in my room.

"I had to go through so much alone!" he said, drying his cheeks, cheering up.

That made two of us, I thought. I tried to answer wisely. "Neither of us will be without either of us ever again. Or something. You know what I'm getting at."

"I agree. I agree." He paused. "Well, then . . . Oh, oh, oh, I know something I should . . . I should share with you," he said enthusiastically, hesitantly.

"It's about another girl! You go, Matt! Give me the gossip."

I said that, and I meant it. I honestly would not be jealous. I would be truly happy when he was, just like our friendship used to be. I was glad we had shared that awful kiss; it had cleared up a heavy worry-load of things.

"You remember Juliana? The girl who dumped me?"

"Grrr," I said. She had hurt him last year.

"She's been calling me a lot lately."

"You are such a lady-killer!" I teased.

He turned bright red. "She said she made a mistake when she broke up with me," he said.

"She was right," I assured him.

"I know she's going with her band friends to the prom. Maybe I'll hang out with her. I mean, it looks like Cherry will be with Kevin, and that's fine with me. She's a handful, Katie."

"Yes, she is," I said, thankful to have taken the anti-itch pills she brought for me. "Just be careful, Matt," I added. "I'll kick Juliana's ass if she breaks your heart again."

"I'm a lady-killer now, remember?" He rubbed his head. "She's the one who should be worried."

"You're right." We laughed.

"So what about you?" he asked. "Which one of your guys is the lucky one? You can tell me, I won't get weird or anything."

And just like best friends do, I told him my secret thoughts on my unrequited crush.

Say Cheese

Still Saturday, May 10

My friends got ready in an excited frenzy. I had learned a lot about makeup, and I convinced Frankie that a little black eyeliner would complement her tux. Renee didn't have to be convinced. She asked me to fix her hair, which was flat under the bandanna, and do her eyes up. Kevin and Cherry got ready together in Vikki J.'s room. I straightened Matt's bow tie, then asked him to go down to the laundry room and get my Ivy League Barbie. I put her back on my dresser.

"I'm gonna get me some lay-dees," Eugene proclaimed just as I was coaching him on what *not* to say to girls. Kevin promised to introduce him to some freshmen.

My friends all snuck cookies — like they couldn't eat them in front of me — and before they left, I took their pictures. For the couple photo, Frankie and Renee cheesed it up, grabbing each other's butts when I snapped, I could totally tell. In the picture I called my All-Male Revue, Kevin stood tall in the middle. I hoped he'd be voted Prom King. They were running late; they didn't leave till eight even though the dance started at seven. Before they left, they made a big deal of taking a picture of me, the rashy mess that I was, all by myself. So what if I was solo? That, for the first time ever, suited me fine.

After they were gone, I cracked open a light beer and slipped it into Vikki J.'s can-huggie. I ran a hot bath, pouring instant oatmeal in the steaming water and hoping that honey flavor would feel the best. I cranked up the chanting monks — Eugene had put my stereo back into my room. I slid into the water, and I sighed.

The drama had ended. The plan and prom were over. I hadn't accomplished my goal, but maybe that's because the goal was screwed up in the first place. No one could fall in love on cue the way I'd hoped. That idea had been silly. Who got to choose when they met the right person? No one. I had learned a lot about love even though I hadn't found it. I'd had all kinds of trysts, good and bad. And, most important, I'd finally come to terms with my ex. Those were huge accomplishments. I was proudest, though, that I had found — and kept! — friendship. Matt, Frankie, Kevin, Renee, even Eugene and Cherry were all a part of it. And since that was the case, I decided that the whole to-do had been brilliant.

I had one regret, of course. But I decided to dwell on it tomorrow.

At about nine o'clock, the doorbell interrupted the serenity I had struggled so hard to create. I hopped out, threw on a thick white robe, and opened the front door at the same time I bent over to scratch my ankles.

And just like that, there he was. Blue. Sparkling.

It couldn't be true. Surely, I'd drunk too much beer. But he was really there, standing in front of me.

"Put on your dress, Katie James," he said. "I am taking you to the prom. I don't care how much you itch. I will scratch you."

"What are you doing here?" I gasped, pulling my robe together to hide my splotches.

"Matt gave me the tip," he said. Blue had the whitest smile I'd ever seen. "He's a good kid." And he looked incredible in a navy-blue tuxedo and bowling shoes.

"He did?" Matt was amazing.

Blue nodded, reaching his hand out for mine. He didn't even flinch when he saw the welts on my fingers. Instead, he rubbed them, which felt really good. "We don't have much time left. Hurry."

"Don't you have another date?"

"She ran off with Eugene," he said, smiling.

"Are you kidding?" I yelled. "You have to be kidding!"

"I introduced them and, well, they hit it off."

"You've got to be kidding," I repeated, worried that I sounded like a ding-a-ling.

"It was the second-best thing that happened to me all night," he said, never breaking our stare. "The best was finding you here. Now hurry."

In the last six weeks, I'd been through way too much to argue. Besides, I was a sucker for those eyes. I dashed upstairs to my bedroom, threw off my robe, and slipped the silky gown fabric over my fancy underwear. I forced my curls — the moisture from the bath twisted them into tight knots — into a ponytail. Rashy red splotches lined my arms, legs, and shoulders where glitter would've looked nicer. At least my face had been spared; it was the only part of my body that hadn't been under attack.

265

"I wouldn't miss this night for the world," I said, heading out the door, holding Blue's hand while I scratched my shoulder. We hopped into the purple Bug that Jesse had left at my house. I killed the little stick shift twice before we even got off my block.

"You want to drive?" I asked while he tried not to laugh.

It was my final date, and I shut my eyes as he steered down the street. What would happen? I would not plan. I would only imagine.

love
sex
friendship
betrayal
depression
revenge!

Ellen's boyfriend is cheating on her…with her best friend. Her sister is bratty. Her mom is having an affair with one of Ellen's most hateful teachers. And her second best friend is ruining their relationship by falling in love with her.

At first Ellen just wants to climb into bed and never get out again. But she comes up with a better idea: revenge. She's getting off and getting even—and she's going to find out how sweet (and sour) revenge can be.

www.thisisPUSH.com

IWST

PUSH

YOU ARE HERE.

www.thisispush.com

Meet the authors.

Read the books.

Tell us what you want to see.

Submit your own words.

Read the words of others.

this is PUSH.